Also by J Melvin Smith:

MULTIPLES

Praise for MULTIPLES.

Good solid story. I greatly enjoyed the cast of characters. The story was fast paced and I was taken on a thrilling ride. The novel needs a bit more editing as there are a few careless errors. All in all, well done

My husband and I thoroughly enjoyed Multiples by this first-time author. It was suspenseful with interesting twists and turns. We have been anxiously awaiting his second novel.

Excellent first novel from J Melvin Smith. Great story and character development will keep you involved and entertained. Exciting look inside the health insurance industry and plenty of mystery keeps this novel rolling. Anxiously awaiting sequel!

A RICHARD MOORE NOVEL

FUNDS

J MELVIN SMITH

JMelvinSmith.com

Woburn, MA

For Jackie

J. Merlo [signature]

© All rights reserved.

Printed in the United States of America.

This is a work of fiction. Any resemblance of characters to actual persons, living or dead, is purely coincidental. The Author holds exclusive rights to this work. Unauthorized duplication is prohibited.

Acknowledgments

To Bernie, my brother: your professional editorial skills comments, suggestions and your continuing support have kept me working on the series. Knowing you are available for help is very comforting and greatly appreciated

Many people helped and encouraged me to continue writing. I am privileged to have their comments, suggestions, editing, proofreading, designing and other assistance. Please forgive me for not mentioning all of you individually.

To my son, Christopher Allen, and daughter, Stephanie Lyn: Thanks for developing into better offspring than I deserve, and for allowing me to use your names in the book. I hope that I did justice to them.

To Gale, my wife: You have always encouraged and supported me, regardless of the endeavor. You have been a true companion.

1

As Richard Moore focused on the face of his long time and closest friend, his mind traveled back in time to a place thousands of miles away.

The United States government was also very interested in capturing this particular terrorist, as he was wanted in connection with several attacks on US interests. When El Salvador offered refuge to the terrorist, it was seen more as a direct slap in the face of the US than a helpful hand to a friend.

When El Salvador made contact through back channels, the US State Department began tripping over its own feet trying to offer help to El Salvador in removing the terrorist. It was, as many administration officials would say, a perfect opportunity to show El Salvador that the US could be a valuable and helpful friend.

Richard stayed at Enrique's one-hundred-thousand-hector ranch. It was here that he planned the operation to capture the terrorist, gathered vital intelligence, staged for the jungle incursion, and met Salina, Enrique's only daughter. Richard and Salina quickly developed an intense friendship; one that Richard hoped would evolve over time.

Often the international political benefits so sought after before an operation, are not realized with a successful operation. Richard's successful removal of the terrorist from El Salvador was no exception. Richard left the country wondering if he would ever enter El Salvador or see Salina again.

Richard and his twelve-man team were back. In the mountain jungles of the northeastern part of El Salvador, they prepared to make a cold camp and wait until nightfall before advancing on the camp where the senator's idealistic missionary son and his friend were being held.

"All right, people, we're four klicks east of the bandits' camp. We'll rest here. Bear, take the north perimeter. Spider, go west, but stay away from the camp."

"Richard, I'll take a position south."

Richard turned to face Salina. "No. I want to go over a couple of details with you."

The real fact was that they were very close to the bandits' camp and Richard did not want to let Salina out of his sight. Although he tried to fight the feeling, he was very protective of her.

Richard vehemently protested when informed by Enrique that Salina would be the guide on this mission. He told Enrique that if she as the only guide available, the team would operate without one. Enrique was insistent. No rescue attempt unless Salina was the guide. She was fit, proficient with a variety of weapons, knowledgeable of the area where the bandits' camp was located, and could be very persuasive with the local villages if necessary. Richard was left with no real choice but to agree to have Salina as the guide.

Richard and Salina spent some time reviewing a map and the plan as his men kicked back for a brief rest. Shutter Bug was moving about taking pictures of the area and the team. Photography was a hobby, and, in some cases, an assignment. His digital camera recorded much that was not meant to be recorded.

Bear radioed in as Richard turned and walked away from Salina. "Leader this is Bear. Be advised patrol one klick north of your position. Six, I repeat, six, bandits."

Richard was about to respond when Salina pulled a smoke grenade from her pack and tossed it into the center of the cold camp. She then pulled out a fragmentation grenade. One of the team radioed, "Frag. She's got a frag."

With this news and the smoke, Richard pivoted while taking out his silenced pistol. He fired one shot. Salina collapsed like a rag doll. She had one hole in her head.

"Leader, what the hell is happening down there? Bandits are progressing on your position." Bear's voice was clear and steady with just a bit of panic laced in.

"Listen up, people. Time to move. We have company coming from the north. Shutter Bug, take point, we're heading south. There's a road one and a half klicks from here. Bear, can you join up?"

"Negative. I'll follow behind the bandits."

"Roger that. We will take up position on the south side of the road. If the camp sends out a truckload of troops, they'll head toward the smoke. If we're lucky, we'll be behind them."

The team proceeded to the road. Shutter Bug crossed first then signaled for the rest to follow. As Richard and the rest of the team broke into the clearing, a column of heavily-armed bandits appeared from the south side of the road. Out in the open and boxed in, Richard and the team were in no position to engage the bandits.

The Bear watched as the fifteen or so bandits lined up Richard and ten men in the middle of the road. Some of the bandits were dancing around as if they had just won the lottery. Richard and his men were instructed to kneel with their hands behind their heads. "A truck will be here shortly to bring you and your men to our camp," the leader of the band said.

Spider and Bear never joined up with the team. They were behind the six bandits as the team headed to the road. Now within eyesight, Bear signaled his plan to Spider. As Spider acknowledged, each of the team heard the Bear through his earbud speaker. "On three, go prone on the ground. One, two, three." As the word three came out of his mouth, Bear squeezed off a short burst from his silenced MP3, hitting the bandit leader and several of his men. As Richard and the team hit the dirt, Bear and Spider opened with several long controlled bursts. In seconds, the bandits were history.

Richard and the others quickly grabbed their weapons and set up a defensive perimeter. Richard turned toward movement coming from the woods. He gazed at Bear as the man leaned against a tree. The ever-present smile spread across his dark-brown face. The twinkle in his eyes brighter than Richard had ever seen it

2

"Richard. Richard." The sound of someone calling his name brought Richard back to the present. He did not divert his yes from the face of his friend: A face no longer smiling; eyes devoid of any twinkle; the brown skin noticeably pale.

Bear was lying face up on wet leaves between a tree and several bushes just off the parking lot of an office building. Two bullet holes identified the method of Bear's death. The person calling Richard's name was one of the State Police crime scene technicians.

"Richard, you can take a closer look if you want. We're about finished. It appears to have been a mugging gone badly. Sorry," the technician said as he walked away. He knew Richard from the days when Richard worked for the Boston Police Department. The technician also knew Bear and the close friendship Richard and Bear shared.

"What the hell is Small-town doing here? Partner, will you look at this. It isn't bad enough that we have to respond to a murder late on a Sunday, but we have to find our old buddy, Small-town, at the scene."

Kelly and his partner, Nelson, detectives with the Massachusetts State Police Homicide Division, had just pulled their unmarked car up to the curb and gotten out when Detective Kelly spotted Richard. "Hey, Small-town, what are you doing stomping all over my crime scene? This isn't your jurisdiction, so get the hell out of here."

Richard ignored the detective's ranting. He had met detective Kelly and his partner a year earlier. Richard had been at the scene of a sniper shooting which took place at a state park called the Sheep Fold. Richard had reacted poorly to the detective's questioning and comments. Although Richard had forgotten about their heated conversation, the detective apparently had not.

Officer Garvey of the Stoneham Police Department walked up to detective Kelly. "Detective, that's Richard Moore—"

"I know who he is, and he isn't supposed to be here. Who the fuck invited him? Small-town, I told you to get lost."

The officer persisted, "You don't understand, the victim is Jan Pulaski AKA the Bear. He and Richard were very close. They served—"

"Hey, Small-town, I hear this guy was a friend of yours. Sounds like old times. Being an acquaintance of yours is hazardous to one's health."

"If I were you, Detective, I'd put a lid on it."

"And who the hell are—" Detective Kelly started to say as he turned to see who was telling him to put a lid on it. "Oh, hi Chief."

Paul Valentine, Stoneham's chief of police, walked up to Detective Kelly and put his face within an inch of Kelly's. "Richard is a very good friend of mine. He was captain of the Boston PD's antiterrorism unit, the chief of police in Winchendon, and he served this country as a member of the military's elite forces. He deserves more respect than you'll ever earn in your lifetime. If you have something to say to him, I suggest you do it in private. Otherwise, keep your mouth shut. I had Richard called. In addition to being a friend of the victim, he'll do a better job investigating the murder than any of us."

"I doubt that, Chief. I don't mind you telling me to keep my mouth shut, but don't question my investigational skills. I've been at this—"

"Detective, the State Police and my department have limited man-hours to devote to this particular crime. That man," the chief motioned toward Richard, "will bring more man-hours and resources to this investigation than we could bring to ten homicides. He gets our full cooperation."

"With all due respect, Chief, this is a homicide investigation, and, as you well know, since this is Stoneham and not Boston or Springfield it's being investigated by the State Police Homicide Unit just like any other homicide outside those two cities. This case is mine. You have nothing to give him, and Small-town gets nothing from me." The detective walked away from the chief.

Chief Valentine walked up to Richard's side. "I take it you know the detectives?"

"Hi Paul thanks for having Garvey call me." Richard had been in his condominium in South Boston working on a threat assessment report that he had to get to the assistant director of Home Land Security. While working on the report, he had also been waiting for Stephanie to call so he could pick her up at the airport. The patrolman's call changed everything.

"Yeah, I know the detective. He was assigned to the shooting at the Sheep Fold last year. He played bad cop when they interviewed me at the hospital. I lost my cool. I got over it, but it looks as if the detective hasn't"

"Well, Richard, everything we get or find on this, you'll get. I can't say you'll get any information from the state guys. The detective doesn't want to help you."

"That's okay; I prefer running my own investigations."

"I know its personal, Richard, but the crime scene guys said that this was a mugging. You may never find the guy."

"This was no mugging."

"Why do you say that, Richard?"

"First, two slugs in Bear's torso. One looks like it came from a slight side angle, the second more directly from the front. I'd say someone standing off to his left shot him as he passed, then Bear turned to face the shooter and he was shot again. A mugging gone bad usually has one shot and then the mugger runs, or the mugger panics and shoots wildly and indiscriminately. This shooter was cool and calm.

"The shooting took place over here." Richard walked over to a puddle of blood in the parking lot. "Bear goes down on his back right here, but he's moved fifty feet and placed in the treed area."

"The shooter wanted to hide the body so he could have more time getting away," the chief concluded.

"I don't think so," Richard responded. "Bear wasn't dragged across the parking lot and into the trees. His shoes are still on and the heels are not scratched. He was carried. The man weighs two hundred and fifty, maybe two hundred and seventy-five, pounds and he was carried and neatly placed down on the muddy ground."

Richard's mind went through the probable scene as he looked around at the ground. "I'm confident we are looking for at least two and they are in good physical condition. They picked Bear up and carried him. No sign of dragging, dropping, or stumbling.

"They took his wallet out, emptied the contents, and left it on his chest to help make it look like a mugging. His pickup is missing. I looked around the street and it isn't here. His keys are gone. One other thing," Richard stopped and put his words together carefully, "picking up the body and moving it took some time. Add to that the time they took to go through the pockets and stage the mugging. They weren't concerned about someone hearing the two shots and calling the police. No rush to leave before the police could respond. They used silencers."

"Richard, you're saying Bear's murder was planned."

"That's the way I see it."

Chief Valentine worked the scene through his mind. Then he said, "How the hell did anyone surprise Bear? He was a pro and very cautious. What was he doing here in the first place?"

"Maybe Laura can tell me that."

"Laura. I forgot about his secretary. She and her family will be devastated."

"I know," Richard said. "Informing Laura of Bear's death is not a task I'm looking forward to doing."

Richard's cellphone rang. He held it up to look at the caller ID. It was Stephanie.

"Hi, Stephanie. How was your flight?"

"My flight?" Her voice portrayed a high degree of irritability. "Where the hell are you? I called your home telephone but got no answer. I thought you were going to wait for my call and pick me up."

"Sorry, Stephanie, but I had —"

"You had to what? Go out chasing bad guys. My flight gets bumped all over hell and I can't even rely on you waiting for my call."

"Stephanie, please calm down and let me explain."

"Calm down. I am calm. I'm just tired, and instead of finding you ready to pick me up, I find out you couldn't wait—"

"Stephanie, Bear is dead." Richard words were almost loud enough for everyone around to hear.

Silence hung in the digital space of cellphone conversations as Stephanie regrouped her emotions. "Dear, dead. Oh my god, Richard, I'm so sorry. What ... what happened?"

Richard gave Stephanie the shortened version of Bear's death. He would give her more detail the next day, after she had had some time to recover from the shock. Stephanie had only known Bear for a year, but they had formed a close friendship. As Richard thought about that fact, it occurred to him that Bear made close friendships with most of the people with whom he came to know.

"Ah ... listen, Richard, I saw Rob Lee this evening."

"Rob Lee? Are you sure? Where was he?" With the mention of Rob Lee, Richard's thoughts were coming faster than he could process them. Professionals shot and killed Bear and Rob Lee was in the area. This, to Richard, could not be a coincidence.

"I was heading to the bus the airline was putting us in for the return back to Logan."

"Wait. What do you mean for the return back to Logan? Where are you?"

"Boston's Logan Airport is closed due to the storm that passed through. Most of the air traffic was diverted to Manchester, New Hampshire. The airlines are busing the passengers back to Logan from Manchester. I tried calling you from the plane. While I was walking toward the bus, I spotted Rob Lee."

"Are you sure it was Rob Lee?"

"It was him. I'll never forget that man after he tried to have us killed last year."

"Was he alone?"

"No, or at least I don't think so. Two military types were walking with him."

"Military types? Sometimes your descriptions belie the fact that you are a newspaper reporter. What do you mean by military type?"

"I don't know. They just made me think, *Military,* when I saw them. One was tall, about six-three. The other was shorter, maybe five ten. They were average build, but with an appearance of being solid. Both had close cut hair."

"All right, when do you arrive at Logan? I can't pick you up, but I'll have someone meet you."

"No, that's all right, Richard. I'll get a cab. What will you be doing?"

"I have to go see Laura."

"Oh. She'll die on the spot. They were so close. Do you want me to meet you at her house?"

"No, I don't think so. You try to get some rest. I'll handle talking with Laura."

"Hey, you get some rest too, Richard. I'm sorry about Bear and sorry about how our phone conversation began."

"I know. You get some rest. I'll be at Bear's office in the morning if you need to get in touch. I love you."

"Yeah. Talk with you in the morning."

3

Richard left the scene of Bear's murder and headed to Laura's. enroute, Richard called Steve Deschenes. Steve was the owner of an internet development company based in California. Steve had been part of the special operations team with Bear and Richard. The news of Bear's death would hit Steve hard.

"Steve, Richard."

"Hello, Richard. What has you up at this time of night?" It was just after 1AM. in Boston.

"Bad news, I'm afraid. What's all the noise in the background? I can barely hear you."

"One of my employees got married today. I'm at a party," Steve shouted into his cellphone.

"Steve, can you find a quiet place? I need to talk with you. It's important."

"OK, hold on." After several minutes of muffled sounds, Steve began speaking again. "This should be better. I found a supply closet away from the party. So, what's so important?"

Richard gave Steve the news and a rundown of his suppositions about the events of the murder. After Steve's initial shock, he became focused as Richard laid out the facts indicating that Bear was targeted. This information meant that there was work to be done, and Steve was suddenly all business.

"Steve, Stephanie told me that she's very sure that she saw Rob Lee at the Manchester, New Hampshire airport."

"Rob Lee? On the night Bear gets killed? What are the odds on that?"

"Can't be a coincidence. Steve, I need you to do some checking."

"I know. How many flights out of Manchester, private and commercial and where did they land. Cross Rob Lee's known aliases against the passenger lists and track where he went."

"So, why am I on the phone with you? Get busy. You obviously don't need me to tell you what to do."

"You taught me, remember? I'll get back to you as soon as possible, but it could take days. What about the arrangements for Bear?"

"I know it will take some time. I have someone going to the airport to start tracking from there. The Medical Examiner has Bear. When he's finished with the body, he'll release it. Then we can figure out the arrangements"

"All right, Richard. I'll call you in ten hours regardless of what I find, earlier if anything significant pops up."

"OK, Steve. I just pulled up in front of Laura's house. I've delivered bad news many times, but this one will be the hardest."

"Glad I don't have to be with you, friend. Tell Laura we'll find this scum and he won't get off on a technicality."

Steve and Richard finished their telephone conversation, and Richard sat in his car across the street from Laura's white colonial style house.

1

Bear retired from the military shortly after Richard, and headed back to the Boston area. He did not move to Roxbury, the city where he had grown up. Instead, he moved to the suburbs just north of Boston.

His dad was Polish-American, and his mother was African-American. She was an orphan, so all of Bear's relatives were Polish. Bear's grandparents lived on a farm in Poland, and he spent most of his summers there as a child. His parents passed away while he was away on a classified mission.

The Roxbury neighborhood where Bear grew up presented him with many vices all designed to corrupt ones inner values. Bear was on his way to forsaking his values when his parents enlisted the help of a priest from the Catholic parish where Bear lived. The priest taught Bear the value of school, and faith. Bear often commented that the priest most likely saved him from an early death.

Out of the military and back in Boston, Bear started his own security consulting business, and spent free time sitting in the back of juvenile court. He knew he could not save all the youths of the area, but saving just one was all Bear had in mind.

Over seven years Bear became a familiar face in juvenile court. Prosecutors and defense attorneys often called him with the story of a good, but wayward, youth that needed his help. Bear did not take in troubled youths. Instead, he used his network, which had become extensive, to find shelter, jobs, and rehabilitation services for those he chose to help.

Laura was one of those fortunate few. She had been in court a few times on minor offences. Bear spotted a good kid headed toward serious trouble. His first few attempts to convince her to let him help went nowhere. Laura was sure the big black guy was interested in only one thing, just like most men she knew. She would have no part of him.

At two o'clock one morning, Laura was walking home from a night out with several girls from the neighborhood. Her boyfriend, Dom, could not see her that night, as he was busy. Laura rounded a corner and Dom pulled up to the intersection. A man about ten years older than Dom sat in the passenger seat of the boat-sized Chevy.

"Hey, Laura, what you doin'?" Dom yelled out the window.

Laura stepped up to the driver's side window, stuck her head in, and gave Dom a kiss. She held the kiss a little longer than usual, for the passenger's benefit. She backed up, "You done with your business?"

"Yah, I'm giving Dance here a ride home. Come with us. I'll take you home after I drop him off."

Dance gave Dom a very stern look. "You sure you want to do that, Dom?" Dance asked, with a tone in his voice that answered, "No."

Laura smiled, opened the rear door, and got in. "Of course he does; he's my man." She leaned forward and wrapped her arms around Dom, smiled, looked at Dance, and said, "I'm Laura."

A half hour later, the trio drove past the parking area of a chain retail outlet. Dance's apartment was two blocks away. An unmarked police cruiser sat in the parking lot, its lights off, and the occupant's eyes scanning the neighborhood. It began moving before any lights were turned on. The driver took his time following the Chevy, time for a backup to corner his prey.

The three were arrested and charged with murder. An eyewitness saw three people in the Chevy as they left the scene of the murder. The witness could not be sure if all three were male or female. No matter, the cops had their trio.

The next day, Laura sought out help from Bear. He made no promises. If she were involved, he would have nothing to do with her ever again. The police did not go looking for someone else to fill the third spot in the getaway car. They had Laura for that, even though she had friends swearing that she was with them at the time of the killing.

Bear found the third person a week later. Laura was released. Dom and Dance were looking at some serious time in prison. Laura followed all the rules and guidance Bear gave her. She completed her high school equivalency, kept out of trouble, and went to college nights while she worked part-time days.

When his secretary resigned to move to Washington with her husband, Bear gave the job to Laura. Bear walked Laura down the aisle when she married Justin. Bear paced the halls of the hospital when each of the girls was born. Bear was the father that Laura never had.

"Hello." The voice was hoarse and still masked in sleep.
"Justin, this is Richard."
"Richard? What time is it?" Justin's senses started to function normally. He sat up in bed and turned his back toward Laura. She was moving but still asleep. "Richard, what's the matter? Are you all right?"
"Yes, Justin, I'm all right, but I have to talk with you and Laura."
"Now?" Justin's voice betrayed his concern and confusion.
"Yes, Justin, now."
"OK, when will you be here?"
"I'm across the street."

As soon as Justin opened the front door of the house, Richard got out of his car and walked across the street. The front yard of the house was surrounded by a white picket fence. The brick walkway delivered visitors from the sidewalk to the three steps leading to a porch and the front door.

"Hi, Justin, sorry about the hour."
"I'm not as worried about the hour as I am concerned about the reason that brought you here at this hour."
"I brought coffee, muffins, and those doughnut holes that the girls like." Richard handed one of the bags to Justin, and they walked down the hall wall directly into the kitchen.
"I like what you've done with the kitchen," Richard commented.
"What? Oh, that's right; you haven't been in the house for some time."

Richard looked around the room noting the changes: new cabinets of light oak; hard-wood floor; dark-green, speckled-granite countertop; and new appliances. One of the walls had been moved back, adding space to the room. An oak table with captain's chairs was centered below a stained glass hanging light fixture.

"Laura did the preliminary design for the room, and she did the floor pattern. She picked out the colors, cabinets, and appliances. I's sorry, you didn't come by to see this room.

"I'm just delaying until Laura comes down."

They both heard footsteps racing down the stairs and along the hall.

"One of the girls woke up when the telephone rang. She didn't want me to leave her, and I didn't think it would be wise to bring her down," Laura said, as she entered the kitchen and walked up to Richard. They gave each other a kiss on the cheek and a hug.

"I brought some coffee," Richard told Laura, as he pointed to the bag on the counter near where Justin was standing.

"For Christ's sake, Richard, will you just get to the purpose of this visit," Laura and Justin said, almost in unison.

"OK, but sit down." They did as directed. "There was a shooting earlier. The victim died at the scene."

"Bear! Oh my god, Bear's dead," Laura said, as she broke down crying. Justin looked quizzically at Richard. Richard looked Justin directly in the eyes and nodded his head. With that, Justin's eyes filled with tears, he grabbed his wife, and they rocked back and forth.

Richard was prepared to give the couple as much time as they needed before continuing on. He just wished that he had made himself a cup of coffee. He did not want to get up from the table until Justin and Laura were through this first stage of grief.

He did not have to wait long. "Richard, I'm going to have some coffee. You want some?" Laura asked, as she got up and walked to the counter.

"I can get it for both of us, Laura. Why don't you stay seated?"

"No, I have to be busy. You like it black, right?"

"Yes, thanks."

"So, what happened?" Laura asked.

"The police are saying that it was a mugging gone badly. At least, that's their official finding for now."

"You don't believe their finding." Laura said as she placed a cup of coffee in front of Richard.

"I don't. Laura, why don't we go over this at another time? You "

"No. It'll be good to get it out of the way. I don't want to drag it out for days or weeks. The facts will help me come to terms with Bear's death." Tears started running down her face again.

"He spent most of the day with us," she said. "We all went to Barrier Field, and Bear helped the girls fly." Bear's passion was model remote controlled airplanes. "It was such a lovely day." Laura sat and hid her face as she sobbed.

Justin continued for Laura. "We wanted to have a cookout here at the house, but the weather turned bad, so we went to a restaurant. When we left the restaurant, Bear said that he had a meet and had to head home."

Laura regained her composure. "So, let's hear what happened."

Richard gave Laura and Justin as much information as he had about the crime scene and also told them his theory. Laura listened carefully, but Justin had little interest in the details.

"Knowing Bear," Laura started, after Richard finished his summary, "it would be hard to surprise him and get two shots off, without a reaction from him."

"You have to excuse me," Justin finally said, "but I can't sit here and listen to this. Bear was like a brother to me and to you, Laura, or maybe more like a father. He was Uncle Bear to the girls and now the man is dead. These details are enough to make me sick."

"You're right, Justin. I forget that not everyone looks at murder the same way. Surely, not everyone looks at the details the same way. Let's drop this discussion for now," Richard suggested.

"One more question first," Laura insisted. "What about Rob Lee?"

Richard was stunned by the question. "What makes you ask about him in particular?"

"You and Bear have all but branded the man *Public Enemy Number One.* You have been hunting him for over a year. He has to be high on the list of suspects."

Richard told Laura about Stephanie's account, and told her that Steve was doing some checking.

The three spent another hour and a half talking about Bear. They laughed and cried many times while they recounted memorable events. When they ran out of things to talk about, Richard got up to leave. At the door, Laura hugged him. "Thanks for coming by. I know how close you two were, and you haven't had a chance to do your own grieving."

"Maybe that will come later. I have too much to do right now. You take care of the girls. Take as much time off as you need. I'll be using Bear's office for a while and will be able to handle the office during that time."

Richard turned and shook Justin's hand. "If you need anything, just call. Try to get some rest."

5

Richard opened the door to Bear's office at 7:30AM. Before arriving, he had a few hours of fitful sleep and an abbreviated run along the Charles River. With coffee in hand, he roamed the office.

Bear's company, like Richard's, was a one-man operation, although Laura would dispute that statement with facts showing that she was as valuable as Bear. Richard and Bear were silent partners in each other's companies. They liked their independence, and they knew that one could not work for the other. Each took and worked assignments without reporting to or informing the other. When assignments were large enough, they would subcontract with each other. Their extensive contacts within the law-enforcement and private-contractor communities allowed them to expand their workforces to fit the needs of the assignment.

Bear kept a simple office. The reception area accommodated four chairs, Laura's desk, and her lateral file cabinets. Unlike a doctor's office, visitors seldom had to wait. Generally, no one had an appointment to meet with Bear at the office. The conference room took up almost half of the total office space and was the nerve center of large or complex assignments. The room included the standard long conference table and seated twelve. The table also had power outlets and high-speed internet connections for each seat. A projector and a remote controlled display screen hung from the ceiling. Four television monitors sat on hangers mounted on the wall opposite the projection screen.

Richard entered Bear's office and stood surveying his friend's domain. Two computer screens sat on Bear's thirty inch by seventy-inch oak desk. The right side extension was covered with files, while the rest of the desk was clean. A high-back leather chair was positioned behind the desk. The wall behind the desk was one continuous window. Two other walls were lined with modest wooded wall units of shelves and cabinets and the remaining wall was reserved for pictures and framed documents.

A remote-controlled model of a twin-engine B-25 Mitchell bomber airplane hung from the ceiling over Bear's desk. Several of the shelves of the wall units also held remote-controlled model airplanes, although none was as large as the one hanging from the ceiling. Two remote-controlled helicopters occupied the very top of the wall unit. Bear's idea of flying was to grab a remote control unit and a model plane and head off to any field large enough for him to launch and land one of his planes. Flying was his hobby, passion, and stress reliever.

Bear also saw commercial potential in his hobby. He experimented with several designs based on the military's Predator, a remotely controlled unmanned surveillance and attack aircraft. Bear was sure that a market existed for a smaller unarmed version of a surveillance drone.

Richard sat behind Bear's desk and powered up the two computers. It was time to get to work. Richard had to review the assignments that Bear was working on and retrace the man's steps.

Maybe I won't get started right away, he said to himself as he looked at the message on the screen: *Enter User Name and Password*. He rummaged through the draws, files, and file cabinets looking for the user name and password and found nothing.

After twenty minutes of searching and trying a variety of passwords, Richard stepped into the small kitchen area and made coffee. As the coffee brewed, he considered calling Laura but then thought better of it. No doubt, Laura was up all night and then had to handle her girls. As the thought passed, Richard heard the front door open. He had locked it when he came in and the sound of someone coming in put him in survival mode.

"Richard, you in here?" It was Laura.

Richard walked to the doorway between the reception area and the kitchen. "What are you doing here? I thought I told you to take a couple of days off and get some rest."

"You're going to find Bear's killer, so you need to know what assignments he has been working and what his schedule has been during the past couple of months. You need to get into his computers, and you need a synopsis of each of his most recent important cases. Without me, the only thing you can do for yourself is make coffee, so here I am. By the way, the coffee is lousy. Try this," she finished, handing him a cup from a bag containing two cups of coffee.

Richard stared at her. She was wearing well-worn blue jeans, a loose pullover blouse, and sneakers. Her face was puffy from lack of sleep and hours of crying. She had tried to hide the effects of crying and sleep deprivation with a larger amount of makeup than was her norm.

She knew exactly what Richard was doing. It was second instinct for him, Bear, and their colleagues to make mental notes of everything and every person they met, every time they met, and to assess what was going on in the person's head and life.

"Just for the record, I don't usually come to work dressed this way. I figured that if mentally and physically I had to feel like shit, I could at least dress comfortable."

"You'll get no comments from me about what you wear," Richard replied as he held up his hand. "I just rather you go home and rest. This could be a long investigation. It certainly will not be completed today."

"Richard, I know we might never find the guy. I also know that the longer it takes to find his trail, the less likely our chance of success. So, let's get started. If I get to the point where I can't function, I'll go home and rest, but, for now, I have some files for you."

Richard followed her into Bear's office. She sat behind the desk and started typing on the computer keyboard. "I had all of Bear's user names and passwords. Last night I combined them. Now you only need one to access all his files and accounts. This file," she pointed to an icon on the screen, "has a list of the three active assignments, the contacts, and a synopsis. The synopsis is as good as I could do last night."

"You did this last night?"

"Yeah, I know what you need. I've been doing this for some time for Bear." With that comment, tears started rolling down her cheeks.

"Come on, let's stop, and you go home."

"No, Richard. Last night I realized that the tears come at unexpected moments. A sound, scent, thought, words, it doesn't matter; it just happens. It's OK. This file has his calendar for the past year. Now I need contact information for you: if you're out, how best to get in touch."

Richard gave her his home number, office number, and cellphone number. "I think you and Marcella should coordinate my schedule. That might make it easier to contact me. I'm planning to work out of this office until I find the guy. I'll call Marcella later and let her know what happened and what I need her to do."

Marcella was Richard's administrative assistant. She was functional, efficient, and a great asset to Richard. The job functions for Marcella and Laura were very similar. However, while Marcella enjoyed the details of the business functions, budgets, accounting, scheduling, and contracts, Laura enjoyed the hunt. She often participated in the conference room brainstorming sessions and contributed valuable insight to those sessions.

Just before 9 A.M., Richard's cellphone rang. It was Marcella. "Richard. Oh, Richard, I heard on the news this morning. What a loss. When I didn't find you in the office, I figured you must be working to help find Bear's murderer. What can I do?"

"Marcella, I'm at Bear's office. I will probably work out of here until we finish the investigation. It would be helpful if you and Laura coordinate my schedule and any files we might need."

"Of course Richard, I'll set up a network that will give all of us access to the same information. I'll have it active in an hour. I'll call Laura with the details. Why don't I route the telephones calls from Bear's office to here? That way, Laura won't have to deal with all the calls that might pour in."

"Thanks, Marcella. The telephone idea is great. Set it up. How do I get calls that come in for me?"

"Steve set up a nice little routing system here the last time he was out. We haven't had to use it, but I can forward a call to any telephone I want, and the caller will think you're in the room next to me."

"You and Steve could be dangerous if left to tinker with his toy chest. That reminds me, I asked him to track down some flights last night. Rob Lee was in the area, and we need to follow that lead."

"You think Rob Lee had something to do with Bear's murder?" Marcella asked, skeptically.

"He was here, in Boston, and was trying to get out of the area shortly after Deui's death. I never believed in coincidences."

Marcella kept her thoughts to herself. She knew that Rob Lee never pulled the trigger although he had arraigned for someone else to do so. She also knew that Rob Lee seldom watched or got involved in any assignments after he awarded the contract.

"All right, Richard, I'm sure Steve can get a call directly to you but if he calls the office, I'll track you down. Any idea what the arrangements for Bear will be?"

"The police will hold on to the body until an autopsy is complete. If they have everything they need, they'll release his body after that. I figure the end of the week at best."

"Do you want me to make and coordinate the arrangements?"

"In the file under Bear's name you will find his instructions. They include the funeral home, church, and burial. You don't have to coordinate; he expected that I would do that. Relatives on his father's side are too far away, his mother was an orphan with no known relatives, and Bear did not want anyone other than me to assure that his wishes were carried out."

"Well, you have to investigate his murder. I'm sure he won't mind if I take care of coordinating the arrangements, unless, of course, you want to do it."

"I would be grateful if you handle the arrangements. There may be a lot of calls inquiring about the arrangements, and you can respond with first-hand knowledge."

"Done, now let me get busy with the computers and phones. Talk with you later."

6

The main door to the offices opened, and a sixtyish man walked in. Laura looked up from her computer and gave the man a less than welcoming look. She was in no mood for visitors or sales representatives. "May I help you?" she asked.

The man was dressed casually in a blue windbreaker over a light-grey-pullover shirt with collar. His black slacks were creased down the center of each leg, and, except for the wrinkles from sitting, the slacks were neat. Boat shoes finished off the man's attire. "Hello," he replied. "You must be Laura."

"And why must I be?"

The man smiled, "Well this looks like the nerve center of the office. You have the telephone and computer. No one gets in the door without you confronting them. That makes this position the administrative assistant's desk. You are not a temp. Your eyes contradict the cheerful facade. You lack sleep and have cried real tears. So, you are the resident administrative assistant. Richard told me that Laura was Bear's administrative assistant. How did I do, Laura?"

"And who are you?"

"Philip Andrew Tyron, the third," Richard responded for the man. Richard had been standing in the doorway of Bear's office listening to the pair. "Also known as Pat or Ty, depending on whom you are talking with, retired Army lieutenant colonel. He was an instructor with the one oh ninth Military Police Battalion. He taught investigative and surveillance techniques. After suffering a minor leg wound during an as yet undisclosed firefight, he retired and went to work for the New Hampshire State Police. He retired from there after becoming Captain of their Homicide Detective Division. How are you, Phil?"

The men embraced and shook hands. Turning to address Laura, Phil said, "Laura, it is a pleasure to finally meet you. I wish it were under different circumstances."

"Nice to meet you also," she replied and extended her hand.

"So, what brings you to the office?" Richard asked. "When we spoke, you said that you would see if you could follow our man's trail."

"And that is what I have been doing all night. It brought me to the area, so I decided to drop in and give you my findings in person."

"Let's go into the office. Do you want some coffee?"

"No, thanks, I've had nothing but cup after cup all night."

The two left Laura in the reception area and went into Bear's office. Phil slumped into one of the chairs.

"You OK? I haven't seen you limp like that in a long time," Richard inquired of his friend as he took a seat.

"I did a lot of walking last night. The leg will be OK. How is Laura dealing with Bear's death?"

"She's tough. Right now, she's hiding it by working to help find the killer. She should be home resting. She spent all night putting together information I need for the investigation.

"And how is Richard doing?"
"I'm doing fine. Let's get to your report."

"OK, let's," Phil replied. "I talked with a limo driver. He was sitting outside Manchester Airport waiting for a couple of executives to arrive. Their flight was diverted from Boston's Logan Airport. He happened to be in Manchester because he drove three men from Logan to Manchester. He noted the three, because he thought them odd to be together."

"Why was that?" Richard asked.

"One guy he described as a business type: dark-blue or black suite, white shirt, maroon tie, and polished black shoes. The second guy he described as very fit, not necessarily lean, but fit. The man wore a pullover and slacks. I guess he was dressed like me. The third guy was a contrast: black sneakers, black pants with multiple pockets—he probably meant fatigue type pants— white T-shirt under a dark zippered windbreaker. The zipper was open down to the waist. The guy was fit and lean, about six feet tall."

Richard thought about the descriptions then said, "Sounds like Rob Lee was in the suit, his bodyguard was casual, and the shooter was dressed for action. Did the driver confirm Rob Lee's description?"

"He did. You really think that the guy in the T-shirt was the shooter responsible for Bear's death?"

"I do, and that puts Rob Lee at the center of it."

"Richard," Laura stepped into the doorway of the office, "Steve is holding to talk with you."

"Thanks, Laura," Richard said as he picked up the phone receiver. "Steve, you're up early. Is it still dark in California?"

"Actually, it is a beautiful sunrise right now, and I have been up for a long time. I wanted to tell you that I contacted most of the people we know, about Bear's death. I have a database of former unit members, friends, and business associates. What I wanted to do by sending out the information was to put everyone on alert to find Rob Lee."

"I hadn't thought of that, Steve; good thinking. Our whole network of contacts will be on the outlook for him. Interesting approach, I take it that you didn't have any luck with private airline carriers last night."

"No. I struck out, although I did find out that someone chartered a flight out of Manchester but cancelled at the last minute."

"I have Phil Tyron here with me. He tracked Rob Lee's movements last night. I'll let him tell you about it. You might be able to find something about Rob Lee's travels from the tail numbers of the airplane he rented."

Richard moved Phil into the conference room and put him on the line with Steve. Richard then talked with Laura and gave her instructions on what he wanted to do next.

Twenty minutes later, Richard was back in Bear's office. Phil stuck his head in, "I'm heading home for some rest. You call me if anything comes up. I'll be back tomorrow, if not sooner."

"OK, Phil. Thanks for everything."

7

"Good morning, Stephanie. You look radiant this morning."

"Thank you, Phil," Stephanie replied. "You, however, look like you could use some rest. You're limping."

"The boss drives us too hard," Phil pointed at the office Richard was using. "I'm going to get some rest. See you again soon."

As Phil left the office, Stephanie turned toward Laura. "How are you holding up?"

Laura got out of her chair, and the two women hugged. "I'm still in shock. Every now and then tears just start flowing without warning."

"You should be home. Why did Richard have you come in?"

"Oh, no he told me to take as much time off as necessary. I just had to come in."

"OK, but you leave whenever you feel you have to. I take it Richard is in the other room."

"Actually, I'm standing here wondering when I would get to say, 'Hi'." Richard had once again heard talking in the reception area and stood in the doorway to see who had entered the office.

Stephanie walked over to Richard, and he wrapped his arms around her. He went to kiss her on the lips, but she turned her head at the last moment. He kissed her cheek. They walked into the office and sat in chairs facing each other.

"Have you had any word from the police about Bear's murder?"

"No. I really don't think that investigating his death will be a high priority."

"So, you're heading up your own investigation. I take it Rob Lee is your prime suspect."

"Actually, you are correct." Richard paused before asking the obvious question, "Why do you sound so upset about that?"

"I'm not. I just have other things on my mind."

"OK. So, tell me about your interview with the vice president."

"Oh, you really don't want to hear about that. You have more important things to do."

"Come on, Stephanie, I'm always interested in what you've been doing and how you feel."

"OK. Actually, the trip was very productive. He gave me open access to most of his staff. I got time with him in his bus as we traveled from one campaign stop to another. You know, he really is very charismatic. I mean, everyone says that about him, but in person, you really see it."

"So, you got a good interview and a good story to write."

"I did. The story will run in this Sunday's edition. I also got a job offer."

"Oh, did this job offer come from the man himself?"

"It did. How did you know?"

"The man certainly has good taste in women," Richard said, as he smiled to himself.

"What! What was that supposed to mean? You don't think I can handle assistant press secretary to the president when he gets elected?"

"That's not what I said, Stephanie."

"No, but it's what you implied: 'He has good taste in women.' I'll have you know he has some very intellectual and knowledgeable people on his staff."

"I know that. I also know that he has a reputation concerning women. Many are hired, but few stay for long."

"I can't believe this is coming from you." Stephanie was livid. Her face was flush red and she was getting ready to leave. "You remember when we first met you did that cop thing. You assessed me, and I asked for your assessment. I had to tell you then that you left out the fact that I was highly intelligent, that men always leave that part of the assessment out."

"Look, Stephanie, I can't believe that you took him seriously The position might be great, but not with this guy. He's so predictable; I bet I can tell you how the topic came about."

"You think so, huh? All right, go ahead, tell me."

"You had a nice one-on-one interview with the vice president. He made sure you were not interrupted. Maybe only his chief-of-staff was with you. At some point, he mentions that he has to finish up. He has a meeting he has to get to, but first he has to freshen up and change. He suggested that you join him while he gets ready. That way, you can finish the interview. Plus, he has something he wants to discuss. You go to his suite at the hotel. While he's cleaning up, you ask more questions, and he yells back the answers. Only the answers are a little playful, not as serious like during the initial part of the interview. He's testing your defenses. Then he comes into the room and sits down. He has something to ask. Then, he offers you a job. How did I do?"

"I've heard enough. I'm out of here. Richard, I can't believe I didn't see how chauvinistic you are," Stephanie yelled, as she stormed toward the door to leave.

Richard stood in the waiting area and watched as she left.

Laura could not help but hear the exchange between Richard and Stephanie. As Stephanie walked out the door, Laura turned to Richard, "Don't you think you should go get her and stop her?"

"No."

"No! Richard, Stephanie is one pissed off woman right now. I think you should tell her you're sorry or do something to get her to calm down."

"No. Not now. She's not upset about our conversation. That was just an excuse. When she's ready, she'll let me know what is really upsetting her. For now, she's using me so she will not have to address the real problem. Were you able to get me an appointment with any of the tenants of the building where Bear was murdered?"

"You really are going to let her go as upset as she is?"

Richard nodded his head.

"OK," Laura let out a large sigh, "Holly Cook is the president of Higher Credit Score. The company owns the building and occupies the first two floors. The third floor is occupied by a law firm, and the fourth floor has a variety of smaller tenants. Ms. Cook was out but should be back now. I'll give her another call."

When Stephanie left the office, she got in her two-seater BMW, threw it into reverse, and sped out of the parking space. A quick slap to the shifter and a purposeful downward push with her right foot, and the car rocketed forward and down the access drive. The drive bent sharply twice before reaching the street. At the first bend, Stephanie drove the brake pedal to the floor.

"Shit!" she screamed, as she pounded the steering wheel with her open palms. "What the hell was that all about? Why did I jump all over Richard? He was right, of course. That's why I got pissed at him. He's so self-assured, so ... annoyingly right. He missed the fact that the VP not only talked, he brushed up against me as he walked from room to room as he freshened up."

She sat in the car for a few minutes regaining her composure. *The job would be a great step for me, if only the VP could keep his mind on business. Maybe he will once he's president.* Finished talking to herself, she drove out to the street, crossed to Interstate 95, and drove south to her office.

8

At two o'clock that afternoon, Richard entered the first floor of the office building where Bear had been murdered.

"Hi, I'm Richard Moore to see Ms. Cook," he said to the receptionist.

Located on Salem Lane, three blocks South of Main Street in Stoneham, the building was four stories tall and made of tan brick. Parking lots bracketed the right and left sides, and the rear was bordered by a fifteen-foot-deep wooded area. The state owned the land just beyond the wooded area and parking lot on the left. From the building's front door, one could stand and look down a side street directly across Salem Lane. The street was lined by single-family homes, each with a large maple tree on the street side of the sidewalk.

"Mr. Moore," the receptionist lifted her head and looked at Richard; "Ms. Cook will see you now. Will you follow me please?"

Holly Cook's office was in the left front corner of the first floor. The office was furnished with the standard large cherry-colored desk with a right side return, three-foot round table with four chairs, two cherry bookcases, and several four-drawer lateral file cabinets. It was, Richard thought, a modest office for a company president. The only surprise Richard found in the office was the man standing alongside Ms. Cook.

After Richard and Ms. Cook made their introductions and shook hands, Ms. Cook said, "This is Glen Hurshberg of Hurshberg and Stein, Attorneys at Law. The firm occupies the third floor of this building. Mr. Hurshberg has represented Higher Credit Scores almost since our inception."

Richard extended his had to Mr. Hurshberg, "Nice to meet you. Was I interrupting something?"

"No. Ms. Cook asked me to sit in on your meeting. You're not with a law enforcement agency investigating last night's incident, are you?"

"By incident, you mean the shooting death of Mr. Pulaski?"

"That's right. You're not, are you?"

"I'm here to learn as much as possible to help speed the investigation into Mr. Pulaski's ... murder."

Richard looked at Ms. Cook. "Did you ever meet Mr. Pulaski?"

"No, I can't say that I had."

"Do you know if there was any reason for him to be here at this building last night?"

"Mr. Moore," Hurshberg was getting back into the conversation, "Ms. Cook said that she never met the victim. How could she know if there was a reason for him to be here? If you are here to go through the standard questions, why don't you go talk with the police? They were here earlier and questioned Ms Cook. Since you have no legal authority to be here, I think you should leave."

"I certainly do not want to take up a lot of your time, Ms. Cook," Richard said, without looking at the attorney. "Did you give the police a copy of the security tape from your security cameras?"

"What? Why no ... I mean, the cameras are not working."

"Now if you do not mind, I think you should leave. Ms. Cook and I have some business to finish," Hurshberg said as he stood up.

Richard eyed him for a moment, then asked, "Were you present while the police questioned Ms. Cook?"

"Ah ... No I was with another client at the time. Why do you ask?"

"That's what I do." Richard paused. "I ask questions." He smiled, got out of his chair, shook their hands, and left.

9

Back at the office, Richard and Laura reviewed Bear's current client list.

"So, he had three active contracts: Container International, the Archdiocese of Boston, and Congressman Willard."

"Right," Laura responded. "The summary of each is included with each file. We also had two pending jobs: Transportation Security Administration wanted a security analysis and training schedule for Bedford Air Field and Bee Mountain wanted a security assessment of their manufacturing plant in Hargood. Both were on hold until sometime next month."

"I assume that Container International was the real moneymaker; the other two wouldn't have been paying much."

"Actually, both the congressman and the Archdiocese were paying a good rate. The Archdiocese was paying more that our usual rate, and both were current in terms of payments."

"The Archdiocese was paying more than standard rate?" Richard sounded skeptical.

"Yeah, Bear wanted to discount his services, but they wouldn't hear of it. They said that his assignment was very complicated, and they wanted the best results possible."

"OK, I'll take that up with them. What about his schedule the past six months?"

"Oh, that reminds me. I wanted to tell you—"

Richard held up his hand to stop Laura. His cellphone was ringing. "This is Pam Alverez. I need to talk with her, but stay; we'll get back to your comments."

Richard sat in the oversized deck chair. "Pam, how are things in South Carolina?"

"Right now, they're screaming by me. I'm on Interstate 26, heading south. I'm trying to catch up with a black Ford Crown Victoria. I have reason to believe that Rob Lee is in the back seat of the car."

"Rob Lee!" Richard screamed as he jumped out of his seat. The chair was catapulted backward and slammed into the wall. "Are you sure?"

"As sure as I can be without opening the car door," Pam responded. "When Steve sent out the notice about Bear's death and Rob Lee's possible connection, I notified everyone I know. My partner Stu did the same. Stu's uncle is retired but works part-time at the airport as a skycap. Stu's uncle spotted Rob Lee. Apparently, Rob Lee's flight was delayed. The uncle overheard the man driving tell Rob Lee the trip to Highland Park would take two and one-half to three hours down Route 26.

"Stu and I are on 26 now. Rob Lee has a lead on us, but, if his driver is not driving full out, we should catch up with them outside their destination in about ten minutes."

"All right, we need to set up a roadblock." Richard's mind was processing different options for stopping and capturing the man he had been hunting for over a year.

"No, that's not a great idea. If he sees cop cars or a roadblock, he's going to find a way out. I know a contractor doing some work on bridges at that end of 26. When we're close and have Rob Lee in sight, I'll call the contractor. He'll stop traffic while he moves one of his large trucks around. It will look perfectly natural. Stu and I will be right behind Rob Lee's car. We'll get out and grab him."

"Pam, you worked this out quickly. Will the contractor go along with it?"

"He better, he's my brother-in-law."

"All right, but no shoot-out. If you can't grab him clean, I don't want a gun battle. No innocent casualties."

"I hear you, Richard. Now I need you to clear the way for us. I don't want some state cop pulling me over for speeding. We will also need the Feds to take custody of Rob Lee."

"I'll make the calls and get back to you in five minutes. Then I want you to leave the phone line open so I can talk with you as this goes down."

Richard hung up, then called Charles White at the FBI in Washington, DC. Charles and Richard had worked together several times in the past, and Charles had become Richard's go-between at the Bureau. Richard explained what he needed and why.

"Tim," Charles yelled to his administrative assistant, "get me the director of operations in South Carolina. I don't care where he is or what he's doing. I want him now."

A few minutes later, Tim was standing in the doorway to Charles's office. "Sir, the DO you asked for is on the line."

"Thanks, Tim. What's his name?"

"Her name," Tim smiled, "is Kate Winslow."

Tim stood in the doorway as Charles gave Kate a rundown of what was happening on Route 26. "So, tell the state cops to leave the dark-blue Subaru alone, and call Richard and let him know the Staties have been notified. Get someone over to the contractor to help out. Kate, let me know what happens as soon as you can."

Charles hung up. "That will be all for now, Tim."

"Pam, you should have clear travel. The state cops have been notified, although, they aren't happy." It had been a half hour since Kate called Richard and told him that the state police had been notified. "Where are you now, Pam?'

"We should see the car anytime now. We still have ten minutes before we get to the work area."

Rob Lee was sitting in the back of the large car trying to catch up on some sleep. The night had been a series of cab rides. The vibration from his cellphone disturbed his rest. "I haven't had the honor of a phone call from you in some time. Is there a problem?" he asked.

Rob Lee listened to the response. "Thank you for the information. I guess I'll have to reschedule my appointment. Are we still on for our game Sunday?"

The answer was affirmative. "Excellent. I'll see you at 9 AM. Now, you'll excuse me. I have to make changes to my travel plans"

Rob Lee snapped the cellphone shut. "George, we have a dark-blue Subaru trying to catch up to us. Construction up ahead will stop traffic and try to box us in. Notify the other car. When the Subaru catches up, lose them. And tell the other car, 'No gunfire.' They can block, but no shooting."

"OK, boss," George responded. He then called the other car traveling behind them. The other car was additional protection meant for their meeting location.

"Stu, is that the car, the one just ahead of the truck in the first lane?" Pam asked.

"Right model and color. Why don't we pass them and then drop back. We might be able to identify the driver. We're still eight miles from the construction site.'

"Sounds good."

Stu slowed down so they could get a good look at the Ford as they overtook it. When he pulled into the passing lane, however, the Ford also moved left directly in front of Stu and Pam's Subaru.

"What the hell?" Stu screamed as he watched smoke rise from the Ford's rear wheels. The Ford was coming to a stop, and Stu was about to slam into the rear end of it. Stu turned hard right while the Ford was turned hard left.

George had executed a bootlegger's turn. He stepped on the emergency brake while he turned the steering wheel all the way to the left. The car went into a controlled skid. The rear of the car slid right while the front of the car went left into the center breakdown lane. George then released the brake, brought the steering wheel back to center, and accelerated. The car was now headed in the opposite direction while Stu was fighting to get his car back under control.

George drove west into and across the median, then joined the westbound traffic on the other side. The trail car also traversed the median, but emerged headed east against the westbound traffic until the driver spun it around to face the right direction.

Stu regained control of his car, brought it to a stop, turned left, crossed the median and turned west while entering the active traffic. Two fast-moving cars swerved to avoid hitting Stu's slower moving vehicle.

"Over there, heading toward the exit," Pam shouted, as she pointed at the black Ford Crown Victoria.

As Stu stomped on the accelerator, the trail car hit the left end of his rear bumper. The contact put Stu's car into another spin. It turned broadside and traveled right, crossing the path of oncoming vehicles. A tractor trailer driver saw Stu's car sliding out of control and slammed on his brakes. The air mechanism locked the brakes on the trailer causing it to swing left, and the driver turned into the skid. His actions did little to slow the skidding motion of the trailer as it swung like a gate, closing off both lanes of traffic. Two cars plowed into the side of the trailer, pushing it even faster toward Stu and Pam.

As their car continued to slide across the lanes, Stu and Pam watched the trailer lean toward them. The tires of the trailer finally gave up contact with the damp pavement, and it flipped on its side with a thunderous roar, collided with the right side of Stu's Subaru, and drove the car into the right side guardrail.

Richard could only pace in the office as he listen to the yelling and crashing sounds coming from the speaker of his desk telephone. Pam had dropped her cellphone when Stu's car went into its first spin. After that, Richard could hear some of the conversation between Pam and Stu, but he could not determine exactly what was happening. When the telephone went silent, he screamed, "Ah, shit!"

Richard called Charles and told him what he knew and what he had heard.

"Richard, the agent-in-charge is at the construction site. I'll give him a call and call you right back."

For the next forty-five minutes, Richard paced the office while Laura tried to allay his concerns.

When Charles finally called back, he said, "Richard, Rob Lee and your people never arrived at the work site. The agent-in-charge was still waiting for them when I called. It appears as if there was some sort of encounter between your people and Rob Lee eight miles before the work site. The aftermath of their encounter was a crash scene involving a dozen vehicles, including the car your people were in."

"How are they Charles? What's their condition? Are they—?"

"They're alive, Richard. According to my man, Pam has a severe concussion, bruised or broken ribs, and various cuts and bruises. Stu is in better shape. He has cuts and bruises and a fractured left wrist."

"Well, it's better than I imagined, but worse than I would have liked."

"They might not think so after the state police get through with them, Richard. The state cops have a mess on their hands, and, with Rob Lee long gone, they only have your people to blame. Their looking at a half dozen charges to throw at Stu and Pam. They're also going to revoke their private investigator licenses."

"Charles, Stu and Pam were working for me." Richard paused. He was angry with himself for putting others in peril. "You know what that means when it comes to finding, chasing and apprehending Rob Lee?"

"Richard, I know, but you have to understand this incident can cause a major crack in the Bureau's relationship with the state cops. They didn't want to let your people chase the car at all. They wanted to handle it."

"Charles, if you can, I would appreciate it if you would arrange some understanding with the state cops. Stu and Pam shouldn't face charges. I will call the man and see if he can intercede if you prefer."

The man Richard was referring to was D. Adam Yurrikie. In some circles he was referred to as Day, however, he preferred Adam. Adam was the assistant director of the Central Intelligence Agency. Richard first met Adam when they were in Protective Services training with the 145th Military Police Battalion.

Their careers took them in different directions, but they found a way to keep in touch. Adam left the military as soon as his enlistment was up. During his last year in the Army, Adam was recruited by the CIA. Adam and Richard worked on a few assignments while Richard was in command of his Special Forces unit.

As Richard's operation in El Salvador was ending, Adam arrived and requested that Richard remain in the country for a few days to help him, "solve a little problem." Two days later, Richard helped a badly wounded Adam escape a posse of Salvadoran police and get out of the country, an act that left Adam very grateful to Richard.

"No!" Charles said. "I'll take care of it, but you might want to send flowers or something to our office down there. They will not be happy."

10

Early the next morning, Richard was jogging alongside the Charles River. The early morning exercise was a habit built into him during his military days. This morning he was thinking about his conversation with Stu and Pam. He had reached them in their hospital room. The details of the accident and events leading up to it were cloudy to them, but they both agreed on one point: Rob Lee had been expecting them.

Not possible, Richard thought to himself. *There wasn't enough time for Rob Lee to have learned about Pam and Stu chasing him.*

He pushed the thought to the back of his mind and focused on his investigation into Bear's murder. Although he was certain Rob Lee was involved, Richard knew he should not rule out other potential suspects. He would start with Bear's three active clients.

Laura arrived at the office just before 9 AM. She found Richard was in Bear's office and stepped into the doorway.

"Good morning, Richard."

Richard looked up and smiled.

"Hi, Laura, how are you doing this morning?"

"Ah, well, I want to apologize. Most days I'm here by eight, but, if the sitter gets delayed, like today, I can't get here until about this time. I meant to—"

"Laura, don't even think about this. Hell, I told you to take time off. Do not hesitate to change your schedule if needed. End of discussion. Now, how are you and the family holding up?"

"Thanks, Richard. Last night one of the girls asked when she would see Bear. She wants to go flying. It was a difficult moment. We'll get by. We have to. ... Now, what's your plan for finding Bear's killer?"

Richard gave Laura a rundown of the previous day's events and his conversation with Pam and Stu. He did not mention that their professional opinion was that Rob Lee had been expecting them. Then, he told her how he wanted to proceed with Bear's active clients.

"Well, that's good," Laura said after he was finished. "I made an appointment for you with Gloria Stokes. She's the director of loss prevention at Container International Insurance. She engaged Bear's services. You're meeting her at 10:30. Her office is on State Street, in Boston."

"I read the summary you gave me. The insurance company has been hit for loses when some containers came up empty at the final destination," Richard said.

"That's right. Gloria knows it's an inside job, but she couldn't figure out how it was going down. Bear had some ideas, but didn't elaborate to me."

"OK, I'll head out. While downtown I'll stop by my office and touch base with Marcella."

"Not so fast." Laura motioned for him to sit back down. "I also made an appointment for you to see Mary Christensen at the Boston Archdiocese."

"Mary Christenson? You're kidding me, right?"

"Oh, no, it's her real name. According to Bear, she's real smart and very guarded with information. You get to meet her at four this afternoon. First thing tomorrow morning, you get to talk with Congressman Willard."

"If I sit in one place too long, you just remember to push me and keep me going," Richard said, as he smiled and got ready to leave.

When he arrived in downtown Boston, Richard parked his car, met with Marcella in his own office, then walked through Post Office Square to Gloria Stoke's office on State Street.

As he walked, the fragrance of fallen leaves wafted down from the nearby Boston Common, but few trees could be found in this part of downtown. And, though the bright autumn sun was occasionally visible, for the most part, the tall buildings of the financial center effectively blocked it from shining directly on the throngs of pedestrians shuffling to and from their destinations. Where its rays did find their way to the street, Richard could only briefly feel their welcomed warmth before his onward movement thrust him back into the cooler shadows. Wryly, Richard thought to himself that the "heart" of the city around him was made of cement, brick, and asphalt.

Gloria's office was on the twelfth floor of an office building shared buy a variety of businesses. At three hundred square feet, it was spacious. One of the walls was all windows, although it only gave a magnificent view of the side of a building thirty feet away.

Gloria was five feet, six inches tall, with charcoal-black eyes. Her dark-brown hair was pulled tight against her head forming a ponytail that swung between her shoulder blades as she moved. The cuff of her pant legs rested on black patent leather flats. The matching suit jacket was worn over a peach-colored dress shirt. The top two buttons of the shirt were undone. Her full lips had a hint of color and gloss. No other makeup was evident, nor was it needed on her rich brown complexion.

"Mr. Moore, I'm Gloria Stokes." She extended her hand and gave Richard a firm handshake greeting. "I was deeply saddened to learn of Bear's death. I understand from Laura that you and Bear were friends." As she was talking, she directed Richard to a chair positioned near a three-foot round table. She sat in a chair opposite him.

"Bear and I were longtime friends. He saved my life once when we were in the military."

"Such a senseless death: Unfortunately, there are far too many senseless deaths these days."

"Did you know him long?" Richard asked.

"Not really, I met him about four months ago. We were having a problem with missing shipments at the container terminal in Charlestown. He came here to my office, and I gave him an overview of the situation. We worked out an agreement, and he began conducting an investigation."

"You have your own people for conducting loss investigations. Why did you hire outside help?"

"We sent an investigator to the yard to look around and ask questions. As we expected, he got stonewalled. We figured that we might ultimately have to put some people undercover, but that takes some time in a place like the container terminal, and we wanted the thefts stopped quickly. Before going that route, I decided to try a more direct approach. Mr. Pulaski had Homeland Security credentials and he'd done security audits of container terminals. I figured that his involvement might put an immediate stop to the thefts."

"Did it?"

"No. We were hit twice after he started asking questions and flashing his credentials around the dock."

"Did he find anything unusual?"

"None."

"Did he mention anyone in particular that he wanted more information about?"

"He asked me to check out one of the foremen. The guy's name was Dan Sweeney. I didn't find anything unusual in his finances: no large purchases, no cash withdrawals, no unexpected deposits, and no similar activity. He did not have a rap sheet."

"Did Bear have any run-ins with any of the workers or management at the terminal?"

"If he did, he didn't mention it to me."

Richard started to get up from the chair, "Thank you, Ms. Stokes. I appreciate your taking the time to see me."

"It was the least I could do. What will you do next?"

Richard contemplated telling Gloria that he was going to the terminal then decided against it. "I'm retracing Bear's movements of the past couple of months. I'll be talking with some of his other clients." Richard extended his hand, thanked her again, and left her office.

11

After retrieving his car, Richard made the short drive to Charlestown's City Square. A right placed him on Chelsea Street, a street that no longer goes to Chelsea; it veered left at the Mystic River and become Terminal Street, the access road to the Massachusetts Port Authority's Moran Container Terminal. Richard, however, turned right onto a short street called Terminal Way, the entrance to the Cushing Container Terminal. The terminal is located at the mouth of the Mystic River, and is bounded on the east by that river and on the south, by Boston Harbor. The area was once part of the historic Charlestown Navy Yard, one of America's earliest shipbuilding and repairing facilities. In its 174-year history, workers at the navy yard produced over two hundred warships, and maintained and repaired thousands of others. Although Charlestown became part of Boston in 1874, the facility was not renamed the Boston Naval Shipyard until 1945. After its closure in 1974, a thirty-acre section fronting Boston Harbor became the Boston National History Park, and houses, among other things, the frigate USS Constitution and the Fletcher-class destroyer Cassin Young. In a convoluted and controversial deal worked out behind the scenes, the remainder of the Boston Harbor frontage was used to build a container terminal managed by the Massachusetts Highway Commission. Rumors abounded that project was conceived by a small but powerful clique that wanted to bypass the Massachusetts Port Authority and provide themselves with a unique and lucrative source of political patronage and favors.

As Richard approached the guard shack positioned in the middle of the access road, a guard seated inside stuck his head out of a window and asked, "May I help you, sir?"

Richard held up a picture of Bear. "Have you ever seen this man?"

"Who wants to know?"

"I do. He was murdered Sunday night. I'm retracing his steps and talking to the people he met during the past couple of months. Have you seen him?"

"Yeah, I've seen him. Big guy. The picture doesn't show how big he really is ... ah ... was. Said I should call him Bear, everyone does. Murdered you say?"

"Shot twice Sunday night. Do you know who he talked with here?"

"I'm not sure. He was doing some kind of investigation. He wanted to talk with the foremen. I gave him Sal Abbrazzee's name. I don't know if he ever talked with him."

"Is Sal on duty today?"

"Yeah, but he could be anywhere in the yard or dock area."

"That's OK, I'll find him," Richard said, as he started to drive past the guard.

Richard parked his car and started walking around the busy yard. Large forklifts and small mobile cranes moved shipping containers from one location to another. Tractors pulled trailers in and out of parking spaces, and, in the distance, at dockside, the large overhead crane lifted containers from the deck of the ship and placed them gently on waiting trailers.

Richard finally found Sal. The man was talking on a hand held walkie-talkie directing several vehicles and cranes at once. Richard walked up to Sal and introduced himself. Sal held up his hand indicating that Richard should wait. Sal was at least five inches shorter than Richard was, but outweighed Richard by seventy-five pounds. For all the activity going on around him, it was apparent that Sal did little physical work himself.

"Now, who the hell are you, and what do you want?" Sal asked Richard.

"Mr. Abbrazzee, I'm Richard Moore. I have a few questions I'd like to ask you."

"No."

"Excuse me?" Richard had not expected the response.

"I said, no. Now, get lost."

Ignoring him, Richard took out the picture of Bear and held it up so that Sal could see it. "Do you remember talking with this man?"

"No"

"No, you don't remember, or no, you didn't talk with him?"

"I said, no, I'm not answering questions. I'm busy. Now get out of here or I'll have security remove you." Sal was watching a forklift carrying a container pass by. He barked some orders into his walkie-talkie and walked away from Richard. Sal was startled when he almost bumped into Richard. When Sal had started to walk away, Richard moved quickly to block Sal's path.

"Sal, I'll tell you what, I'm going to make this real easy for you. I'm going to walk alongside you and ask some questions. You can answer in between barking into that walkie-talkie. I'll be patient. Tell me no again, or walk away without answering some simple questions, and I'll put you right on top of my list of suspects for the murder of this man."

Again, Richard held up Bear's picture again for Sal to see.

"Are you done? I assume you are. So I'll tell you this. The man in that picture came to talk with me and I told him the same thing I'm telling you now: See that building?" Sal pointed at the administration building at the end of the terminal. "Martin King's office is on the second floor. Talk with Martin. If he calls and tells me to stop what I'm doing and talk with you, I'll be happy to spend as much time with you as you'd like. Until he calls, I'm busy." Sal turned and walked in the direction of a fork truck carrying a container. This time, Richard just watched the man walk away.

Richard found that the administration building had two functions. The administrative offices were on the second and third floors, while the first floor was a maintenance shop. If a piece of equipment was used in the terminal, the maintenance shop repaired and maintained it. The second and third floors extended only half the length of the building, which allowed half of the maintenance shop to have a three-story high ceiling. This provided ample height for lifting trucks and containers so that workers could inspect and repair the underside as needed.

"Hi, I'm Richard Moore. Sal told me that I should talk with Martin King." He was talking with a secretary in the open office area just outside an office with King's name on it.

"If Sal told you to find Martin, then Sal doesn't want to talk with you. He just pawned you off," she said with a slight laugh.

"I'm sure he did. I would still like to see Mr. King."

"He's not here. Should be downstairs in the maintenance area." The woman didn't look at Richard as she talked. Then she got up with some files in her hands and walked the few feet to the desk next to her.

Richard roamed around the maintenance area taking in all the activity. Actually, there wasn't that much activity. The pace in the shop was very slow, a sign of the terminal's poor maintenance culture. When he went over to the heavy vinyl curtains that separated the one-story shop from the three-story area, he saw that, despite its vast size, it contained only one project: an aged container was receiving a fresh coat of paint.

He walked around the benches where workers kept tools and tool boxes. He noticed one of the worker's tool box contained stencils and metal number punches. As he looked more closely at the punches, a worker shouted, "Hey, what the fuck do you think you're doing? Get away from those tools."

Richard looked up to see a man coming at him. Richard's first thought was that this guy must be the legendary Man Mountain Dean. He was over six feet tall, close to three hundred pounds, had white hair pulled back into a ponytail, and a beard that brushed across his barrowed midsection as he moved. His short-sleeved shirt revealed a tattoo of a human skull.

The man extended his arm when he got close to Richard and attempted to forcefully brush Richard aside and away from the workbench and tools. "I told you to get away from here. These are my tools and I don't take kindly to no one snooping around them. Hey—"

The man was startled when Richard stopped the man's arm from brushing him aside.

"I'm just looking around while I wait for Martin King," said Richard in a calm, friendly voice. "I do some restoration of antique cars, and I always like to see what others use for tools. Sometimes I get ideas for handling tricky repairs."

"Well, you get no tools here for fixn' tricky repairs, and you just missed Martin. He left early, so I guess you'd better leave too."

Richard was frustrated but undeterred. He pulled out the picture of Bear. "You ever see this man?"

The big guy standing in front of Richard hardly looked at the picture. "I don't know him, but he's been around here a few times. Likes to be called Bear. What's it to yah?"

"Bear was a good friend of mine. He was murdered last Sunday."

"So you thought, 'Hell, Bear's been around the docks. A dock worker must have killed him.' Like there ain't no other bad people who could have killed him. Why don't you go home?"

"I just want to find his killer." Richard noticed a few workers standing around watching his interaction with the big guy. "I don't care if it was a dock worker or a choir singer. I'm just going to find whoever it was."

"Well, good luck. Now, I have to get back to work, and you have to leave."

12

The drive from the Charlestown container terminal to the Cardinal's Residence in Brighton was not pleasant at three in the afternoon. In addition to the stop and go traffic and rush hour volume, the clear blue sky had turned dark. The rain started at four, just as Richard walked along the curved driveway from the parking area to the front door of the residence.

The residence was a four-story box of a building built from light-tan brick. Richard thought that its most distinguishing and misplaced feature was the portico that covered the main entrance and was apparently used as a carport. The entrance itself consisted of large double-doors that opened into a small foyer from which one set of stairs lead downward to a lower level and another, wider, set ascended three-feet to another foyer. This second foyer bisected a corridor that ran the full length of the building and along which Richard could see doors with brass plates stating the name of a person or department. The corridor seemed to him to be lifeless as well as long, and, indeed, there was no sign of life as he waited, until a nun arrived to escort him to Mary Christenson's office.

Christenson's office was economical at one hundred and thirty square feet. The ceiling, like that of the corridor, was too high. The walls of the office were devoid of any color except for the colored pictures and religious objects hanging from them. Mary's desk was clean, neat, and well-worn.

"Mr. Moore, I'm Mary Christenson. Please have a seat." Mary was five-feet, ten-inches tall. Her light-auburn hair was cut short. *A pixie cut*, Richard thought to himself. Her white blouse was buttoned to the neck. The ruffled cuffs, which matched the collar, extended past the sleeve ends of the blue blazer. The full-length floral skirt brushed the tops of her black leather pumps. A simple wedding band with matching diamond and a wristwatch were the only jewelry.

"Ms. Christenson, I appreciate the opportunity to meet with you." Richard sat in the proffered chair.

"It is my pleasure. By the way, it is Mrs. Christenson or Mary. Ms. has no definitive word associated with it. It was concocted for those afraid to be identified as either single or married. I have no such aversion. I took an oath before God, and I am proud to proclaim that I am Mrs. Christenson."

"I understand. I'm glad you have no aversion about clarifying that point."

"I understand you were a friend of Jan Pulaski. I was shocked to learn of his death. The Cardinal and staff have prayed for his soul."

"The Cardinal knew Bear?"

"He …" Richard watched as Mary formulated her response. "Actually, he knew of him. I do not believe that they ever met. Several discussions have come up where Mr. Pulaski's name was mentioned."

"Bear was investigating claims of abuse and the priests that were accused; is that correct?"

"Yes, it is."

"Why did you hire Bear? I mean, why a private investigator and why Bear?"

"The insurance company was getting very nervous about the number of claims. They felt that, with so many claims, it would be very likely that some would be fabricated. Our attorneys were also concerned that some of the claims would be fraudulent. Of course, they were only concerned with the amount the fraud would add to the final settlement expense. The Cardinal wanted to be open about identifying any priest guilty of abuse. He also wanted to exonerate those falsely accused. So, it was agreed that an independent investigator would look into the claims.

"Your friend was willing to investigate the claims. He made two demands, however. If he determined a claim against a priest to have merit, we were not to transfer the priest within or out of the Boston Archdiocese. If he found a claim to be without merit, the claimant was to be prosecuted. We agreed, and he went to work."

"Mrs. Christenson, did Bear ever mention any claimant that gave him a particularly hard time, maybe someone who threatened him or members of the Church."

"He ran into some very angry people, both claimants and their families, but he found that their anger was largely directed toward the Church. I think this was due, in a large part, to the professional, yet empathetic, way Mr. Pulaski handled himself when explaining his involvement. Most understood the need to verify facts."

"Did he uncover any fraud?"

"Yes, he did."

"How many cases, and what were the claimants' names?"

"I'm afraid I can't share that information with you. We are very cautious about the privacy of the claimants and their families."

"I understand that, but there is a possibility that one of the claimants saw Bear as the enemy, especially if their claim was denied because of what Bear uncovered. One of them may be responsible for his death."

"You may be correct, Mr. Moore, but even if you are, this is a matter for the legal authorities, and, as far as I know, you have no legal standing in it."

"I'm not sure that 'the legal authorities' will bring the killer to justice unless I find out who it is for them. If I am to find Bear's killer, I need to talk with anyone that might have had a reason to kill him."

"Mr. Moore, you may think that you can act as your own law enforcement agency, but that does not give you the right to this information, and it certainly does not give me the right to divulge it to you. Rightly or wrongly, I have to trust that the police are doing their best to pursue Mr. Pulaski's killer. You could use a little more trust yourself, Mr. Moore: trust in God. We all face God's justice in the end, and even if the police fail to pursue or find Bear's killer, the Lord will take care of him in His own way."

"I really disagree with you, Mrs. Christenson, not with your beliefs, but with the need to pursue the killer. You agreed to prosecute fraudulent claimants. You should be willing to help find and prosecute Bear's killer."

"Mr. Moore, I and the Archdiocese will render the proper legal authorities any assistance that is legally required in the matter of Mr. Pulaski's murder. We are more than willing to cooperate in the pursuit of justice, but not in the pursuit of vengeance, and, Mr. Moore, I must honestly say that it seems to me that it is the latter rather than the former that is motivating you."

Christenson got up from her chair. The meeting was clearly over.

"Mr. Moore, we will continue to disagree, and I will pray for your enlightenment, but I will not reveal the names of the claimants, those either whose claims were deemed legitimate or whose claims were not. Have a nice evening. Sister Patrice will show you out."

13

Richard drove to his condominium in Boston's South End. Housing in the South End is predominately composed of rows of mid-nineteenth-century, five-story, redbrick structures known as *brownstones*

Richard's building ran the length of Willow Street and was one of four that surrounded a courtyard housing first-floor patios, parking spaces, some ancient thick-trunked trees, and an open-space garden. Except for a few brick patios, all ground surfaces were dirt and stones.

Richard turned right on to Willow Street and immediately turned left into the paved alley leading into the courtyard. The alley pitched downward sharply and was barely wide enough for one car. Four such alleys, one at each corner, provided access to the courtyard and off-street parking. The pavement gave way to dirt, and, making two sharp right turns, Richard parked his car facing the back of his building.

Walking around to the front of the building, he climbed the steps and opened the outer door. In the vestibule between the two entry doors, he checked his mailbox then unlocked the inner door and entered the second lobby.

"Regis, how are you this evening?"

Regis was the evening security guard. At sixty-two and slightly out of shape, he was not going to wrestle many thieves to the ground. However, he was passionate about his job and told everyone willing to listen, *No one's going to get burglarized or injured on my watch.*

"Mr. Moore, you look like you could use a drink or two. Had a tough day, did you?"

"Something like that; but no drinks. How was your day?"

"Just fine. me and the missus had the grandkids for the afternoon. We spoiled them rotten and then sent them back to their parents. Life is grand.'

"Good for you. Say 'Hi' to Gwen for me."

Richard walked up the stairs and down the hall to his condominium. The front door opened on a hallway that lead left to the living room at the front of the building and right to the kitchen at the back. The kitchen entrance was on the left of the hallway, and the stairway to his second floor was on the right. Diagonally across from the front door was the entrance to the dining room in which Richard, who preferred to eat in the kitchen or to go out to eat, had haphazardly stored unopened and partially opened moving boxes.

Richard strolled into the living room and slumped into his favorite chair, which he had positioned in the left corner of the room. While sitting, he often looked down the hallway toward his front door, a habit he hardly knew he had. Now, the hallway was dark, the last of the September evening light having given way to the early dark. Richard sat in the gloom and watched the shadows move across the walls and ceiling.

He thought about the day, his friend Bear, and Stephanie. Except for Gloria Stokes, no one greeted him warmly, and no one was open about Bear. *Hostility was the norm for the day,* he thought to himself.

"Hey, Bear, what the hell is up with these people? I thought you always left a good impression." Richard paused. "Now I'm talking to myself. I really can't believe you're gone, friend."

Becoming melancholy or remorseful would only create problems. The investigation was just starting, and he knew that there was much to be done: many to be interviewed, and deceptions to be culled from truth. He also knew that he was more vulnerable now that Rob Lee was above-ground.

As frequently happened, the thought of Rob Lee brought images of Stephanie to his mind. He had met her, worked with her, and nearly been killed with her while investigating the statistically improbable deaths of a series of municipal employees and employee dependents. The investigation eventually led to Rob Lee and the truth about the death of Lori, Richard's wife

Next to his chair, a table supported a lamp and a telephone. Richard picked up the telephone receiver and started to dial Stephanie's number. Halfway through the dialing, he changed his mind and hung up the phone. Whatever the problem with their relationship, Stephanie would have to initiate the conversation.

Richard had some ideas about what might be troubling Stephanie. She was thirty-eight years old, intelligent, attractive, and quite possibly, ready for a commitment. She had mentioned children several times recently. She did not bring the subject up directly. She usually moved the conversation around to her mother talking about grandkids. Since Stephanie was an only child, her mother pushed more than most.

Richard was not sure how he felt about commitment. His whole life had revolved around Lori when they were married. When she died, he could not imagine letting anyone in his life again. At times like this, when he was alone with his thoughts, he would admit to himself that he was deeply in love with Stephanie. However, he could not allow himself to think that he could have the same kind of intimacy with Stephanie that he and Lori shared. Such a thought seemed disrespectful to Lorie and, in a way he could not fathom, somehow dangerous.

Richard knew that part of what was troubling Stephanie was concern for her father. Stephanie and her parents were very close. Stephanie was particularly close to her father. She could sense his moods and see through his smile when things were not going well. She had recently told Richard that she thought something was wrong with her father's business. "Dad's concerned about one of his business investments. He hasn't told me directly, but I can see it. He's not like that. Only one in ten investments actually works out for venture capitalists, so he's not concerned about a company failure. I just can't get him to tell me what's troubling him. He has never shut me out before."

Richard continued thinking about Stephanie and her concern for her father. His thoughts kept coming back to questions about his relationship and feelings for Stephanie. As he thought about Stephanie, the darkness enveloped him. He fell asleep in the chair.

14

Across town, Stephanie also gave consideration to making a telephone call. She wanted to talk with Richard, but decided that their talk should take place face to face. Instead of making the phone call, she went to the gym for an intensive workout.

It was nearly nine-thirty when she arrived back at her apartment. She showered and dressed in sweatpants and a thermal button-front shirt. In the kitchen, she made a sandwich and a cup of green tea.

The pleasant late September night was changing: The temperature outside had dropped fifteen degrees, and clouds blacked out the quarter Moon and surrounding glare. The wind was picking up, and the forecast called for it to increase to howling speeds accompanied by heavy rain later in the night.

Stephanie took her dinner into her home office, sat in the armless desk chair with her left leg folded under her, and turned on her computer. She began surfing the news wires. She wanted to get back to investigative reporting. The interview with the vice president had been assigned by her editor. "We've been after the campaign manager for an interview for months. Now they approved the interview with one condition: you. They want you to do the interview. If you don't do the interview, no one else will, so get going." So she went. It was not as bad as she had envisioned it might be, but it was outside her norm. The chief political writer was outraged.

The interview left Stephanie fascinated with the vice president. She had never met the man and had little interest in politicians in general. "When you're an investigative reporter, you see the seedy side of politicians," she told friends and colleagues who thought it was "cool" that she got to meet influential politicians. However, her time with the vice president was different. He was charming, courteous, direct, and open. Except for his overtures in his hotel suite, he was nothing like what she had expected.

Just after ten, her telephone rang. The caller ID told her that the number was blocked, and she considered leaving the call to her voice mail. On the fourth ring, however, she picked up the receiver.

"Hello."

"Hello, Ms. Lynn?"

"Yes. Who is calling?"

"This is the White House operator. Please hold for the vice president. Mr. Vice President, I have Ms. Lynn on the line. Go ahead."

"Stephanie, I hope I'm not interrupting you."

She was pulling her composure together. Although she had sat with the vice president while she conducted the interview in his limousine, and again in his hotel suite, it was daunting to have him contact her via the White House operator.

"Not at all, Mr. Vice President. I'm just doing some background research in my home office."

"That's good. I was a little nervous about calling you at this hour, however, it was the only time I had a few minutes clear."

"I understand, Mr. Vice President. I generally work late at home."

"I read your article. I must say, my staff was correct: you're thorough and tough, but fair. You did not agree with everything I said, but you didn't tear me apart just to get readership or notoriety. So, I had to call and tell you personally how pleased I was with your article."

"Well, thank you, Mr. Vice President. It is very flattering that you would take the time to call and comment. I imagine that if you did that in response to every balanced article written about you, you would never be able to get the work of the nation accomplished."

"Nonsense, most stories or articles about me are based on the reporter's or editor's preconceived agenda. No one has written or reported with the openness, objectivity, or impartiality that you have."

"Again, thank you."

"I also wanted to assure you that my offer was sincere. I want you to join my administration as assistant White House press secretary."

"As I told you, Mr. Vice President, I'm not sure I can accept your offer—"

"Yes, Yes. I know, but I want you to consider it. Don't just blow it off. We have some time before I take the oath of office, so think about it." His voice changed and assumed a conspiratorial tone. "Off the record, Clint is thinking about resigning shortly after I take office."

Clint Abrams was Vice President Lampert's press secretary and had been with him since his first run for governor of Georgia. He was in his late fifties, lean, balding, and haggard looking. Rumors abounded that his health was failing him.

"Charlene, his wife, has been after him to slow down. She wants more time with him. I guess she's concerned about his health. I want you on board so you can take over as White House press secretary when he goes."

"What? Oh, Mr. Vice President ... I don't know what to say. I'm a print reporter not a pool film reporter, and certainly not a live, on-the-air talking head."

"Nonsense, you'll be great: You can't be shaken. You're not easily intimidated, and you'll have my full support. Listen, I have to go. I just called to comment on your article and to stress how serious I am about having you join my staff. Stan will keep in touch with you. Maybe you two can at least get the security reviews out of the way, even if, in the end, you turn me down. Good night, Stephanie, and stay in touch."

Stephanie wanted to respond to the vice president but never got the chance. As quickly as the telephone call interrupted her dinner, it ended. Stephanie sat back and realized that she had been holding her breath. She exhaled loudly. "White House press secretary, that's one hell of an offer. You sure know how to get my attention, Mr. Vice President." This she said as she stared at the ceiling.

"White House press secretary, that was a nice carrot to dangle in front of her." Stan had been in the hotel suite with the vice president during the telephone call with Stephanie.

"Not a carrot at all. Clint is beginning to look like death. If Stephanie stays out of harm's way, press secretary is a good possibility.'

"You can't be serious. The woman has no experience in front of a camera. She's also dangerous; she likes digging up dirt and exposing skeletons, and she's not a team player."

"Stan, don't be so hard or short sighted. The public will love her; she's intelligent, well spoken, and has one hell of a body. Sex sells, remember, and she'll deliver the party line because she'll be too busy to find another line.

"Stay in touch with her. Develop a ... I don't know ... an adviser, mentor, a sounding board I don't care what just be there in case something come up. Someone fucked up in Boston and I don't want any more surprises."

"Don't worry we will find the kid and that will be the end of the problem."

"I don't worry. That's your job. Just don't give me any more surprises or it won't be you job much longer."

15

Richard was heading west on the Massachusetts Turnpike. The sun was behind him and occasionally shined into his rear view mirror. The Boston bound traffic going in the opposite direction was heavy as thousands of commuters scrambled to get to their destinations before some mishap shut down the morning commute. Richard was aware that the smooth driving he now enjoyed would change as he got closer to Worcester and became part of the inbound Worcester traffic.

He flexed his shoulders to help relieve a mild yet persistent muscle ache. At 1AM, he had woken and found himself in his living-room chair. He went to the kitchen, poured a glass of milk, and downed it in short order. He then went upstairs to his bedroom and slept until five. His usual morning run took him across Storrow Drive near the famous Hatch Memorial Shell where the Boston Pops plays every Fourth of July. He altered this every day by crisscrossing the river using different bridges.

"Richard Moore." He answered his cellphone as he continued driving.

"Oh, good morning, Richard, I hadn't heard from you yesterday and decided that I should call and remind you that you have an appointment to see Congressman Willard."

"Laura, you sound tired. Are you all right?"

"I guess so ... I think the reality of Bear's death is setting in. The girls asked a lot of questions last night. I don't think I slept soundly. I feel beat."

"You want to go home? Marcella can handle the telephone calls."

"Not now. If I don't think I can function, I'll call Marcella."

"OK, you make the call. I'm on the Mass Pike. I'll be at the congressman's office on time. I'll see you after the meeting."

Richard left the turnpike at exit ten and followed Route 146 through Worcester and headed west toward the regional airport and his destination, Goddard Memorial Drive. Goddard, which is named for the Worcester rocket pioneer and Clark University professor, Robert H. Goddard, is home to a variety of warehouses, research and development companies, and a few office buildings. Congressman Willard's office was on the third floor of one of the latter, a bright brushed aluminum building.

Richard pulled into the parking lot, parked as far away from all the other cars as possible, got out, and looked around. *Not exactly the kind of place I'd expect to find the office of a congressman*, he said to himself.

As he walked across the parking lot, the sun cast his movements as shadows on the asphalt. The temperature was a pleasant sixty-eight degrees, at least six degrees warmer than Boston. It was, Richard thought, a lovely late September day.

White stencil letters on a solid glass door set in an aluminum frame told the unaware that this was Congressman Willard's office. Richard preferred wood instead of glass for office doors. He also preferred stairs to elevators and had taken the stairs to the third floor.

The office was disproportionately long to its width or maybe the other way around. The effect was less than warm or inviting. The waiting area was similar to many physicians' waiting areas. Several uncomfortable chairs lined the far wall, and a small table was covered with outdated magazines. At least the corners of the magazines were not dog-eared. Apparently, no one visited the congressman, or, if they did, they did not read the magazines.

The nearest desk was surrounded by a fabric partition forty-eight inches high. The receptionist, who looked to Richard like a young woman still in college, was busy typing and watching the computer screen. Richard cleared his throat and said, "I'm Richard Moore. I have an appointment with the congressman."

The young lady looked up. "Hi, I'm Cindy. I know the congressman was expecting you. Let me check with him?"

Cindy picked up her telephone headset and dialed a number. "Mr. Moore is here for Congressman Willard." She listened to the response. "I'll tell him."

"Mr. Moore, Congressman Willard will be with you shortly. Would you like some coffee while you wait?"

"No, thank you. I had my fill during the drive."

"Just as well, I hear the coffee is really bad. I don't drink coffee myself. I'll be right back." Cindy walked down a long corridor flanked on each side by desks holding computer monitors, telephones, and stacks of paper. A staffer at each of the eight desks was intently occupied searching through the paper and talking on the telephone.

Richard took his time surveying the office and activity. He then turned to the window and surveyed the view of the surrounding area.

"On a bright, sunny day such as this, it's really a beautiful picture." Richard turned and found Cindy behind him. When he had heard her approaching, he wondered if she would tap him on the shoulder or step around in front of him before announcing that the congressman would see him now.

"The area is very nice. Looks as if it has recently gone through a phase of development," he commented

"Yes, it has. That area to the right across Goddard Memorial Drive was built four years ago. The congressman was one of the first to purchase a house. You can see it from here. He loves it here. He can walk to and from the office and the airport."

"Very convenient.. Have you worked for the congressman long?"

"Off and on for four years. I helped when he moved the office in here. I'm a student at WPT, so I only work here when I have time off from my studies."

"Did you ever meet Jan Pulaski?"

"Ms. Wingate should be ready for you now. Are you sure you don't want something to drink?"

"No, thank you." *That was a quick change*, he thought to himself.

At the end of the office suite, four doors, all closed, brought their walk to a stop.

"This is Ms. Wingate's office," Cindy said as she pointed to the first door on Richard's left.

"That one is the congressman's office." She was referring to the last door on the left.

"These two on the right are the conference room and our break room. The break room was supposed to be another office, but we haven't needed it yet so the staff gets to use it." She knocked on Ms. Wingate's office door and a voice from the other side said to come in.

Cindy held the door as Richard entered the office. She then closed the door and headed back to her desk.

"Mr. Moore, I'm Eleanor Wingate. Please have a seat." She motioned toward a chair but did not offer a handshake greeting.

Richard sat and stared at Eleanor, doing his usual quick assessment: Five-feet, six-inches tall, one-hundred-and-fifty pounds, auburn hair cut shoulder-length, too much make-up, off-the-rack skirt and jacket, married, and not pleased with this meeting. "Ms. Wingate, thank you for seeing me today. Will the congressman be joining us shortly?"

"No, he will not. He had an urgent meeting. It is election time. His schedule often gets moved around. It gets hectic as Election Day comes closer. I am his chief of staff; anything you need, I will be able to handle. What can I do for you, Mr. Moore?"

Richard was certain she knew why he was there. "Sunday night, Mr. Pulaski was shot and killed. I'm investigating his murder. I understand that he was hired by the congressman to investigate some threats against the congressman's life. It would be logical to assume that if Bear had gotten close to identifying the person threatening the congressman, that that person may have been Bear's killer. I would like to know what progress he might have made and reported to the congressman. I would also like to have a look at the letters you received."

"Are you here in an official police capacity?"

"I am not. I am a licensed investigator."

"Well, Mr. Moore, I believe your information is inaccurate."

"Oh! And how is that?"

"Mr. Pulaski helped provide security at a couple of political rallies. The local police felt they were understaffed and needed additional help. Bear, as you call him, was hired to augment the local police. He arraigned for additional security. That's all, and, since you are not here in official police capacity, I don't think I want to go into his employment further."

Richard watched her very closely. He was not sure if she really expected him to believe what she just told him. Her movements under his eye contact and the flush coloring of her face told him that she hoped he would.

"Fair enough, but, before I leave, let me tell you what I know; Bear was investigating threats against the congressman. Those threats were received in this office by mail. Bear has been murdered and the murderer may have been the person or persons who threatened the congressman's life. Ms. Wingate you can tell me you never received threats against the congressman and that Bear's murder had nothing to do with his investigation, but the police investigating his murder will eventually come calling. You will have to tell them or you will be obstructing justice. I feel an obligation to notify the FBI and other Government agencies about the threats just to make sure that the congressman's life is not in danger and that Bear's murder was not related to the threats the congressman received."

Richard noticed that the yellow light on Ms. Wingate's phone set went out. Within seconds, a door in the wall behind her opened, and a man entered the office, walked over to Richard, and extended his hand.

"Mr. Moore, I'm Kiel Willard. I apologize for the change in schedule. Election time can be devilish on my schedule. I hope Elli will be able to help you. I wasn't able to brief her before you arrived. Mr. Pulaski was a good man. I was very distressed to hear about Bear's death. Anything that we have that you think will be of help in solving his murder we will be pleased to provide. Just ask Ellie; she runs this place. She knows all the details and knows where everything is filed. Just one favor, I would prefer the threats be kept confidential unless they prove to be germane to the investigation. That's why I hired Bear: to help keep them quiet. I have to run. Call me. I would like to have some time to sit and talk with you."

As they shook hands, Richard said, "Thank you, Congressman. I appreciate the help, and I will call."

"Good. Good. It's set then." Turning to Ellie, he continued, "Ellie, anything, anything at all, get it to Mr. Moore.

16

An hour after Congressman Willard left his office; Richard was traversing the streets of Worcester heading back toward Boston. Ellie had answered most of his questions and given him copies of the threatening letters and Bear's reports. His initial impression was that Bear had made little progress in identifying the source of the threats.

Richard pulled into a rest area on the Massachusetts Turnpike to get some coffee and make a couple of phone calls. He avoided talking on his cellphone while driving as much as possible.

"Laura, Richard."

"Hi, Richard, how did your meetings go?"

"I'm not sure. Not well, I guess. I have to think about them before I render an opinion. How are you and the girls doing?"

"I think the girls are doing better than me. What happened at your meetings? Why did you say they did not go well?'

"I'll fill you in when I see you later. I'm on my way to the morgue to pick up Bear's personal belongings and to talk with the pathologist. Any messages?"

"Steve called. Said he is taking the red-eye out tonight and would like you to pick him up at the airport at seven-fifteen."

"I didn't think he would come to Boston until the funeral. Tell him I'll see him in the morning."

"OK. David Lynn called. She wanted to remind you about lunch today. He will meet you at the Copley."

"David. I did forget. Tell him I will be about an hour late. He or you can call me if we have to reschedule."

"That's it for now—oh, no, wait, I almost forgot. Phil called and said that he found the car of your dreams. You should call him when you have a chance. Will I see you after your lunch?"

"I'll call Phil. I have some items he can take care of for me. I should drop by my office and see Marcella since I will be downtown. It may be late, four or four-thirty, before I get to Woburn. You don't have to hang around."

"OK. We will see how the day goes. Anything else?"

"No, thanks, I'll talk with you later."

Richard pulled into the small parking area at the side of the building that housed the Office of the Chief Medical Examiner. The sandstone-colored-brick, five-story building gave little exterior clues about the importance of the work performed inside. Most people would refer to it as the morgue.

The autopsies were performed in the basement of the building and that is where Richard headed. Doctor Amanda Lee Ash had just finished an autopsy on the teen victim of a drive-by shooting. Amanda and Richard had known each other since his time with the Boston Police Department.

"Richard, what brings you to the basement of the dead? I haven't seen you in, what, five years?"

"Hi, Amanda," he said, leaning forward to give her an imaginary kiss on each cheek. "I'm picking up personals of a friend. Do you remember Jan Pulaski, the Bear?"

"No. I don't ever remember meeting him. I do remember you talking about him, however. If I remember correctly, you and he were very close. I'm sorry for your loss."

"Thank you, Amanda."

"If you're here for his things, it must have been bad. When did he come in?"

"Last Sunday night or early Monday morning, depending on when the log was filled in. Gunshot, two rounds."

"I remember that one. I almost did the post, but Shillings got the call."

"Shillings, I thought he retired. Four years ago, he had to worry that if he laid down on one of the tables, someone would mistake him for one of the dead bodies. Where can I find him?"

Doctor Nate Shillings was in Room Four performing an autopsy on a middle-aged white female. The woman's two teenage children waited patiently in their respective lockers for their turn on Doctor Shilling's table. Her husband was down the street recuperating on the seventh floor of Boston City Hospital. Something they ate hastened their death.

Shillings raised his head and saw Richard watching through the wide glass observation window. He waved at him, signaled for him to enter the room, and returned to his work. Without taking his eyes off his work, when he heard the door close, he said, "The family went to a local restaurant for dinner. Two hours after they returned home, the father calls 911 and everyone gets a ride. Three came here to me and one went to the hospital. They ingested a nasty case of poison. My bet is the husband did it. What do you think?"

"Nate, do you see murder behind everybody that gets brought in here?"

"Not everybody, only the unusual, like this one. So, what do you think?"

"The odds are with you. Unexpected death is usually caused by a family member, spouse specifically, or close friend."

"Yes. I will find the poison then I'll find out if it had been in the food or ingested some other way. Later we will see why the husband didn't ingest enough to die along with his family. Always a spouse or close friend, except for the one yesterday." Shilling raised his head and looked at Richard.

"I was told you did the post on Bear. Did you back me into that corner for a reason?"

"No, Richard, I meant no such trickery; I was concentrating only on this woman and her family. Bear is a different matter entirely." He removed his gloves and stepped back from the table. "I'm sure you came to talk about Bear, not this woman, so let's get a cup of coffee, shall we?"

A room at the end of the hall was used for breaks. Inside was a counter with a small stainless-steel sink. A coffee pot and toaster flanked by a refrigerator were on the opposite end of the counter. Four stackable chairs surrounded a round, Formica-topped table. Shillings and Richard sat down and placed their cups on the table.

"I can't tell you anything you don't already know, or that you don't already suspect."

"Maybe not yet, Nate, but possibly later?"

"Yes, possibly, first let me confirm what you already know. Bear was shot twice by a nine-millimeter handgun. I pulled two slugs out of Bear, but I doubt they will ever be matched to the weapon used. He took some time to die. Not much, couple of minutes anyway. I found a blade of some kind in his hand. It fits into his belt buckle."

"Bear had that buckle specially made," Richard recounted. "The blade is balanced so it can be thrown, and it is concealed as part of his belt buckle."

"Yes, very ingenious and excellent workmanship. He obviously lived long enough to stab or cut his assailant. The blood on the blade and his hand was not his type. I sent a sample of the blood out for DNA testing. Other than that, there is nothing to report."

"The state investigators labeled it a mugging gone bad."

"Ha! Mugging? Richard you and I know this was a hit by a professional. Maybe. Bear's money, credit cards, and car were taken, but he was killed first, then mugged. This was not a mugging gone bad. Also, they moved the body. What mugger do you know who would take the time to move a body?"

Although Richard had been working on the presumption Bear had been the target of a hit and not a random victim, Nate's confirmation, removing, as it did, any doubt, still sent a jolt through him and eliminated whatever reservations he may have had. However, all he said was, "OK, Nate. I really came by to get Bear's personal belongings and find out when the body will be released."

"We won't have the results of toxicology for another week. Detective Kelly hasn't signed the paperwork to release the body. He told me he would wait until the tox was back."

"Nate, any idea why he is delaying the release? You don't need the body. Even if the lab lost the samples, you have backup. Don't you?"

"No idea. I told the detective we didn't need the body. He said he would get to the release later."

"Thanks, Nate," Richard said somewhat absently. His head was already working out contingency plans, some of them illegal.

"What are you thinking, Richard?"

"How to motivate Detective Kelly and get Bear's remains released."

17

Entering the restaurant in the Copley Plaza, Richard tried again to reach Detective Kelly or his partner. Both were out and neither had called. He left another message.

David Lynn was seated at a table next to a window with a view of James Street. He rose as Richard approached the table. "Richard," he greeted openly, giving Richard a strong handshake and a pat on the back. "I'm glad we got this opportunity to have lunch. We don't get together as much as we should, I mean, given the fact that both our offices are downtown here."

"David, you are absolutely right. We do not get together as much as we should. I think we have been unusually preoccupied."

"Yes, I only wish you did not have to investigate the death of your friend. So tragic."

"Thank you. And you, you have had some problems that have been consuming your time."

"My problems have been insignificant compared to the loss of your friend, but you're correct, they did consume me. I'm sure that's why you wanted to talk."

"David, your daughter has been very worried about you. She's very concerned that you've had to borrow large sums to fund your operations, and she thinks that she's losing touch with you."

David sat quietly for a few moments after Richard finished talking. Richard could see the concern crossing David's face. David's eyes reddened and Richard thought for a moment that he might cry.

"I know of Stephanie's concerns about my financial dealings, and I knew she was not satisfied with our conversations. I did not, however, realize she thought we were losing touch. That fact hurts me. To think I left her feeling shutout or that I didn't want her input." He paused and shook his head.

"The things we do, Richard, without contemplating the impact on loved ones." Again, he paused, this time turning his head to look out the window. After some time, he turned back to look at Richard. "You know, when we decided to have lunch, I thought this would be great. I have good news: my financial problems are behind me. From what you just told me, however, my problems are larger than I imagined. It seems I have more work to do, but don't worry, Richard, Stephanie's concerns about losing touch will be alleviated. I guarantee it."

The waitress came to their table and took their order. David ordered a substantial lunch, while Richard ordered a half sandwich and soup.

"So, your business problems are behind you?" Richard asked as the waitress busied herself setting silverware and plates on the table.

"I won't bore you with the details, but the biotech company I funded finalized a deal with the Government. The return on investment will not be as great as I had hoped for, but at least I can repay all the investors and provide some return on their capital."

"Stephanie told me that you branched out into biotech but never mentioned that the Government was involved.'

"I didn't know until this past weekend. The founder met with me over the weekend and told me he had completed a deal and that I would be receiving a visit and a check. With all I have been through, I was very pissed at him. The founder doesn't get to sell without the investors reviewing the deal and giving their approval. He told me to take it up with the Department of Defense, cocky little ass.

"The deal was good enough, however, and now I can go back to a normal existence. I think I'll find a pet-care chain to invest in." He smiled and laughed a little. David had started out with his own pet store many years before.

"So, now Stephanie will only have to worry about you, and staying alive." David looked Richard in the eyes. His stare hardened, and his whole body stiffened. "In case you haven't realized it, Stephanie is concerned about what might happen to you and to her if you continue chasing … what is his name? … Lee something."

"Rob Lee," Richard responded. "She told you she was concerned about her safety?"

"In so many words? No, but two attempts on her life have left her scared and vulnerable. She frequently talks about those incidents like a person who is anticipating more of them."

Richard went blank. He was careful about dealing with Rob Lee but not overly concerned about his personal safety. His training taught him to be cautious, prepared, and self-confident. Richard and Stephanie came out of the two incidents David mentioned without a scratch. Richard always worked as though the results would be as he planned.

Stephanie had never mentioned her concern about her safety. Their daily routine just moved on. It was not as though they were being hunted or stalked. Richard was the hunter and the stalker.

David did not wait for Richard to respond. "Stephanie is also concerned about where she will be five years from now, assuming that she survives. She has a birthday in a couple of days. It is a reminder that she is running out of time if she is to have a family, a family that includes children." David watched Richard closely as the information sank in.

The server brought their lunch, and David started cutting his lamb as though he was giving Richard time to work through his reply. When Richard started to speak, however, David held up his hand and said, "I understand your desire to bring in the man responsible for the death of your wife, but you are consumed with finding Rob Lee. If you are, are you prepared for the cost? Do you expect Stephanie to mark time in her personal life while you pursue this man?"

David wiped his mouth with his napkin, took a deep breath, and continued, "This is my daughter we are talking about. While I would like to see Stephanie get married and have children, I'll be content whether she does or doesn't marry and does or doesn't have children, as long as she is happy. If she stays happy and never has children, I'm OK. Her mother would be disappointed, but I can't change that. Richard, I am sure that when it comes to Stephanie's welfare, you have nothing but good intentions, but as long as Stephanie's relationship with you puts her life in danger, I don't want you to have any intentions toward her at all. I would rather you fade off into wherever you Special Ops fade off to. If you think I'm overreacting or that Stephanie's fear is overrated, think about what happened to your friend, Bear."

David stood up and put his hand on Richard's shoulder. "I have to leave now. I have said more than I should have. Stephanie will be very upset with me for telling you all this. Richard, I have gotten to know you, and I really like you and value your friendship, but Stephanie comes before you."

David left Richard sitting at the table. Neither man had eaten much of his meal. The server came by, and, when Richard asked for the check, said, "Mr. Lynn took care of the check. He said the next one is on you."

Richard left the restaurant and tried to keep focused on the investigation. Several more calls to the state detectives went unanswered. He gave serious thought to tracking the detectives down and confronting them, but decided that, in his present state of mind, such a confrontation would only lead to trouble. *Tomorrow. If I don't hear from either of you by tomorrow morning, I will find a way around you.*

While in Bear's office in Woburn, Richard called Stephanie. Laura had left shortly after four-thirty. Stephanie answered the phone on the third ring.

"Hey, you; I was about to call you. You have ESP?"

"If you mean are you on my mind, always."

"That's nice to know."

"How was your day?"

"Boring; I spent most of it reviewing records from contractors who worked the Big Dig."

"Why would you do that?"

"Those leaks in the tunnel, I got word that there were fraudulent invoices for material and labor that may be connected with the defects causing the leaks."

"A lot of money was involved. You could make some people very unhappy."

"I don't write to make people happy. Let's talk about this over dinner. How about Lucia's?"

"That sounds good. How long before you leave?"

"I'm headed to the car now. I have two stops along the way."

"See you in an hour."

18

    Richard emptied the contents of the manila envelope onto the desk. Bear's personal items: billfold, loose change, gold necklace with a gold crucifix, and one pen. He took the billfold and removed the items from it: one gas receipt, health-insurance card, gun-club membership card, driver's license, and gun permit. Missing were Bear's car keys, credit cards, paper money and cellphone. As Richard spread the items out neatly across the desk, he wondered if anything was missing from that night.
    Richard studied the items on the desk. The killer had held some of the items, but none of them screamed out the killer's name. "I hadn't expected you to but I was hoping for more help," he said as he got up and left the office.
    Lucia's is a neighborhood restaurant in South Boston that serves Boston seafood, Italian dishes, and fast-fare specials. Richard and Stephanie were regular patrons.
    Stephanie had arrived first and was seated at a table in the left-rear corner. Richard walked to the table, leaned over, and gave her a kiss. He then sat down next to her, his back toward the main room. It was not a comfortable feeling for him.
    "I don't think I have ever seen you sit with your back toward the door or the main activity in a room," Stephanie said with a smile.
    "I didn't want to sit across from you, and there is only a wall on the other side of this table." He was working very hard not to look over his shoulder.
    "I had lunch with your father today."
    "You did? And how was dad today?"
    "He was in a good mood. Apparently, the problem with the company he funded has been resolved. His finances are back on track, or will be soon."
    "Really! That is such good news. I have been so worried about him."
    "I know. He thought he was the only one feeling the problem."
    "He did? How do you know?"

Richard related his conversation with Stephanie's dad. He left out all of the conversation about Richard and Stephanie's relationship.

"I think he will have more information for you. I would be surprised if he doesn't call you by tomorrow morning."

"That is such good news. What a relief. So, any update about the investigation into Bear's murder from the police?"

"None, It is not a priority for the detectives. They haven't even started contacting his former clients."

The server stopped at their table, and they ordered wine. Richard seldom drank alcohol.

"You're joining me in a drink. What's the occasion?" Stephanie asked.

"No occasion, we've had wine together before."

"Oh!" A sly smile crossed her face. "We share wine in a different setting." The server placed the glasses of wine in front of them. Stephanie picked her's up and, looking over the top of the glass, asked, "You planning on getting lucky tonight?"

"I got lucky when I first met you." They clicked glasses and each took a sip. The server returned to their table, and they ordered dinner.

"So, what happens if the police will not investigate Bear's murder aggressively? Are you going to pull some strings and get them to change their priorities?"

"The two State Police detectives assigned are not going to respond well to pressure. I'll have to find out who and why Bear was murdered on my own."

"You still think it was Rob Lee?"

"I do. But I don't know why, and I can't rule out any of Bear's clients."

"So, call Charles at the FBI or the spook at the CIA and have them track down Rob Lee. If the detectives have a problem working the case, we have enough contacts to have them replaced. Let's make the call."

Richard noticed a change in Stephanie's body language, but before either of them could say anything further, dinner was served, and they ate in silence

When they had finished, the server suggested desert and both declined. Richard ordered coffee; Stephanie ordered scotch on the rocks. She was avoiding eye contact with Richard.

"What's the problem, Stephanie?" Richard asked after the server had brought their drinks.

Stephanie took a gulp of scotch and stared at the glass while she rubbed her index finger in circles on the rim. She continued this for some time as she tried to control her emotions and respond in a noncombative way. The effort was minimally effective as she said, "Why do you have to investigate Bear's murder yourself? Why are you obsessed with tracking Rob Lee? Why don't you let the police and other agencies do their jobs? Why—"

Richard cut her off by raising his right hand in the universal stop sign. "Rob Lee was responsible for my wife's death and the death of many other people, sick, vulnerable people whose only error was to be insured by Rob Lee's company." He paused, collecting his thoughts and emotions. "I owe my wife and the others peace by bringing Rob Lee to justice. Now it looks as if I owe it to Bear to find Rob Lee. Using your skills to correct a wrong can hardly be called an obsession. Part of my contract with the Government and my decision to operate a private company is based on pursuing Rob Lee. I—"

This time it was she who interrupted

"Yes, you! Bear and who knows how many others have been chasing this guy for a year, only to find out where he has been after he's left the scene. Now Bear is dead, possibly because he was hunting Rob Lee with you." Stephanie's complexion changed noticeably red. "The last time you and I saw him he was saying, 'Goodbye.' Why, because his men were about to shoot us." Stephanie's voice had become louder, her tone more sarcastic. "Now it looks like Rob Lee might have killed Bear. Who's next? Me?"

Richard's expression conveyed his dismay at her last comment.

She continued, "Oh, you didn't think about me as a possible target, did you? Why was it easy for him to get Bear and the others, and why will it be easy to get me? I'll tell you why. We live out in the open. We're easy to find. You can't find Rob Lee because he's hiding. He's hiding behind fake passports, fake credit cards, and a dozen new names. He doesn't even have to come out of the shadows to get at us; he has people to do it for him. All he has to do is make a phone call."

"OK, Stephanie, I know all of that. You're right, but it's the same for any investigation."

"Any investigation; this isn't any investigation. It's the continuation of a manhunt, a manhunt for a former spook with the CIA. He's cunning, allusive, dangerous, and probably still well-connected."

"Sounds like some of the guys who worked on the Big Dig." His attempt at humor only brought a cold stare from Stephanie.

"I'm not trying to put them in jail or a coffin ... but let's not go there. We could discuss this until the next ice age, and we would not see eye to eye. I need to get home and finish some research."

"OK." Richard stood and held Stephanie in his arms for a moment. "We still on for the theater on your birthday?"

She lifted her head and looked in his eyes. *God, I love you so much*, she wanted to say. "Yeah, sure. Maybe we'll get lucky. Just don't bring any company."

19

At six-forty-five the following morning, Richard was waiting outside Terminal C at Logan International Airport when Steve Deschenes came through the door of the terminal. He had a carry-on suitcase hanging from his right shoulder, and each hand carried a cup of coffee and a waxed paper bag. As he approached Richard he asked, "What the hell is this?"

"What is what?" Richard replied with a grin.

"You know what; this ... this ... Where is your BMW?"

"It is in the shop for regular maintenance. Besides, it is a beautiful fall morning. The top comes down on this, and we can enjoy the ride."

Steve had dropped the carry-on to the pavement and was walking around the car. "How old is this? And does it run? I mean, it looks great, but is it reliable?" He handed Richard a cup of coffee and one of the bags.

Richard placed the coffee and bagel on the front seat, opened the trunk, and tossed Steve's carry-on in. "This, my friend, is a classic 1966 Mercury Comet Cyclone GT with a three hundred ninety cubic inch V-8 engine and a four speed stick. It runs because I personally rebuilt the engine and transmission. I put in some modern accessories."

"How do you find the time to work on the old cars you get?" Although he started out sarcastically about the car, Steve admired Richard for his craftsmanship and his ability to shelve day-to-day stuff and unwind working on a hobby. Steve wanted to be able to bury himself in a hobby for a couple of hours a month, but knew he would never get to that point.

"I like the work: no deadlines, no administrative reports, and no one's life hanging in the balance. In reality, I do not get as much time to work on the cars as I would like. This one took me over two years." Richard maneuvered the car through the jumble of traffic around the airport and descended into the Ted Williams Tunnel.

"I haven't been to Boston in years," Steve said, as he worked on his coffee and donut. "I assume this is part of the Big Dig for which I helped pay."

"It is, and you haven't stopped paying. You may never stop helping to pay for this scenic, underground, leaking tube. I'm taking you to your hotel first."

"If you don't mind, I would like to see where Bear was killed first."

This caught Richard by surprise, and the surprise showed on his face. "Why in the world would you want to see where he was killed? There isn't much there except the building and street."

"A very smart investigator and tactician once taught me to gather as much intelligence and background as possible. The information helps to identify plausible scenarios and gives a base for developing a picture of events." Steve let out a sigh of relief as they exited the tunnel: the wall had not given way and they did not drown.

"It has yet to be proved that he was, or is, a smart investigator. As for being a tactician, based on current result, the objective might not be obtained," responded Richard.

"Self-doubt is not an operational prerogative. That's a saying from the same smart guy."

Richard pulled up to the curb in front of the building where Bear was shot. He and Steve got out, and Richard described the events, as he knew them.

"What about those security cameras? Did they get any useful images of what happened?

"The owners of the building are new. They said the security system was in place when they purchased the building, but they never connected it."

"Do you know when they purchase the building?" Steve asked, as he walked from side to side looking up at the cameras.

"The records indicate four years ago. Why do you ask?"

"These cameras are Action 1500 series outdoor, day-night IP Bullet cameras. They're motion sensitive and produce high resolution images. Either the person answering your question about the system was misinformed, or they lied to you."

Richard knew he was out of his element when talking technology with Steve. When he had been assigned to Richard's Special Operations Unit for a mission designed to *retrieve* a foreign diplomat, Steve neutralized some of the most sophisticated detection, communication, and security systems the unit had ever encountered. Steve Jobs had tried to recruit Steve shortly after Steve left the military. Steve chose instead to start his own company. Still, Richard had to ask, "Why is that Steve?"

"Simple. The technology is expensive, is virtually tamper-proof, and it was not available until three years ago. The system had to have been upgraded by the new owners, and no one would do that and then fail to use it. If the system was disabled, then it was disabled by the new owners. If it wasn't, then those cameras should have recorded the shooting. The system logs will tell me the answer."

"It will take a search warrant to find out the answer. I'll talk with the Stoneham chief of police. Seen enough?"

"Yeah, it was worth the stop, but I am tired. I'd like to get some shut-eye before I head over to the office."

It was a ten-minute ride to the King's Castle hotel. Richard scanned the lobby while Steve went to the front desk to check in. The area was set up as an indoor courtyard. Skylights formed the ceiling seven stories above the umbrella-covered tables. The guest rooms encompassed slightly more than two-thirds of the courtyard.

Steve turned from the front desk and said, "I'm all set. Room is on the fifth floor with a lovely view of the access road to the front of the building."

Richard went up with Steve to the room. He wanted to check out the accommodations. "No telling how long you might be living here. Might as well make sure it's comfortable. You want to call me when you're ready to come to the office?"

"I really am tired. I hate that red-eye flight. Don't know when I'll be ready to come to the office. I'll pick up the rental and get to the office on my own."

20

After Richard left, Steve turned on the TV and listened to the morning commentator as he watched the access road below. "Vice President Lampert is in an unprecedented position. Ahead in the polls by ten percent and still raking in millions of dollars in campaign contributions, he is outspending his opponent four to one. The vice president cannot lose unless he makes a monumental error, and, with only six weeks left in the campaign, that is not likely to happen."

Steve had heard the same analysis by different political analysts from the West Coast. He paid little attention to the one on the TV in his room. He was waiting for Richard to appear. *There he goes. Nice car Richard.* Steve was talking silently to himself. *In that car, you could be found from a mile away, even in Boston's noted rush hour traffic.*

Steve walked over to his carryon bag and opened a zippered flap. He took out three cellphones and two file folders. He then went downstairs to the car rental desk and rented a car.

He drove south on Interstate 95. His first meeting was scheduled for the lobby of the Double Tree Hotel in Waltham. As he walked through the lobby, Steve saw Craig sitting in a plush chair in front of a bar. Steve and Craig shook hands and sat. A pot of coffee and two cups were on the table in front of the men.

"I could use more of this," Steve said as he poured himself a cup.

"Long flight?" Craig knew the answer. He knew the flights and the layovers Steve took to get to Boston.

"It isn't the length, I can't sleep on a plane, and I was up at four yesterday." He took another gulp of coffee. "You got my e-mail?"

"I did. It seems pretty straightforward. Not a problem. I actually think I might get bored." Craig smiled

"Well, don't, and don't get macho either. Just handle the assignment. If you need any help," Steve reached into his pocket and brought out one of the cellphones, "hold down any two buttons. You will be immediately connected to me. The phone has GPS positioning, and the connection between us is encrypted."

"I don't need help. Just give me Richard's itinerary. I'll do my job."

"Use the phone." Steve now took out a file folder. "Here's the data: car license number, telephone numbers, favorite restaurants, et cetera. If I missed anything, call on that phone. I'll get you what you need."

"When do I get started?" Craig was moving in his chair. He didn't enjoy sitting in one place in the open for long.

"I'll know later today."

They departed by going in separate directions. Steve's next meeting was at the Marriott in Newton, just two exits further south on 95.

When he arrived, Steve found that Hawk, the man he was meeting, had chosen to sit at a table in the restaurant that gave him a commanding view of the lobby and the entrance to the hotel parking lot. As Steve sat down, Hawk said, "I ordered you some iced tea. I think you had too much coffee."

"And what would make you think I had too much coffee?" Hawk, Steve knew, was one of the CIA's best trackers. Once Hawk had a target in his sights, it was nearly impossible to shake him. Steve assumed Hawk had been following him all morning.

"Am I right, or not?"

"OK, Hawk, you're correct."

"Good, but we will not be here long. What do you have for me?" Hawk's eyes never focused on Steve. They were in constant motion reviewing every detail of the restaurant, wait staff, and grounds outside the window.

Steve gave him the file folder. "Stephanie's data, she's usually in the office early." He took out the cellphone. "Use this phone to communicate with me." Steve gave Hawk the same instructions as he had given to Craig.

"All right, Steve. I know this is important to you. It will be done your way, but you owe me an explanation when it is finished."

"I know, Hawk. I know."

Steve went back to the hotel and fell asleep.

21

After dropping Steve off at the hotel, Richard went to Bear's office. Laura greeted him when he arrived.

"Hey, stranger, how has your investigation gone?"

"I really don't know. I just haven't been able to make sense of my conversations with the three groups. I think I need to get away for a couple of days." He went into the Bear's office and sat at his desk.

Laura followed him into the office. She wanted to ask more about his conversations with Bear's clients but decided to wait until later.

"Here's a receipt for gas Bear had in his wallet," Richard said, as he held it up for Laura to take.

She studied the receipt. "Oh, this is from one of the times Bear disappeared."

"What do you mean disappeared?"

"Bear always told me where he was going even when he was leaving on vacation. Six months or so ago, he told me he would be gone for a couple of days. I asked him where he was going, but he didn't say. He didn't ask for travel assistance, and I didn't see any charges on his credit cards."

"Was that the only time he did that?"

"No. Two times after that, he was gone for two days each time. I thought maybe he found himself a female companion."

"But, he didn't, or he would have told you. You have no idea where he went or why?"

"None."

"Check out that receipt, and find out where the station is located. I think I'll pay them a visit."

Richard piled several spiral bound notebooks from one of the drawers in Bear's desk. Bear had a habit of writing notes to himself in the notebooks and lining them out when the task or issue they referred to had been resolved. In some instances the note was just a name, location, or company. Richard paged through the books looking for any unusual notes, but nothing caught his eye.

"The gas station is located on Route 79 in South Dakota, a little more than half an hour's drive south of Rapid City."

"South Dakota! What the hell was he doing there? His notebooks make no reference to South Dakota. Did you come across anything referring to South Dakota?"

"Until now, nothing. This receipt is the only indication he might have been in that state."

"The date corresponds to when he was missing?"

"Yes, it does."

"OK. Can you get me to Rapid City?"

"If you can get to the airport in two hours, you can be in Rapid City by four this afternoon. I can get you a late flight out of Rapid City tomorrow, and you will arrive at Logan Airport around eight thirty tomorrow evening."

Richard thought about the quick turnaround. "Well, I don't have any more leads here, so I might as well find out what I can in South Dakota. Besides, I did say I needed a couple of days away. I can use the flight time to sort things out. I'll see you in forty-eight hours."

22

Richard's flight to Rapid City was uneventful and unproductive. He had hoped the flight would provide the opportunity to sort out the events of the past several days and allow him to piece together some of the information he had gathered. He had accomplished neither. Whenever he tried to concentrate on the events of the previous week, his mind became a jumble of images of Bear, the friend he had lost, and Stephanie, the woman he appeared to be losing. By the time the flight ended, he was wondering if he would be able to resolve either situation successfully.

Cruising along Route 79 South from Rapid City, did nothing to eliminate the mental flashbacks. The road split the flat terrain into two equal slices of boredom. Farmland spread for miles on either side of the four-lane highway. The sun was low in the sky to his right but still cast a bright glare across the landscape.

An hour after leaving the airport terminal, Richard spied the service station where Bear had stopped for gas. He also saw something that made him believe that his mind was still playing tricks on him: a model airplane was flying in the sky just ahead and to his right.

The plane was doing loops and diving low before angling almost straight up to repeat the performance as Richard pulled into the service station's parking area. In the office, a young man in his late teens sat in a chair and watched Richard's car drive in. He had not gotten out of his chair by the time Richard walked into the office.

"You work here?"

The young man looked at Richard with an *Are you serious?* expression on his face. "I wouldn't pick this place just to hang around."

"I'm looking for someone who might have seen a friend of mine a few months ago, large man, six feet six, around two hundred and seventy-five pounds, black, looks like a football lineman."

"Don't play football and can't stand watching it. Maybe the owner's son can help you."

Richard waited a few seconds. "Is the owner's son around?"

"Yeah, out back in the field. He's playing with his models."

Richard spotted the owner's son about three hundred yards southwest of the station. He watched the plane doing tricks in the air as he approached the young man.

"Hi, I'm Richard Moore. I hope you might be able to help me."

"Hold on for a minute. I have to bring the plane in for a landing."

As the young man manipulated the remote controls to land a model of a British WW II Mosquito, Richard took a close look at him. While the youth's face was pockmarked from severe acne, and he was overweight, his jeans, shirt, and jacket were stylish and clean. It was, however, the intensity and care the youth showed as he used the controls and watched his model plane react that impressed Richard most.

As the plane taxied to their feet, Richard was sure he recognized it.

"There she is, safe and sound. Sorry about that. I'm Rick. How can I help you?" Rick asked, as he held out his hand to shake with Richard.

"I had a friend who loved flying those models. I was wondering if you might have met him a couple of months ago. He was a big guy, around two hundred and seventy-five pounds, six feet—"

"Bear. Black guy goes by the nickname, Bear, right?"

"You know him?"

"That plane was from him. He stopped here a few months ago, like you said. He got gas. Didn't really need any, but stopped for directions and, when he saw me flying my model, asked if he could fly 'er. He sure made my simple plane do some tricks. Next time he came out, he brought me this plane. Taught me how to push it right to its limit. He spent hours teaching me. Can't wait to see him again. You said he's a friend of yours?"

Richard did not want to tell the boy that Bear was dead. He did need to know where Bear was heading when he asked for directions. "You said he asked for directions; where was he headed?"

"Actually, he asked me if I knew Father Grant. He's the priest at Saint Andrew's in Buffalo Gap."

"Did he say why he wanted to know if you knew Father Grant?"

"Just said he had an appointment with Father. He knew the church was off 79 but wanted to get specific directions."

"And where, exactly, is Saint Andrew's?"

"About fifteen minutes down the road you will come to 656. Turn left and follow it into Buffalo Gap. Turn left on to Third. The church is on the corner of Third and Oak. I thought you said Bear was a friend. How come you didn't ask him?"

Decision time, Richard thought. *How will this kid take the news of Bears death?*

"I couldn't. Bear died last Sunday."

The young man just fell to a sitting position on the ground. A blank look overtook his face as his mind processed the information. "Shit!" He said it more to himself than to Richard. "He said he was coming back again." A long pause was accentuated by the quiet of the surroundings. "My mom always said that there's a reason we meet people. I really enjoyed learning to fly with Bear. Now I have to figure out why he and I met."

"Maybe it was so you and I would meet," Richard said, with less conviction that he intended.

Rick apparently did not catch the lack of conviction. "You may be right. You goin' to see Father Grant?" Rick got up and stood near Richard.

"I am."

"Good. Tell him I said hello, and that I'd appreciate it if he would say a Sunday Mass for Bear."

23

Saint Andrew's was a single-level, stone building with a steep, tiled roof. The three front doors were in need of paint, but the grounds around the church were well maintained. At that moment, in fact, a man was raking the leaves into a huge pile. He was in work boots; jeans with holes, paint, and a hint of grease; and a turtleneck shirt under an orange-hued plaid jacket only a hunter could appreciate. His hands were covered with cowhide gloves.

"Excuse me. Could you tell me where I might find Father Grant?" Richard asked, as he approached the worker.

"That depends. Who wants to know?"

Richard extended his hand, "I'm Richard Moore. I'm looking for Father Grant."

"Nice to meet you, Mr. Moore. Am I supposed to know you?"

"No, but you know a good friend of mine; assuming you are Father Grant."

"I am. I am also Grant the gardener, painter, mechanic, and landscaper, as you might have guessed. Who might your friend be?"

"Jan Pulaski, also known as the Bear, I believe he came to see you a couple of months ago."

"And if he had, what brings you here?"

Maybe it was Richard's imagination going wild again but he was quite sure the temperature had just dropped ten degrees. He was certain that the priest had just gotten colder.

"I'm retracing his final steps, as I investigate his murder." *Maybe the direct approach will warm things up a touch*, he thought.

"May God have mercy on his soul," Father Grant said as he made the sign of the cross and quietly said a prayer.

When he was finished praying, he looked at Richard. "I could use a cup of tea. Would you like to join me?"

Richard followed him around the church building to the back door of a house. "This is the rectory. The parishioners built it themselves in 1956. A generous donation was made to update wiring, heating system, insulation, windows, and appliances about ten years ago. It is really quite comfortable."

They entered the kitchen. Richard was impressed. The kitchen was indeed modern, with dishwasher, gas double oven, oak cabinets, stone counters, oversized double door refrigerator, and a microwave.

"The parishioners hold breakfasts, dinners, and holiday functions in the church, but they come in here to cook and prepare the food. That's why we have the large oven and refrigerator. The original church building was wood. It burned down in nineteen fifty-six and took the attached rectory with it. That is when they erected the stone church. It has a beautiful interior; so beautiful that it put the project over budget before the rectory could be built. So, the parishioners went ahead and built the rectory with their own hands."

He placed two cups of tea on the table and took a seat across from Richard. Neither said anything as each sipped his tea. Each man waited for the other to break the silence. In the end, Father Grant was the first to speak.

"You say you're investigating Bear's murder. What brings you to South Dakota from Boston?'

"I never said I was from Boston, but you are correct. I'm following any lead I uncover in hopes of finding who killed Bear and why. I know he came here to visit you. Want to tell me why?"

"I'm afraid I can't."

"Can't, or won't?"

"Does it make a difference? You came all the way out here looking for information. Unfortunately, I really can't help you. I feel bad; you've wasted your time. You will not get what you are looking for from me."

"And why is that?" Richard found Farther Grant to be a likable person. The priest's demeanor and body language were open and not combative. His face was red from weather; his dark-blue eyes were large and friendly. *So,* Richard thought, *why do I have the urge to choke the shit out of this man and get some answers?*

"I gave my word that I would not discuss anything associated with Bear. In this region, and in my profession, my word is sacred."

"Look, Father, let me reiterate something to you, Bear was murdered. I will find out who and why. I know he was investigating priests accused of child molestation and the people who accused them. If you are one of the accused priests he was investigating, I can assure you that anything you say to me will be kept in strictest confidence. I'm not working for the archdiocese or any plaintiff or any law-enforcement agency. I'm just a man trying to find out who murdered his friend. You can help me, Father, by telling me why he came to see you."

"I can assure you I'm no pedophile; I am not under investigation, and no one has ever accused me of improper behavior. I cannot, however, be of any assistance to you."

Richard got up from the table. "If that is your last word, I'll be on my way. I'm staying at the Point Hotel in Rapid City if you have a change of mind. Bear was a good Christian. I know he attended church regularly. I think he would have been disappointed in our conversation."

Richard's words did not draw an angry response from the priest who got up and courteously escorted Richard to the door. As Richard was about to leave, the priest suddenly took his hand and said, "Richard, I am sorry that your friend is dead. I think he was a good man and a likable one. I did not know him well, but I do believe that he was a man of his word, and will not be disappointed that I am a man of mine. I will pray for him and for you as well. Have a safe trip back."

24

The following morning Richard once again experienced the self-doubt that occurred during his flight from Boston. It was a new feeling for him. The success of his entire career was based on his confidence and decision making. Lately, however, he was unsure of the next step to take. He was tired after a night of fitful sleep. He had cut his morning run short because it did nothing to help and took too much energy. He was packed but not sure he wanted to catch an earlier flight. He decided to go out for breakfast, when the telephone ran.

"Richard Moore."

"Mr. Moore, so glad I caught you." It was Father Grant. "A friend of mine, Mr. Davenport, would like you to join him for breakfast. He may be able to answer some of your questions."

"Why would he be able to answer my questions and you cannot?"

"That is a question you will have to ask Mr. Davenport. Will you meet him?"

"Yes. I have nothing to lose."

"Good. The Rapid City Hunt Club is located on the eastern edge of the city. Mr. Davenport will meet you at 8:30. I believe he will have his daughter-in-law with him. Would you like directions?"

"Not necessary. I'll get directions from the hotel desk."

"Good. Mr. Moore, you will get some answers, I just don't think they will be of help in identifying Bear's murderer. I hope you will call me when you solve the case."

The Rapid City Hunt Club was a large, charming, wood building bordered by a field of plowed cornstalks on the left and a heavily wooded area on the right. A portico on the right of the building protected cars and guest from some of the elements.

Richard pulled open one of the thick, wooden double doors and stepped into the foyer. The second set of doors led into a waiting area. Capturing the attention of anyone entering the waiting area was a replica of a wooded scene. Shrubs and short trees lined three sides of a shallow pond fed by a babbling stream. Several stuffed animals, a fox, doe, pheasant, quail, and bobcat, were positioned in various places throughout the scene.

To his left, at the end of a short walk, was a wide doorway through which he could see a vast hall filled with round tables and accompanying chairs. One and one-half stories above it was a ceiling supported by a timber beam and truss system. Richard assumed the club did a brisk event business.

Richard had his back to the entry doors when they opened. Richard turned as a man and woman entered.

"Dick, I'm Earl Davenport." Earl extended his hand.

As Richard shook Earl's hand, he replied, "Mr. Davenport thank you for inviting me to breakfast."

"Please call me Earl. It was my pleasure."

"And please call me Richard."

"Oh, I meant no offence by calling you Dick."

"None taken."

"This is my daughter-in-law, Vivian."

"Richard, it is a pleasure. I'm glad you were able to meet us."

As they walked down the corridor to their right, Richard did his usual assessment of people he meets for the first time. Earl's voice was loud and his handshake forceful enough to be uncomfortable. He wore a three-thousand-dollar, custom-tailored, dark-blue, Armani suit. His white cotton shirt was accented with a silk striped tie and gold cufflinks. Patten leather shoes rounded out the image of a wealthy individual.

Richard estimated Earl to be six feet tall and to weigh one hundred and ninety pounds. His shoulders were broad and proportioned to his general physique. He stood ramrod straight and walked with a purposeful gate.

Vivian was different. Her grey plaid Brooks Brothers pantsuit, white blouse and sensible black pumps, complimented her features. The thin lines of gray in her short, light-brown hair and other signs led Richard to estimate that she was in her late thirties. Her eyes held steady as she addressed Richard. Her voice was measured with a tone of intelligence and force.

"Richard, do you hunt? Animals in the wild, I mean. I know you hunt criminals."

"No. I can't kill for sport. Nor can I pull the trigger on anyone or anything that's unarmed."

"I grew up hunting. I had a rifle in my hands when I was six. I'm a good shot. Lost interest in hunting some time ago, nothing philosophical, just lost interest. Most of the members of this club are hunters. They get to take two kills home for meat. The rest of the kills are given to needy families as food."

"That's very commendable," Richard responded.

When they were met by the maitre d' at the restaurant's doorway, Richard saw that twenty booths lined three walls, while the floor area was occupied by square tables that seated four. Six tables and four booths on the left were occupied when they arrived, but Earl and his guests were escorted to a table on the right, away from the entry door and the other customers.

When the three were seated, Earl said, "Richard, there are no menus or price lists. Anything you want, just ask. I haven't yet found anyone who could order something that the cook couldn't provide."

A server came to the table. "Angie, how are the children?" Earl asked.

"Just fine, Mr. Davenport. The youngest is showing a talent for drawing."

"Well, you make sure I have first bid on any of his paintings." Earl turned his attention back to his guests, he said, "Viv, you having tea." Richard noted that it was a statement and not a question. Vivian nodded her head to Earl in acknowledgement. "Richard would you like coffee or is milk your specialty this morning?"

"Coffee will be fine."

When the server had left, Earl looked at Richard and said, "Richard, Skip ... Father Grant, told me about Bear. I'm sorry about your loss."

"Yes, Mr. Moore," Vivian said, "It must have been a terrible loss for you."

"Thank you both. Earl, did you know Bear?"

Earl smiled. "Skip told me about your visit yesterday and your conversation. I know you have some questions, and Skip didn't give you answers. I hope to rectify that for you this morning."

The server brought the coffee and tea. "Will there be anything else, Mr. Davenport?"

"I think I'll have some juice and a Bagel. It's unfortunate Skip couldn't make it this morning. He loves the sweet rolls here. Richard, you might try one. They are very good. Actually, Angie, bring a plate with an assortment of breakfast breads, muffins, and things. Richard, Viv, anything else?"

After Angie went off to get their order, Earl said, "In answer to your question Richard, I hired Bear some months back. I'll let Viv give you the background. Viv."

"My maiden name is Noonan, Richard. My father was Senator Dexter Noonan. He was killed in an auto accident six months ago. He was driving from here to Buffalo Gap on 79 South when his car went off the road. The Highway Patrol said it was an accident. He probably fell asleep or some animal jumped out in front of him."

"And you don't believe their explanation?"

"I think they believe it, but me ... no, not for a second. I wanted an independent investigation conducted."

"Did you have reason to believe the Highway Patrol didn't do their job investigating the accident?"

"None at all. They were confronted with a set of circumstances they see all the time, and they came up with a plausible explanation that usually fit those circumstances. I wanted someone to go beyond the usual." Vivian stopped and sipped her tea.

"Richard, Viv told me about her concerns. I have no problem telling you in front of her now, because we have had the conversation, I thought she was being emotional. But I love her like the daughter I never had. I have one child. My boy is the love of my life, but I always wanted two children, a boy and a girl. Fate didn't allow it but gave me Viv. I'd do anything for her." He took some juice.

"Viv wanted an independent investigation. I agreed on one condition: No one outside of the small circle of people involved was to know about it.

"Despite my skepticism, I wanted the best investigator I could find. I am very well-connected, politically. I didn't want anyone local, so I made inquiries through my Washington political contacts and the FBI. Several names were presented. Your name, Richard, was on the top of each list, but I was convinced to drop your name. Seems you are hunting someone important, and no one wanted you distracted."

Richard was aware that Earl was sending a clear message, *I know you. I know more than you think I might.* Richard wondered who Earl's source might be.

"Bear was second on the list. Given his association with you, I figured I'd get the top two picks for the price of one. Not that the price meant anything to me."

"I know you didn't want anyone local, but Boston is a bit of a commute." Richard had some real problems with Earl's explanation. Besides, Earl was annoying him with inside knowledge.

"Well, I have to give you the other side of the story. His Eminence, Winston Cahill, Cardinal of the Boston Archdiocese, is an old friend of mine. We roomed together in college. Boy, I could tell you some stories about Winston."

"You were in the seminary with Cardinal Cahill?" Richard asked.

"Ha Ha! That's good Richard. Me in the seminary. Hell, no! Winston decided to become a priest after he finished his degree in biology. Winston and I have stayed in touch. When the molestation issue dragged on, Winston once commented to me that he really should hire an independent investigator. Apparently, no one believed the Church when they found a priest to be innocent of an accusation. Winston hoped an independent investigator's findings would lend credibility to the findings.

"It was perfect for me. I could pay Bear for investigating the senator's death by funneling money through the Boston Archdiocese. At the same time, I paid him to investigate the priests and accusers."

"So that's why it appears the Archdiocese is overpaying for Bear's services."

"Could be. I don't know what his usual rate might have been. The last piece was Skip. He went to high school with my wife's brother. My wife and I are members of Skip's parish although we don't attend regularly. Skip was an intermediary between Bear and me."

Earl looked at his watch. "Listen it's later than I thought. I have another meeting."

He was getting up from the table. "Viv will fill in the rest. If any questions come up that she can't answer, she can call my cellphone. I want you to have all the information we can provide."

He kissed Vivian on the cheek then turned to Richard. "Richard, please walk me to the car; I have something else to cover with you."

Richard got up and excused himself to Vivian.

Earl and Richard walked in silence to the foyer. Once closed between the two sets of doors, Earl turned to Richard and held out an envelope.

"This is a retainer. I want you to work for me. I want you to find Bear's killer, and I want to know if his investigation into Viv's father's death had anything to do with Bear's murder."

Richard held the envelope without opening it. "I can't work for you. I'm working for Bear." He handed the envelope back to Earl.

Earl did not take the envelope. "I don't want it back. Look, if Bear was killed because of his investigation into the senator's death or because of his involvement with the Boston Archdiocese, I would blame myself. Use whatever resources you need; this will defray some of the costs."

"What did you mean his involvement with the Boston Archdiocese? Did Bear run into something that might have been dangerous?"

"I'm not sure. I have been told a group is very angry with the Church. The group believes the Church continues to downplay the effects on the victims and that it is still protecting the priests. Rumor has it that several of the members are advocating a militant response."

"That's helpful information. Does the cardinal know who these people might be?"

"I don't think so, but someone in the Archdiocese or his staff might. I really am running late. Take the check. I want Bear's killer found at any expense."

"Sorry. Bear's my client, and we have an agreement. I can't take on another client. Why the secrecy about investigating the senator's accident?"

Earl thought for a few seconds. "Viv will tell you more about her suspicions. That might answer your question. I'm trying to help Viv because I love her dearly. I also have to be conscious of how my political contacts might perceive my involvement with any investigation. Being politically connected is sometimes a burden." He held out the envelope for Richard again.

"You know I can't take that."

"Well, please keep our conversation about the investigation into the senator's death confidential. If that investigation had anything to do with Bears murder, I'll personally divulge our investigation and Viv's reason for it. In the meantime, keep me posted on what you find. I may be of help if obstacles need moving."

Richard watched as Earl got in the back seat of a black Lincoln Town Car. The chauffer closed Earl's door then went around to the driver's side and drove off. Richard went back to talk with Vivian.

25

As Richard sat down at the table again, Vivian asked, "Did my father-in-law try to hire you?"

"Yes, he did."

"And you turned him down." It was a statement, not a question.

"I already have a client."

"And that would be Bear. Am I right?"

"Very good. I don't think your father-in-law got the message."

"The only message Earl gets is the one that meets his needs or expectation. He is a smart businessman, expert political manipulator, generous benefactor, and mean-spirited loser."

"I'll remember that. Now, if you don't mind, tell me why you thought your father's death was more than an accident."

"Well, I could tell you all the reasons that the state accident investigators would not apply to my father: He was a careful driver. He never got tired while driving. It wasn't very late for a man accustomed to working until 4 A.M. But I won't. I will tell you this: At the time of his death, dad was the most powerful member of the Senate Banking Committee pushing legislation to reform consumer loan and credit-card fees. Do you have any idea how big a business the fees on loans and credit cards is?"

"No, I don't."

"A little history first; in 1980, the president of Citibank contacted Bill Janklow, the governor of South Dakota. He had a proposal for the Governor: pass legislation removing interest legal caps and Citibank would relocate from New York to South Dakota. With it, Citibank would bring thousands of well-paying jobs.

"At the time, money was costing Citibank around twenty percent. Under New York law, it could only charge twelve percent to its customers.

"A December, 1978 Supreme Court ruling permitted national banks to charge interest rates on consumer loans up to the maximum allowed in the state where credit decisions were made. The ruling gave the credit card issuing banks the ability to exceed interest rate limits set by the state where the borrower lived.

"The governor got the legislation passed. To this date, South Dakota has no cap on consumer interest rates. The deal saved Citibank from extinction.

"Credit cards are the most profitable sector of banking. In early 2001 the total was approximately ten billion dollars. The most recent figures available put that number at thirty-six billion." She waited for the number to take root in Richard's mind.

"Thirty-six billion dollars of consumers' money and not a single product or service provided. The fees just get jacked up anytime the industry decides it wants more revenue. And no one stops it. Consumers complain, and news agencies report on the complaints, but, in the end, the companies get the fees."

"So you're saying someone killed your father because he proposed legislation to curb these fees?"

"In a nutshell, yes. But, before you object or call me crazy, let me tell you a few facts. Six years ago, the chairman of the House banking committee died when his twin-engine airplane crashed in the mountains of Alaska. He was heading home after a cantankerous session on escalating consumer loan fees. He opposed the escalation.

"Four years ago, Senator Rubenstein of Ohio and Representative Dole of California died in office two months after joining a coalition of lawmakers pushing banking reform. Rubenstein was shot by a thief who entered a convenience store right behind him. The store surveillance tape showed the thief panicked and shot the clerk and Rubenstein. Dole slipped and fell in his bathtub.

"Two years ago, Vermont representative Baker, an avid skier and physical fitness fanatic, died in a skiing accident. He was leading a banking reform movement.

"Six months ago, my father, died in a single car accident. He had finished a meeting with local merchants. The meeting focused on changing the state's usury laws. Under the current law, most of the credit card companies avoid legislation passed by other states. We are a safe haven for unchecked consumer loan fees."

"Have you brought this summary of events to anyone's attention?"

"It was dad who originally put the information together. Dad said he talked about it with someone at the FBI. They are the most logical ones, right?"

"They are one choice, but I might go to the Secret Service. The Secret Service is in charge of protection for the members of Congress."

"Well, dad went to the FBI. They did not find his summary credible." Vivian stared off past Richard as she slowly sipped tea from her cup.

"Who did your father talk with at the Bureau? Did they do any investigation? If they did, did they give him a report?"

She thought about his questions, and then replied, "I don't know who he talked with. He did indicate that they conducted an investigation. He got a report, but I don't know how or when."

Richard's mind was turning over details and questions. "You're concerned that your father might have been killed, and you haven't tracked down the FBI agent your father talked with? You think your father received some communication from the agent but haven't looked for it? Why did you really hire Bear?"

The look on Vivian's face portrayed amazement or shock. She looked for and found the server and ordered coffee. After she took a drink of her coffee, Vivian looked Richard in the eyes.

"I like to think I'm a fairly intelligent and logical woman. I know when something might be beyond my abilities or knowledge, and I am not afraid to admit it and ask for help. I believe the deaths of my father's colleagues and of my father were not accidents. Now that you have pointed out something I have missed, something I can do, I will work on it. If dad left any information identifying the FBI agent he talked with, I will find it."

She took up the cup. Her hand was trembling slightly. As she replaced the cup, she again looked Richard in the eyes. "Investigating my father's death *is* the real reason your friend was hired. You miss your friend maybe as much as I miss my father. Both men were taken from us unexpectedly. If their deaths are connected … well, I'm sorry, but do not question my motives just because I'm not a detective." She started to get up and leave.

"Don't run off so quickly," Richard said. However, he did not look at Vivian. He was fixing himself another cup of coffee.

"You see, Father Grant doesn't answer my questions. I get an early morning invitation to breakfast. I learn about an investigation into your father's death, an investigation that has to be held secret. You tell me a plausible story about multiple deaths of members of Congress, but no one else has connected the deaths, and you haven't looked to find the FBI agent that might have checked on your theory. You're intelligent. What would your first assumption be if you were confronted with the same facts?"

Vivian had sat down. Richard now looked her straight in the eyes and waited for an answer. She hesitated before answering.

"I think we are both emotionally distracted due to our loss. We have a common goal but different circumstances and different talents. I don't expect you to investigate my father's death, and I cannot investigate your friend's death. I just hope we can stay in touch and exchange information."

She got up again. This time she extended her hand. As they shook, she said, "I enjoyed our conversation, Richard. As much as I liked your friend Bear, I wish Earl had hired you. I think you would have had quicker success."

26

Before heading to the airport, Richard found the Highway Patrol Headquarters. There he spoke with the director of the Traffic Fatalities Investigation section. Richard told him about Bear's murder and asked about the senator's death. "I can assure you Mr. Moore, Senator Noonan's death was the result of an unfortunate auto accident. I told Mr. Pulaski the same thing."

While waiting for his flight, Richard called Laura from the airport. "Laura, any messages?"

"Steve thinks he has found the charter airline Rob Lee used to get to Boston last Sunday. He is sending someone to talk with the owner of the charter company. He said he should have some information by the time you get back."

"TSA called. They want to know if you will handle the Bedford review and training or if they should get another company."

"Why don't you handle it for Bear?"

"What?"

"You know the drill. You know the players. You can handle it. If you don't want to go out there yourself, make the phone calls and put the team together. You would have done it for Bear."

"I don't know, Richard. We miss anything while I'm running it; I'll never get over it."

"Think about it. Do it under my name. I won't have the time. Meanwhile, I want you or Steve to look up any organizations that are vocal about the Boston Archdiocese's handling of the pedophile priests. Check the background of Senator Noonan of South Dakota and his daughter Vivian Davenport. Put together a file on Earl Davenport and Father Grant now assigned to Saint Andrew's in Buffalo Gap, South Dakota. I have to run; they're calling my plane. I will see you in the morning."

"Wait, Richard! Tomorrow is Saturday. I have to run the girls around, so I don't know if I will be in, but Steve will be here."

"OK. Sorry, I lost track of days. Don't think about coming in, just enjoy the weekend. Tell Steve I'll I'm going home from the airport and I'll see him in the morning."

27

While Richard was in South Dakota, Stephanie was at the Massachusetts State House going through invoices submitted by contractors who had worked on the Big Dig project. Errors by the engineering company had resulted in nearly two billion dollars in overruns. Although the errors had been widely publicized and attributed to the engineering company, the company never paid for any of its mistakes. In fact, the company received additional payments for producing plans to correct the errors.

Stephanie was not looking for additional errors or charges by the engineering firm. That story had run its course. She was more interested in the myriad of subcontractors associated with the project.

The Central Artery Project, or Big Dig as it became known, was designed to place Boston's busy central thoroughfare underground and increase its capacity. While the road itself was approximately one point two miles long, connecting the central artery to feeder streets and the existing airport tunnels, along with adding a third tunnel to the airport resulted in a total of seven point five miles of underground roadway. To produce that many miles of underground roadway required the removal of sixteen-million cubic yards of dirt. The average load of the dump trucks was twelve cubic yards. One point four-million truckloads needed to be moved. Removing that dirt required the services of many truck drivers. Theoretically, all of those truck drivers should have been union members, but, at the height of construction, with over five thousand people working on the project, the unions just could not fill the demand. Almost from the start of the project, therefore, just about anyone with a commercial driver's license and access to a dump truck could become a trucking subcontractor earning union rates without paying union dues.

Stephanie was looking for two specific items: the total number of truckloads billed and the amounts paid to the nonunion drivers. An informed source told her the total number of truckloads was nearly twenty-five percent higher than required, and that nonunion drivers received lower pay rates than required by contract.

As she had expected, Stephanie did not immediately find evidence confirming the allegations in the paperwork. She knew that, in the end, she would have to take her computerized notes home and crunch some numbers if she were going to find something worth writing about.

28

After landing in Boston, Richard paid his parking fee and headed home. At eight thirty on an early October night, the air was clean and a pleasant fifty-five degrees.

Steve had told Craig Richard would be heading straight home from the airport. Craig was in his car in the central parking garage of the airport. He watched as Richard paid his parking fee then followed behind. He decided to pass Richard and watch from behind Richard's condominium rather than risk following in the brightly lit Ted Williams tunnel.

Richard pulled into his parking space behind the condominium, grabbed his overnight bag, and got out of the car. As he reached the back of his car, someone called out.

"Mr. Moore."

A man stepped into the circle of light cast by the spotlight over the parking space. He was about five feet, nine inches tall with a full head of brown hair. His Red Sox windbreaker appeared to be holding his gut in place over a pair of clean jeans and two-toned sneakers.

"May I help you?" Richard asked as his eyes scanned the shadows for movement, his ears alert for the slightest sound.

"No, but we're here to do you a favor." A second man joined the first, and two others came from around the fence on either side of the parking area. All three held baseball bats in their hands. Richard now had two men blocking his forward path and a man on each side of him. As they all came in a little closer, Richard watched and calculated.

Richard kept his face centered toward the man doing the talking while his peripheral vision sought out the men on either side. The man on his right was immense, and Richard recognized him as the disagreeable giant he had met in the repair shop at the container terminal. The man on his left was partially beyond his vision, but Richard could see that he was bald and had a medium to large build. The man now standing next to the talker reminded him of a model from GQ magazine. Both he and the talker were about the same height, but the newcomer was trim and fit and wore a tank top shirt to show off his muscular frame. Richard decided the man was more show than action. It was too cool to be standing in a dark alley with just a tank top.

"Skull, this the guy?" The first man, apparently the leader, was talking to the giant on Richard's right. Richard did not turn his head.

"Yeah, that's him. Came nosin' around the shop askin' about his friend that got killed like we had som'tin' to do with it."

The talker spoke up again. "You shouldn' be nosin' around the docks. We're here to tell you to stay away. We don't like people coming around trying to pin murders on dock workers."

Richard did not think a simple message was intended, so he challenged, "OK, not a problem. No one saw my friend Bear so I moved on to other places. Thanks for the favor." Richard took a step forward and to his right.

"Not so fast. We're gonna make sure you got the message good." The leader gave a slight nod of his head.

Skull reared up, his bat held with two hands. The motion caught Richard's attention, but he kept his eye on the leader. Everyone was taken by surprise when Richard, who was still looking at the leader, sidestepped into Skull and grabbed the giant's hands with his left hand while swinging his right arm around the back of the man's neck. In a continuous flow of motion, Richard then moved his own right hip right and upper torso left. The force of Skull's forward swing and Richard's pull and push on the man propelled Skill over Richard's hip.

The bald man on Richard's left, who reacted more quickly than the others, moved in and took a batter's swing before he realized Skulls body was shielding Richard. As Baldy's bat connected with Skull's ankle, there was a sickening crunch followed by a bellow of pain. Richard let the giant fall, directing Skull's landing so that his head would take the brunt of the impact, while, at the same time, allowing his own body to bend at the knees.

Thinking that he must have somehow hurt Richard as well as his friend, Baldy moved in, raising his arms high to deliver the coup de grace. As his arms came down, Richard drove up with his legs from a crouched position, and his right shoulder collided with Baldy's left underarm. As the force of the impact tore Baldy's shoulder out of its socket, Richard smashed his elbow into the back of the man's head, and Baldy went down for the count.

Richard now faced GQ who was standing flat-footed and staring at Richard. He dropped his bat and appeared to be pleading no contest with his empty hands at belt level, when he suddenly lunged forward, deftly pulling a knife out from a concealed belt sheath. Richard had underestimated both the man's cunning, and his willingness to fight, and was momentarily caught off guard. As he reflexively sidestepped the lunge, he stumbled over Skulls bat and the knife caught his shirt and cut into his right side.

GQ had expected the knife would plunge deep into Richard's exposed gut thereby slowing his own forward motion. In spite of his stumble, however, Richard had twisted his frame enough that the knife had hit a rib and glanced off. The glancing cut did little to slow the man, and he was off balance as Richard grabbed hold of his knife hand and pulled the hand and arm back and up while looping his left arm around GQ's neck. As Richard pulled the man's arm up behind his back, he expected the assailant to drop the knife. Once again, however, GQ proved tougher than expected; he did not let go even when his arm broke. It was not until Richard adjusted his grasp and broke the man's wrist that the knife fell to the ground, and GQ fell with it

At this, the leader of the group turned and ran for his truck. Richard picked up one of the bats and tossed it at the running man. Spinning like the blades of a helicopter, the bat flew just twelve inches off the ground until it was tangled in the man's legs, and he went down hard. Richard was on top of him a moment later, picking up the bat with his right hand and grabbing the back of the man's collar with his left.

He pulled the man to his feet, spun him around, and bent him backwards over the left front fender of his truck. The left side of his face was red, scraped, and bleeding. When he threw up his hands to protect himself, the heels were cut and scraped and had small pebbles embedded in them.

"I have a few questions for you," Richard said as calmly as possible. "Let's start with your name."

The man continued to cower and covered his face, but remained silent. Richard tapped the man's left shin with the end of the bat, and he gave a cry of agony as the already battered limb sent a surge of pain rocketing up to his brain.

"A little sensitive are you?" Richard asked. "Maybe you'll listen to me now, and answer my questions. What's your name?"

"S ... s ... Sean ... Sean."

"OK, Sean, who sent you?"

Sean appeared confused. Richard assumed he was trying to decide whether he should answer, and if so, how. Richard helped him along with another tap of the bat on his shin. "The name, Sean, now."

"No one, I got the guys myself. I don't like people snooping around—Ahhhh."

Richard hit the shin hard. When the man stopped shouting, Richard moved in close and said, "In case you hadn't noticed, I've had a bad evening. So, don't fuck with me. I want to know who sent you, and why." He moved the bat so the Sean could see it.

"All right. All right. One of the foremen said to get a couple of the guys and pay you a visit. Said he wanted you out of action for a while. That's why we had the bats."

"Why did he want me out of the way for a while?"

"I don't know. Ahhh." Richard hit the shin again. "I really don't know; He never said."

"Who is he?"

"I don't—don't hit me again. It was Dan Sweeney."

Richard thought back to his meeting with Gloria Stokes of Container International Insurance. She had told him that Bear had asked her to run a check on a container facility foreman named Dan Sweeney.

"Ever been to Dan's house?" Richard asked.

"What? ... His house?"

"Yes, have you ever been to Dan's house?"

"Sure. He has a cookout every year. He invites most of the guys on his shift."

"Good. You can drive."

"Drive? Whereto?"

"You're taking me to visit Dan.

"Hey, Richard, are you OK?"

Richard turned to see Regis, the condominium's evening security guard. "Hi, Regis, yes I'm OK, but those three guys on the ground need medical attention. Call 911 and get an ambulance down here."

"I already call 911. The police should be here any minute."

"Well, then my friend and I need to be going. Will you do me a favor and take my overnight bag in? I'll pick it up when I get back."

"I will. What about these three? What should I tell the police?"

"Just tell them you heard some noise and found them as they are. See you later."

29

As Richard and Sean got in Sean's truck, Craig started walking to his car. He had been hiding in the shadows. "Amateurs. Fucking amateurs," he said as he got into his car and started following Sean's truck.

Daniel Sweeney's house turned out to be a small, white, two-story colonial on Essex Drive, and within walking distance of Livermore Memorial Hospital and the Middlesex Fells Reservation.

Richard was familiar with the area. The previous year, a former member of Richard's special ops unit, a rouge operative working for Rob Lee named Ghost, had shot and killed a horseback rider not far from there. Also nearby on the Middlesex Fells Reservation was the Sheep Fold, a recreation area where Ghost had tried to kill Richard and a young man named Stuart Scott, wounding both of them and several others in the unsuccessful attempt.

Richard took the keys to the truck out of the ignition. "Let's go."

A two-foot-high brick wall kept the Sweeney's front lawn from spilling on to the sidewalk. Two steps bisected the wall and lead to a short walkway that cut across the lawn to the porch. Richard stood off to one side of the door as Sean rang the doorbell.

A man opened the door and looked at Sean in amazement. "Sean!"

"Hi, Dan."

"What the hell? ... I hope that Moore guy looks worse than you do."

At that moment, Richard stepped out of the shadows, propelled Sean past the man in the doorway. Sean fell down on to the polished wood floor of the hall.

"Actually, Dan, Sean looks worse than me, but not as bad as the other three."

Dan looked at Richard as if he were sizing him up for a confrontation. Deciding that a physical encounter would be a bad idea, he said, "Get off my property or I'll call the police."

Richard stood on the porch holding the storm door open. Sean started to get up. Richard said, "Sean, stay down on the floor and don't move until I tell you to."

At that moment, a woman appeared in the doorway that led into the living room.

"Trudy, call the police," sputtered Sweeney to his wife.

"Mrs. Sweeney," Richard looked at Trudy, "I am sorry to have come to your home unannounced and frighten you. You can call the police if you want. If you do, I will file a complaint against your husband and Sean for attempted murder."

"Murder!" Dan shouted. "No one's trying to murder you. You're the one pushing people around."

"One of the men you sent to attack me pulled a knife and stabbed me. That's attempted murder, and you ordered it.'

"My god, Dan, the man is bleeding."

During the ride from his condominium to Dan's house, Richard used the first aid kit Sean had in the truck to mend the stab wound. Richard was only able to get the wound cleaned and placed a couple of band-aids over it. The band-aids came off when Richard pushed Dan against the wall. The wound was open again.

"Maybe you better go in the living room, Trudy. Don't call the cops yet."

Trudy hesitated but left the men in the hall.

"Who told you to have Sean and his men come pay me a visit? And don't jerk me around; I'm in no mood to play twenty questions with you."

"The director of operations, Martin King."

"What did he tell you? Why did he want me out of the way?"

"He just told me to get some of the guys and have them pay you a visit. Wanted me to make sure Skull was one of the guys. He didn't tell me why, and I didn't ask."

"And you just did it out of the goodness of your heart, or was there an incentive?"

"He said there would be five hundred each for the guys and a grand for me."

"How did you know whereto send your men?"

"He gave me an address. Said you'd be arriving around nine."

"Does King work Saturdays?"

"The office operates six days a week. He or one of his assistants works half a day on Saturdays."

"What about tomorrow? Will King be in?

"I don't know. We're backed up. The shipping lane has a couple vessels waiting to come in. Most of the day shift has been working the past couple of Saturdays.

Richard looked at Sean. "You can get up now. You might want to have your face cleaned up. I'm taking your truck to get home."

"What? When do I get my truck back?"

"It will be parked out in front of my place. I'll put the keys under the back seat. No one will steal it, but it might get towed."

30

At eight thirty the following morning, Richard walked up the stairs to the second floor of the administrative office building at the Cushing Container Terminal. A young woman in a sweatshirt and jeans had just hung up her phone as Richard walked over and stood in front of her desk.

"Hi, I'm Richard Moore. I'm here to see Martin King."

The woman glanced at a closed door to her left, and, with a hesitation in her voice, asked if Mr. King was expecting him.

"Absolutely," Richard said, as he turned and headed toward the closed door. The nameplate said Director Martin King. "In fact, I'm late."

Richard opened the office door and stepped inside.

"What the hell is this?" The man behind the desk said as he covered the mouthpiece of the telephone headset. "Tiffany," he yelled.

"My name is Richard Moore. I'm sure you have time for me."

"Yes, Mr. King." The young woman in the sweatshirt was now standing in the doorway through which Richard had just entered.

"Never mind, Tiffany," the man said, then, spoke into the telephone, "I just had company arrive … Yes, that was a good guess … I don't know … You'd better cover." He hung up the receiver.

Looking at Richard he asked, "Do I know you?"

"Nice try. What shall we do: press charges for attempted murder or answer some questions?"

"I'm still not sure who you are, and you're talking in riddles."

"OK." Richard pulled out his cellphone and dialed. "Sergeant Petelle, Richard Moore. How is the family? … Good to hear. And your son? … He did? MVP, you must have partied all night after that … Yes, is detective—Wait."

Martin King was trying to get Richard's attention.

Richard covered the mouthpiece on his phone and asked, "You want something?"

"Hang up. I'll answer your questions."

"Sergeant, something came up. I will have to call back … Thank you.. You have a good day also."

Richard put his cellphone away and looked at Martin. "OK, start talking."

"Truth is, I don't know who told me to send the guys after you. He said I could call him Joe."

"How did you meet Joe?"

Martin was fidgeting in his seat. "Look, you have to realize this terminal is operated by the State Highway Commission, not by Massport like all the other terminals are. There's a reason for that. On paper, it says that I report to the highway commissioners, and they report to the governor. The fact of the matter is that the commissioners know little about running a container facility and care less; however, there are powerful people in the state who are very interested. As far as they are concerned, this place was built to meet their needs, and I work for them, not for the commissioners, the governor, or even the state. When they want a favor from me, they expect to get it. If they don't, they can make my life miserable, and even have me fired."

Richard waited for Martin to continue. He did not, so Richard decided Martin needed some prodding. "Martin, a good friend of mine is dead, and I was attacked last night by several of your workers under instructions from you. Keeping your job will be the least of your troubles. So, tell me how you met this Joe."

"OK. OK," said Martin getting up to pace back and forth in front of the oversized window behind his desk.

Richard looked around the room and focused on a collection of pictures hanging on one of the walls. Martin apparently liked the political scene. Pictures of him with various political figures made up the collection. As Richard watched Martin pacing, he could see a ship coming up the inlet, and, off in the distance, on the other side of the inlet, rows of condominiums.

Martin continued his story. "Four, maybe five months ago, I got a call from a politician. He told me he had a friend that needed a favor. I figured the friend needed a shipment passed though quickly or that maybe the paperwork was missing or filled out wrong, and he wanted me to get the shipment processed without any problems. I mean, you'd be surprised at how often we have to circumvent normal procedures to get a shipment processed for a politician's friend or constituent.

"I told the politician to have his friend drop by, and I would take care of his problem. He said no; his friend wanted to buy me lunch and a beer. So, I agreed to meet the man at O'Tooles down the street for lunch."

Martin paused and stared out the window as though he was lost in thought. It was the first time he had stopped pacing since he had left his chair. After a few moments, he started pacing again.

"When I entered O'Toole's, the bartender pointed me toward a booth near the back of the pub. One man sat in the booth. I walked over and introduced myself. Joe, as he said I should call him, was very friendly. We talked about a lot of things: sports, kids, weather, and so forth I started to think he was a really nice guy.

"After we finished lunch, I told him I needed to get back soon, so we should discuss his problem. Damn. I should have left before that discussion."

Richard noticed that, although the room was not particularly warm, Martin was sweating. His long-sleeve polo pullover had a dark spot at the top of the outward roll of his stomach. Martin's dark-brown hair had been the picture of neatness when Richard arrived. Now after rubbing his head, Martin's hair gave the impression he had just gotten out of bed.

"I don't know ... maybe I shouldn't tell you the rest." Martin was now facing Richard.

"Let me guess: he didn't need a shipment processed, did he? He wanted you to switch containers, hiding the ones with the merchandise, and forwarding the empty replacements."

Martin was dumbfounded. He just stared at Richard. Then he asked, "How ... how ... did you know?"

"The other day when I was here, your people were painting a container a different color than the original. They painted over the name and numbers. Your man Skull had stencils and number punches. It was obvious you were substituting empty containers for the originals. The stockpile of containers coming and going provided a good cover for hiding the original. So, keep talking."

Martin wiped his brow on this shirt sleeve. "Yes. You're right. He asked me to divert some containers. He said there would be substantial money involved. He wanted me to oversee the operation and select the men. I told him to get lost and started to get up ... he said I should look at something before I turned him down."

"Jesus, Richard, I have a wife and three kids."

Martin sat down and placed his head in his hands. He was beginning to shake.

"You want some water? You want to go outside for a walk?' Richard asked as Martin fought back tears.

"No. Let's get this finished." He wiped his forehead, and eyes. Then he ran his hands through his hair and took a large breath. He got up and started pacing. "Joe handed me a manila envelope. Inside were pictures of my kids at play in the school. A couple other pictures were of my wife coming and going from the supermarket. I had no choice. I did what he wanted."

"Who set you up with this guy? Did he know you would be threatened?"

Martin ignored Richard's questions. "Yesterday, Joe called me. We got together for an early lunch. That's when he told me to get some guys to rough you up. He wanted Skull involved. He said he wanted you disabled for a while. He didn't say why. He just told me to take care of it."

"What about Bear? Did you have him roughed up? Did Joe tell you to kill him?"

"No! No! I only met Bear when he came here asking about the shipments. I was nervous as hell. I was sure he noticed. But I never heard anything from Joe except through e-mail. And the e-mail just told me which containers I was to switch. No one ever mentioned your friend."

"All right, who was the politician who called you?"

Martin stopped pacing. He stared out the window as he thought how to answer Richard. "I may be in a shit-load of trouble, but I'm not burning my political bridges just yet."

Richard stood up. He wanted to grab Martin by the throat and shake the information out of him. Instead, he said, "Your political contact may have sold you down the river. If Bear figured out what you were doing, he may have mentioned it to the wrong person. It may have gotten him killed. I have to talk with the politician who put you in touch with Joe. If I don't, you may take the fall for Bear's murder all by yourself."

"I didn't kill anyone. I don't know anything about his murder. I—"

"Martin, I connected the dots and found you. The detectives investigating Bear's murder will eventually do the same. I haven't told the detectives about last night, but eventually I will have to. They will assume you had something to do with Bear's murder. At the very least they will charge you with accessory to murder, maybe even murder for hire. You and your men will all be charged. Now, tell me who put you in touch with Joe."

Martin turned and watched the cargo ship prepare to berth. "All right, but I want some immunity. I can't give you everything and not receive something in return."

"The containers are still here. I'll help prove you were coerced into helping. If you didn't have anything to do with Bear's death, there will be no charges for last night. You will probable walk away with just a slap on the wrist."

Martin thought about said that for a bit. For months, he had felt trapped, and now, maybe there was a safe way out. He turned to Richard and started to speak. "All right, you sure you can—"

Richard heard the glass break. Without hesitation, he leaped across the desk toward Martin. Papers, phone, computer monitor, and other contents flew off the desktop and bounced off the wall before landing on the floor. Richards's open arms grabbed Martin, and his momentum propelled both of them to the floor. As they went down, a second shot ripped through Martin's chest and passed Richard's ear.

"Martin, stay with me. Martin can you hear me? Martin, who put you in touch with Joe?"

Martin took his final breath, then his body went limp.

31

"Richard, Are you all right?"

He was sitting on the edge of a desk just outside of Martin King's office. The State Police crime team had arrived. Boston Police officers were interviewing the office staff. Tiffany was having a hard time concentrating on the police officer's questions. She was too hysterical to listen to anything. Richard was drinking coffee from a Styrofoam cup.

"Hi, Linda, I think I'm OK. No, check that. I'm really pissed."

Detective Linda Pollard of the Boston Police Homicide Department walked up to Richard. They had not seen each other since Richard left the Boston Police Department.

Damn, he still looks good, she thought to herself.

"I don't care if you're pissed. You're bleeding through the right side of your shirt. Did you get hit during the shooting?"

Richard looked down at his shirt. "Aah, another shirt ruined and maybe another pair of slacks." Sitting on the desk had pushed blood from the shirt to the leg of his pants.

"No. A round went past my head, but nothing hit me."

"So, is it from last night?" Linda asked, as she looked him in the eyes. She had an *I know what you did,* expression on her face.

"Yeah, Small-town, was it from last night? Maybe another body we have to investigate?"

Detective Kelly and his partner Nelson were entering the open office area. Richard looked up to face him. Linda turned in Kelly's direction.

"Hello, Kelly." Linda extended her hand.

"Hi, Linda." He did not offer his hand. "Small-town, is this another one of your friends or just an acquaintance? Looks like knowing you could be hazardous to one's health."

Kelly's comment brought Richard up short. The previous year, a young man named Bryan Hayden had used the same words when Richard confronted him in the open at Copley Square Park. A short time later, Bryan took a fall from the fiftieth floor of the John Hancock Tower.

Linda was looking at Richard's bloodstained shirt again.

"I don't like the looks of that shirt. You're bleeding quite a bit." She looked around the room. "Hey, Günter, take Richard down to the ambulance and have an EMT patch up this wound."

"He's not going anywhere," Kelly said to Linda.

"What? Do you see his shirt? He should have someone look at that wound."

"Not happening. It's not a bullet wound, and he said this didn't happen today or here. He should have had it taken care of when it happened. Right now, I want to talk with him."

"Kelly, you know better that that. Richard is a former Boston cop. He deserves more respect and courtesy. I'm having him transported to the hospital. Günter—"

"You're not doing anything but leaving."

"What?"

"This is state property. That means it's my crime scene. You can leave. Thanks for looking after Richard for us, Linda." Kelly was really enjoying himself.

Linda looked incredulous, and then said, "OK, boys, the Staties are here, and they don't need our help. Pack up and get back to whatever you had been doing before you got called in here."

She turned to Richard. "Get that side taken care of as soon as possible. I'll see you later." She walked away.

As she started to walk away, Detective Nelson yelled to her, "Hey, Linda, what about the statements from the office workers? We need them before you and your people leave."

Linda turned and smiled. "Nelson, didn't you hear? This is state property. You have to get your own statements." She turned and walked away.

"Thanks, partner," Nelson said to Kelly.

"OK, Small-town, now that we are alone, you can tell me what happened, and what you were doing in with Mr. King"

"Bear, Jan Pulaski, my friend who was murdered last Sunday, he had been investigating the disappearance of merchandise from some containers. The containers came through this terminal. I wanted to talk with Martin King as part of my investigation into Bear's murder."

"Your friend's murder is my responsibility, state jurisdiction. Stay out of it.'

"You will find, should you decide to check, that I am a licensed investigator. I don't need your approval to conduct my own investigation into Bear's murder."

Kelly leaned close to Richard as if he wanted to whisper in his ear. In a low voice he said, "If you interfere with an ongoing investigation I can pull your license and make sure you never get it back. Interfere, as in cause the death of a witness like Mr. King."

Kelly straightened up and continued in a normal tone of voice, "Now, what did you and Mr. King talk about?"

"Let's see, we talked about a pub down the street. Martin liked to go there for lunch and a beer—"

"Don't be a smart-ass, Small-town. I'll throw you in a cell and forget about you."

"You want to know what we talked about; I'm telling you."

"Yeah, right! Any idea why someone would take this time to shoot Mr. King?" Kelly asked.

"None. I have no idea why anyone would take any time to shoot Mr. King."

"Did what happen to you last night have anything to do with you being here this morning or with Mr. King being murdered?"

"I'm not sure. What happened to me?"

"Don't fuck with me, Small-town. I may pull your license just for the fun of it. That bleeding wound on your right side. How did that happen, and does it have anything to do with King's murder?"

"Not unless he installed the sidewalk near the Boston Commons. I tripped over a broken section and landed on some glass. I can show you, if you'd like to take a ride with me."

"I'm not taking a ride with you. You can go with Trooper Zimmer. He'll take you to the office. You can dictate a statement. But don't disappear. I'll want to talk with you again."

Outside, Richard told Trooper Zimmer he would follow in his own car. When they reached the heavy downtown traffic, Richard simply disappeared from the trooper's rearview mirror.

32

A brisk southeast wind caused many of those jogging northwest along the Charles River to cover their faces against the cold. A half hour of this had drained Richard of much of his energy, and he was grateful when he finally turned and headed in the opposite direction. *I wonder what the problem is*, he thought. *I've run in much colder weather than this without any energy loss.*

As he approached the parking area for the Hatch Shell concert stage, another jogger appeared at his side and began to keep pace with him.

"Almost too cold to be out here jogging," the man commented, affably.

"Almost," Richard replied, "but the alternative is sitting at home and wasting away."

"Or maybe running indoors at a gym. This cold will freeze the sweat when we start walking."

"Well, you have a good run. I have a bit further to go. Have a nice day." Richard did not like to talk while he ran, and he wanted to get away from his chatty companion.

"You should walk with me," the man said, and Richard felt the tip of a silencer in his left side. They both slowed to a walk.

"What do you want?" Richard asked, as the man prodded him toward the parking area.

"What I want is for you and your priest-loving friends to burn in hell. What I want is for the true victims to be treated with dignity and respect. What I want is for us to walk calmly to that white van," he said, pointing toward a small, windowless cargo van idling about a hundred yards away in the parking area. He then stepped behind Richard, prodded him with the gun he held in his right hand, and they began to walk forward through a small park with trees and concrete benches.

"So, why are you interested in me? I don't have anything to do with priests," Richard said, turning to give the man behind him an anxious look. As he did, the cold wind blowing off the river hit him full in the face, causing his eyes to tear, and blurring his vision.

The man pushed the gun into Richard's back near the right side. "Just keep going. You lie like all the rest of them. The Church teaches it's a sin to lie, but everyone working for it lies, especially when it comes to the priests who molested kids."

"I don't know what you're talking about. I don't work for the Church," Richard anxiously said.

"You work for the Church, just like your big black friend. Question everyone making a claim of abuse. You're helping the Church hide the guilty priest. No more, you hear. We're going to put a stop to it."

As he spoke they arrived at the concrete bench that marked the end of the park, and the side door of the van suddenly opened to reveal a man aiming a silenced sniper rifle in their direction.

"Who is *we*? Did you put a stop to my friend?" Richard's voice now had an edge of panic.

"Ever hear of the Catholics for Equal Justice? You will. Then again, maybe you won't."

Richard stopped and began to turn his head, as if to say something. In response, the gunman shoved the gun into Richard's back, and Richard began to stumble forward. As he did, he angled his left hip slightly outward, reached his left hand across his body, and grabbed the gunman's now exposed right hand at the wrist. Continuing with his stumbling movement, Richard pulled the startled man off balance, and he fell to the ground. Without any perceivable break in motion, Richard jammed his foot into the armpit, and then pulled up on the arm while pushing down with his foot. With a pop and a scream of agony, the shoulder separated from its socket and the gun fell to the ground.

The swiftness of Richard's attack had not only surprised the gunman, it had taken the sniper in the van off guard as well. When he did respond, as Richard had anticipated, the wind blowing into his face had caused his eyes to tear, and his view of his target was blurred. He took two shots, but they ricocheted off the pavement as Richard grabbed the gunman's pistol and dove behind the cement bench. Two more ricochets and Richard dashed to the nearest tree. He looked around the side of the tree and saw two men in the cargo van doorway. They seemed to be arguing, then suddenly, the new man yanked the rifle from the original shooter and pushed him to one side. The new shooter took aim and fired.

Instead of the thunk of a slug burying itself in the tree, Richard heard the unmistakable thump of a bullet ripping its way into human flesh. As he turned to see where the shots were directed, he saw blood coming from his attacker. One round had hit him in the chest. The second round opened the top of his skull. Blood squirted from the man's head as his heart pumped for its last remaining moments. Richard looked back at the van. The two in the back were arguing as the second shooter closed the cargo door. A third man drove them away.

Craig had watched most of the action through his rearview mirror from the other end of the parking lot. As the van passed him and made its way onto Storrow Drive, he shifted to drive and followed. He was shaking his head as he commented to himself, "Amateurs. Everyone these days is an amateur."

33

Richard looked at Linda Pollard as she approached him. "Hi, Linda. What brings you here?" Richard was wrapped in a blanket supplied by the EMTs. Perspiration had saturated his sweat suit, and he was shivering in the cold wind.

"When I heard you were the one attacked and someone was dead, this is what, two bodies in three days, I figured my boss would have a lot of questions for me. Not my team. I decided I would interview you personally."

As Linda looked around, Richard took careful note of her. He knew she was about his age, forty-seven. She was five feet, ten inches tall. Her slacks, boots, and long coat were designer labeled, and tailored to her well-proportioned figure. Her dirty blond hair was cut in a practical but stylish coif, the right finishing touch for a self-assured and physically attractive woman.

"Unfortunately, I have few answers for your questions, Detective Pollard."

Ignoring his comment, Linda asked, "Who shot the victim?"

"One of his partners. This one was guiding me to a white van parked here. When a man in the van realized my abduction was not going to happen, he shot this one. He probably wanted to make sure he did not talk."

While Linda listened, Richard described the entire incident, stopping only to answer her questions, or when they were interrupted by a crime scene tech or one of the other investigators.

When he finished, she said, "OK, Richard, I think I have enough for now. I need you to come downtown and give a sworn statement." She smiled at him and added, "And I'm not going to let you follow me. I'll give you a ride home. You can clean up and change. Then we'll go downtown. I'll bring you to your car when we're finished."

They decided to have coffee before leaving Richard's condo. Sitting at the kitchen table, Linda asked, "So, what have you gotten yourself into? Is Martin King's murder and today's attack related?"

"I really don't know if they're related to one another, or even to Bear's murder. Remember, I am trying to find Bear's killer, not specifically solve these homicides."

"But they sure are connected to you, Richard, and, if not with his murder, with Bear himself. What did the guy today say to you? He was a member of what, the Christians for Justice? You did say Bear was investigating allegations for the Church."

"He said he was a member of Catholics for Equal Justice. That's just it." Richard was looking off and thinking. "The guy did too much talking. He may have been a fringe fanatic, in which case he would have talked a lot." Richard paused and thought about the man's ramblings. "I think he wanted to make sure he told me what he wanted me to hear. I can't place it. Something was wrong with the whole incident."

Linda's cellphone rang. "Detective Pollard ... What have you got, Jake? ... Who called? ... Nine, one, one couldn't trace it? ... Where are they? ... I'll leave now and meet you."

Linda stood up and started putting her notebook in a carrying case. "The gut who attacked you was Warren Salvador. His brother, Eli, was probably the first shooter. Their cousin, Vern, was probably driving. Don't know who the second shooter was."

"And you found this information, how?"

"Officer Neace ID'd Warren. Neace arrested Warren a few years ago. We received an anonymous call notifying 911 about two bodies behind a warehouse in Jamaica Plain. The detectives who responded to the report recognized Eli and Vern. They had been shot, and they were still warm despite the cold. The three usually worked together, and, since they were all killed within an hour or so, it's highly likely that they were together in the van. Anyway, I have to get over to Jamaica Plain. Can I trust you to go downtown and provide a sworn statement?"

"Yeah you go do what you have to."

34

Late that afternoon, Richard was in Bear's old office giving Laura and Steve an overview of his trip to South Dakota, the attack behind his condo, the shooting of Martin King, and the morning's incident at the Hatch Shell.

"All these events relate to Bear's murder?" Laura asked skeptically.

"I don't know," Steve added. "If Rob Lee was involved, I can't see these events associated with Bear's murder. Rob Lee doesn't scare people off. That is what the attack behind your place was about. If he wanted you out of the way, he'd have sent professionals, not those amateurs that came at you near the Hatch Shell"

After listing the events and dates on a whiteboard, Richard studied them for a moment, and then said, "I don't know what is associated and what might be background noise. Something said while I was in South Dakota bothers me. It was one of those items where, you know, you want to pursue it, but something else crops up and you can't remember what the first item was later on. That is what happened. I wish I could put my finger on it." After a moment, he shrugged and continued to write on the board.

The office phone rang, and Lora answered it. "This is Lora. How may I help you? ... Who's calling? ... Sheila. Hold on." Laura placed the call on hold and said, "Richard, Sheila Hotchkiss. She says it's urgent. She sounds very excited."

"Sheila, Richard ... Hold on; let me put you on speaker." Richard pressed the button and returned the headset to the cradle. " Sheila, I have Steve and Laura here with me. Laura runs this office."

"Richard, a Sherriff's Deputy I know, received a phone tip that a man in one thirty-seven Airport Drive is Rob Lee. The deputy works with me from time to time, and I had told him about Bear's murder and our suspicions that Rob Lee was behind it."

"Sheila, how does he know the tip is legitimate?" Richard's mind was planning as he asked his questions.

"The tip is legit. He took a picture of the guy the tipster described. I looked at the picture: the man in the photo matches the photo of Rob Lee Steve sent out when he told us about Bear."

"Sheila, do you know what the layout is? How do we get to where you're located?"

"It's a farmhouse off 340 in Clarke County. The house is in a small wooded area. There is one drive going in from the dirt road. Pasture and farmland line three sides. If you can get into Winchester or Warren County airports, we can pick you up."

"We need as much intel as possible; security, sensors, cameras, and floor plan. Sheila, do not attempt to get any of it if you might be discovered. Rob Lee and his men are very dangerous. Just get us what you can without getting hurt. I'll be down as soon as possible. Do not alert the locals. Good work, Sheila. We all owe you."

"Laura, will you get Charles on the phone, please? Steve, you want to go to Virginia?"

"Yeah, they probably have sensors around the house. I'll gather my gear."

"Richard, Charles is on the line."

"Thanks, Laura," Richard replied. He switched lines and began briefing Charles. When he completed the briefing, he asked Charles, "I need transportation. Can you arrange it for me?"

"Richard you should stay where you are. Our people will handle Rob Lee."

"No way, I have two people recovering from the last time. If people are going to be at risk, I'm going to be with them."

"I can't let you run this op. The men have to come out of the DC office. The assistant director in charge down there would have a fit."

"I know but I have to be involved. I'm responsible for capturing Rob Lee. I can't sit back while others are at risk."

"OK, but I'm on record as objecting."

"Noted, now what about transportation."

"I'll handle it and call you back."

"Good, and call Sheila with the arrangements."

35

Charles was waiting for him as Richard walked down the steps of the government Leer jet. "Charles, what are you doing here? You're no field agent."

"Hi Richard, I figured I better be here in case you and the agent in charge get into a contest about who is running this operation. Plus, if this goes wrong like the last one, I can at least say I was here before they send me into the field as dogcatcher. By the way, you lucked out. The ADC is on vacation."

"Do you know Steve?" Richard asked.

Charles and Steve shook hands. "I never met him, but I have heard some stories."

Steve laughed. "If the stories came from Richard, don't believe any of them."

As he was putting his overnight bag in the back of the SUV, Richard asked, "Charles, I see the Hostage Rescue team has already arrived." Richard was looking at the helicopters that were parked on the tarmac. "Where are we meeting the team?"

"At the parking lot of a small hotel not far from Route 340."

As they drove toward the meeting with the team, Richard noted the weather. The night air cooled with showers and occasional spurts of heavy rain. The thick clouds blocked any light from the Moon or stars. Just the type conditions he liked for an operation.

The SUV pulled into the parking lot of a single-level motel. All the doors to the rooms faced the parking lot. Several of the room-doors had a beat up car or pickup parked in front. The majority parking area, however, was now filled with black SUVs, a Hummer, and County Sheriff's patrol cars.

The special agent had fourteen men, all dressed in black tactical uniforms. Simon and his chief were in regular uniforms and Sheila was wearing a black tactical uniform.

When Steve saw Sheila, he pointed her out to Richard and asked, "Ah, who the hell is that?"

"That's Sheila. Haven't you two met?"

"Never, we just communicated when necessary, but we have never been on the same job together. I'll have to change that fast."

"Steve, is this going to be a problem? I mean, no one can be distracted on this mission."

"Distracted? Richard, are you kidding? She's like Angelina Jolie without the lips. Does she know what she's doing?"

"Her mother was a beauty queen of some kind. Miss America, I think. Her dad was a prominent attorney. She had an uncle who was an investigator for her father, another worked for the FBI, and another one in the CIA.

"Her mother wanted her to participate in the beauty contests. Her dad wanted her to be a doctor. She liked the investigative end of law enforcement. She has a degree in criminal justice and a law degree. As a girl, she entered and won a few beauty contests, but she also won more than her share of martial arts contest. She still competes in martial arts. I never counted how many black belts she has."

"And, if I hit you, you will not be saying, 'Come to daddy.'" Sheila had walked up behind Steve and Richard. "Hello, Richard." Sheila gave him a hug. "It has been a while. Sorry about Bear. I know how close you two were."

"Thank you, Sheila. I understand you never met Steve."

"No, I haven't." She smiled and shook Steve's hand. "Sounded like Richard gave you my resume. Just so you know; I'm not looking for a job. I have my own shop just outside Washington DC"

Introducing the man with her, Sheila said, "Richard, this is Special Agent Natalie. Natalie, this is Richard Moore." Richard and Natalie shook hands.

"What do we know about the farmhouse?" Richard asked.

Sheila responded, opening a laptop computer. "The property is clear for one hundred feet around the building," she said as she pointed out the terrain on the computer. "The next two hundred plus feet is wooded, with underbrush. The driveway winds from the dirt road to what was a barn and is now the garage. No clear line-of-sight from the road."

"What about trails, access to the fields?" Richard was looking at a picture of the two-story colonial farmhouse.

Pointing to the computer image, Sheila responded, "In addition to the main house and garage, here and here, there's a larger barn to the right rear of the house here. A path cuts through the woods. It must have been how the farm tractors got into the fields. The path is blocked by a gate. It's heavy and reinforced. That was done recently. The gate was also wired for motion."

"Was?" Steve asked.

Sheila looked at him. "I bypassed the motion detector while I was looking around."

"Any other motion detectors?" Steve asked.

"Motion detectors would be a problem for them. Too many deer, fox, occasional wild cat, and other wildlife for the detectors to be effective. They have pressure sensors in the ground. Three of my men are sweeping the area now. We'll have a couple of clear paths when we decide to go."

"That brings us to our man, Rob Lee. Where is he and how sure are we?"

"Ah, Richard, I'm Sheriff Cutter. This is Chief Buckwell." Richard shook hands with Cutter and Buckwell.

"I took that photo of your man earlier today. Sheila confirmed he's the one you call Rob Lee." Simon put another picture next to the first. "We also got this photo of him as he left the farmhouse. He went to town and had dinner with someone."

"Richard, Simon persuaded me to allow this operation. It's a matter of jurisdiction. If you have any doubts about the identity of this individual, do not proceed with this operation."

"Thank you, Chief. Your concern is the same as mine."

"All right, listen up. This man has a habit of slipping away. A military special ops squad cornered him in a home, and he managed to get away. That time he used an elaborate network of one-way doors in the basement and a tunnel that got him to a hidden garage.

"Tonight, we will send a three-man team down the cellar; I want four up to the second floor, and six on the first floor. I do not want anything tipping our hand. We hit hard and fast. We will not smoke them out; we go in unannounced. Rules of engagement.

"People, keep this in mind: Rob Lee hires only former military personnel. Only combat veterans. They are not to be taken lightly. They do not know this man is wanted by the government. They think he is a businessman. Most of them have not broken any laws and probably will not as long as they work for Rob Lee. So, we have combat vets in that house who are law-abiding citizens. Treat them with the respect and caution they deserve."

Richard turned to talk with the Special Agent Natalie. "This is your team. You take them in. When it's clear, I will come in. I reserve the right to override your orders. I'm in charge. If things go wrong, I'm in charge."

"Richard, this is a crack team. It will not go wrong."

"OK, let's move to the jump off point."

Three of Sheila's men met the team on Route 340, a quarter of a mile from the farmhouse access drive. "Your man returned about half an hour ago." One of Sheila's men informed them. "The driver left again ten minutes ago. We have a tail on him."

"What about sensors?" Richard asked.

Another of Sheila's men spoke, "Here's a rough map of the area. We didn't have enough time to check the entire area, so we concentrated on access lines your men could use to assault the house."

"Got extra copies?" Special Agent Natalie asked.

"Yes. Here you go." He handed a dozen copies to Natalie.

"If there is nothing else, Natalie, it's all yours," Richard said.

36

The operation went off flawlessly. The six men found in the house were taken by surprise and, once the agents identified themselves, showed little inclination to resist. When the all clear was given, Richard entered the living room and found all six men sitting handcuffed on the floor. "Where's Rob Lee?" Richard asked.

When there was no response, he spoke into his communication mike. "Natalie, this is Richard. Our man is not among those in custody. I repeat, our man is not in custody here. Are there any other prisoners?"

Natalie appeared at his side just as he finished. "Richard the team reports that there are no signs of others in the house. The place is secured and these are the only ones found."

Richard took a deep breath and let it out slowly. "Rob Lee could not have gotten out of this house. Natalie, please ask the team to double-check the cellar, garage, and barn. Sheila," Richard said into his mike, "Sheila, where is the driver?"

"Hold one, Richard."

As Richard waited for a reply, he looked at the six men and asked, "Where is Rob Lee?"

One of the men looked up at Richard. "Who the fuck is Rob Lee, and why are we handcuffed?"

"Rob Lee rented this house. He is also your boss."

"Look, man, I don't know who rented this house, and there's no Rob Lee in this outfit."

"Richard." Shelia was back in communication. "We lost him. Our man followed the car out to the Interstate and then it just disappeared."

"Natalie, issue a BOLO on the car, please."

Turning back to the men, Richard again looked around. Five of the men seemed calm and comfortable. One was nervous. He fidgeted and his eyes were red. "You, what's your name." Richard was looking at the nervous one.

"Me?" The man looked around at his fellow captured.

"Yes, you. What's your name?"

"Ah, Chives sir."

Richard noticed it right away. This guy was recently in the military. He had no idea what was happening or how to respond. It made him nervous.

"Come with me," Richard commanded.

In the kitchen Richard said, "Have a seat."

"Sir, I'd rather stand."

"Suit yourself."

They had walked through the dining room and into the kitchen. Chives walked in front of Richard and turned at the kitchen table to face him. Richard had his back to the dining room. To his left and behind was an opening that led to a hallway. The hallway went to the front door and stairs to the second floor.

Directly across from Richard, the rear door lay splintered on the floor: evidence of the violent nature of the entry made by the assault team. Left of the door was a section of wainscot cupboards and broom closet. The sink, stove, and refrigerator were on Richard's right.

"Chives, where did Rob Lee go?"

Chives stood silent for a moment then replied, "Like the guy in the other room told you, there is no Rob Lee. You guys raided the wrong house."

"We didn't. Rob Lee is wanted for some very serious crimes. He has left guys like you out to dry more times than I'd like to count. Now I want to know where he is."

"Look, I don't know what you're talking about."

"OK how about some real time. Harboring a fugitive. We found some interesting weapons here. You'll do time for that too."

"Hey, man, I just got here. I haven't been in this house before."

"If you haven't been here before, how did you happen to be here now?"

Beads of sweat had formed on Chive's forehead. He was trying to think faster than Richard and losing. "Oh fuck. All right, I got out of the Army six months ago. I finished two tours in Iraq and I had had enough. I've been looking for a job since I got out. You know how many employers want to hire a combat vet? None, nada, zero. They all ask 'Can't you be recalled if the government wants?' Sure it can. Once it has a sucker on the hook, why let it go?"

He was pacing a little. "A friend of mine told me this guy hires combat vets. The job is physical and personal security. So I call the number my friend gave me and I had dinner with the man."

"Is this the man you had dinner with?" Richard set down the photos taken earlier.

Chives looked at the photos and started laughing.

"What do you find so funny in the pictures?" Richard saw no amusement in his current situation.

"This one here," Chives dropped the picture of Rob Lee getting into the car. "That's the man I had dinner with. He offered me a job. This one," he dropped the photo purported of Rob Lee getting out of the car and entering the house, "this one's me."

"What? What do you mean it's you?"

"The guy said his name was Joe Turner. We had a nice dinner but I was too nervous to eat much. You see my wife is pregnant. I don't have a job or health insurance. I really need this guy to hire me.

"We were about to finish the interview. We both had coffee and I was responding to names of guys he knows in my old unit. His cellphone rang and he answered it. Then he excused himself and walked away for a couple of minutes. I see him talk to a guy at another table. Then Joe comes back to our table and told me I was hired. I mean, just like that. Starting right then. He said the guy at the other table was his driver and would take me back to the house to meet some of the guys.

"I was like on cloud nine. Wow, six months looking, and now finally a paying job! He said he had to go down the street for a meeting. He asked if he could borrow my rain slick and I could wear his jacket. I was so happy; I didn't care if he asked if he could have my pants."

Chives finally sat down and put his head in his hands. "It was a fucking trick. He must have known you guys were waiting for him so he traded jackets and sets me up. Now what am I going to do?"

"Who put you in touch with Rob Lee?"

"Martinez. He's the only guy here I know."

"He's here?"

"Yeah. Sitting in the living room with the others."

"Natalie, you have a guy named Martinez sitting on the floor. Please bring him into the kitchen."

Richard had turned to look in the dining room as he made his request to Natalie. As he turned back to look at Chives, he saw the broom closet door open. "Hit the deck," he shouted at Chives, as he kicked the chair out from under him.

The man in the broom closet opened fire with two three-round busts from his assault rifle. As Richard was heading to the floor, he aimed his Glock at the shooter and fired four rounds. It was over quicker than it started.

Two men came rushing in from the dining room and two came down the hallway from the front door. The communications network Richard and the team were using became a symphony of questions, comments and orders. Richard ordered everyone to stop. "You said this place was secured." He was shouting and knew he had to control himself. More quietly he continued. "I want this building cleared top to bottom again. I've got two men down. Get the EMT in here as soon as possible."

Chives had taken two rounds. One in his calf and another grazed his hip. Richard started to lose his balance. He had been hit twice in the bulletproof vest.

As the team raced through the room, a beeping sound was heard throughout the building.

"What is that sound?" Richard asked.

"Richard, Natalie. The fire detectors are beeping. I think they are responding to the cordite from the gunfire."

The beeping went from slow to frantic, and then stopped.

"Natalie, I never heard smoke detectives respond that way."

Richard's words were followed by a high-pitched whistle. The covers of the smoke detectors popped open and a loud bang, like a firecracker going off in a can, was heard from each of the smoke detectors. The noise was followed by a stream of confetti shot out in all directions from the smoke detectors.

The heavy rain had been replaced by intermittent light showers. A heavy cloud cover continued to darken the night sky. Charles,

Sheila, Steve, and Natalie were standing around the ambulance. An EMT was attending to Richard.

"Someone sure has a warped sense of humor," Natalie was commenting.

"You never met Rob Lee," Richard replied. "It wasn't meant as a joke. He was sending a message."

"And that would be, what?" Natalie asked.

"Think about it. The smoke detectors could have been real bombs. Where would all of us be now if they had been?"

Steve shuddered at the thought. "What about the shooter? That was no joke or message."

"Don't know. We'll never know. He didn't make it."

Richard stood up and adjusted his shirt and jacket. He looked at Natalie, "If there is nothing else"

"Special Agent Natalie." A member of HRT approached. "Sir, the five detainees all stated that they are employed by Global Advanced Protective Services, GAPS. Owner's name is Joe Turner. A California firm is promoting the national tour of *Strawberry Pie*, the current rock sensation out of London England. The promoter hired GAPS. He has hired them before. Said they are very good. All the detainees check out. Clean records and no wants or warrants."

"Well, Chavez positively identified Joe Turner as Rob Lee," added Richard. "So maybe we should take a good look in to GAPS."

Richard shook Natalie's hand. "Nice working with you. Let's wrap this up and get out of here." Everyone headed off to handle their part of the cleanup. "Sheila, hold on for a minute."

Sheila stayed and watched as the others left. "I'd appreciate it if you would run a background check on Chives, the wounded guy."

"Sure. What's up?"

Richard told her about what Chives told him about job hunting and the events of the evening. "His wife is expecting their first child, he's in the hospital with gunshot wounds, and Rob Lee isn't likely to keep him employed. If the guy checks out I'll hire him."

"Richard, I always liked working with you. You can be as kind as you can be dangerous. I'll check him out but my guess you already have an intuitive feeling he's legit. Your intuition is usually accurate."

37

"Boss you can't pull me from this story. I don't care what the vice president wants." Stephanie was standing in front of the editor's desk.

"Stephanie, your story on the Big Dig corruption is old news. It can wait until a slower time. Right now the election is coming up quickly. The vice president may win with a larger margin than any presidential candidate in history. I want complete coverage and the vice president has offered open access if you are the assigned reporter. That, my dear, is a story."

"Boss, you have plenty of political reporters. They would do a better job from outside the campaign than I would do with open access."

"You're not thinking long term. Do this now and you can get us access during the transition and beyond."

"OK, but I'm taking vacation time starting now. Thursday is my birthday and I'm going to the show and dinner with Richard. I'll see you Monday." Stephanie walked out of the office and sat in her cubicle. She was furious. The vice president, it appeared, was manipulating her life. "If he thinks this will get me to accept his job offer, he better prepare for a disappointment," she said to herself.

She went through the stack of documents related to the Big Dig. She noted discrepancies, that by themselves were not a story; however, her intuition told her another issue lay just below the mass of numbers. She just wasn't sure how she would find it.

She decided she needed some help from sources not on the paper's payroll. An accountant friend would help make sense of the numbers, and a computer hacker would help check on information not in the official records. She called them both and then scooped the papers and left the office.

38

"Good morning Laura." Richard entered the office followed by Steve.

"Hi, Richard, Steve. How was your flight?" Steve and Richard had left Washington three hours earlier after meeting with Charles in his office.

"Without problems or delays," Steve commented.

Richard headed straight to Bear's office and sat down. He fixed his eyes on the whiteboard across from him. He had written a jumbled mix of names of people, companies and locations. Some of the people were moving entities while others were dead. The only thing Richard could be certain of was that the people were being crossed off his list not because he was eliminating them as suspects, but because they were dying.

Laura stood in the doorway of the office watching him trying to put it all into order. She had never seen Richard look so perplexed while reviewing and following leads. "Richard the chief of Stoneham Police called earlier. He asked that you call him as soon as you got in."

"Did he give any indication what he wants?"

"None just said he wanted you to call."

"OK. Thanks, Laura, and Laura, the flight was fine. Thanks for asking."

"Paul, how are you?" Richard asked Paul Silverman, chief of Stoneham's Police Department.

"Hi, Richard, are you holding up OK?"

"Yea, I'm OK. You wanted me to call. What's up?"

"We may have a break in Bear's case. The receptionist at Higher Credit Score, a tenant in the building where Bear was killed, reported a worker missing. Apparently, the man has no family in the area and the receptionist has an interest in him. Anyway, after a week with no information about him, and since he worked in the building where Bear was killed, I asked the Cambridge PD to check on him. He rents an apartment on Massachusetts Avenue down the street from Harvard University."

"Did they go in?" Richard was eager to hear what the outcome was.

"They did. No one in the building had seen the man since Friday before Bear's murder. The building superintendent was helpful and opened the apartment. Turns out the super and this guy were friendly. The guy would help the super out with some of the maintenance.

"Inside the apartment they found one of Bear's credit cards, his car keys, and his cellphone."

"Jesus, Paul, why didn't you call me with this before? I would have come right over. This sounds like our man."

"It gets complicated. In addition to Bear's belongings, they found newspaper clippings, schedules, and airplane flight stubs. The guy was tracking the vice president. He had a diary in which he rambles on about how bad the vice president would be for the country if he were elected president. He went on to write that he could not allow the vice president to be inaugurated as president. This information, by the way, is classified. The Secret Service has locked down the guy's room and holding all evidence, including Bear's stuff, until they track this guy."

Richard was thinking about the possibility that Bear's killer was now identified. All he had to do now was track the guy down. He was also thinking about Rob Lee. He wondered what the connection might be.

"Paul you got a file on this guy, what is his name?"

"Marcus McGill. He grew up in Jamaica Plain. I got a thin file on him. I'll fax it to you. I'll send you whatever we get along the way. I'd appreciate it if you would do the same."

"You can count on it. Thank you, Paul."

Richard sat while he mentally put together a plan for dealing with the information he had just received. He would have to skirt the Secret Service. Their only priority was protecting the vice president, soon to be president. If they allowed a killer to go unprosecuted in the process, so be it. Richard would not allow that to happen.

"Laura, Steve, will you come in here please," he called out.

Richard gave them the information he received from the Stoneham chief of police. "Laura, I'd like you to go talk with the receptionist."

"Me? I'm no investigator. I'm a secretary."

"You're more than that and you know it, besides I think you'll get more from her than anyone here. We need names of friends, relatives, coworkers. I also want you to get Phil and tell him I need him here now."

Laura went to her desk and called Phil.

"Steve I want to know more about this guy than anyone else including himself. Scan, tap, or hack, I don't care. No item too small. Start with a criminal background check, then finances, bank accounts, credit cards, and the airlines."

"Richard," Laura called out from her desk, "Phil is on his way. I gave him an overview of what we are doing. He didn't want to come down from New Hampshire until I told him why."

Richard and Steve worked in the office while Laura talked with the receptionist and Phil made inquires at law enforcement agencies in the area. By six that evening, they had a list of friends who lived in the greater Boston area. Marcus's mother and father had moved to Texas. He had one brother and no sisters. The brother is doing time for armed robbery. Aunts, uncles, and cousins were scattered throughout New England. The largest cluster of them was within a six-mile radius of Boston.

"Phil, I hope you have more information for us. Steve came up empty. Marcus has no criminal record anywhere. His last ticket was a three years ago. He sends money to his parents apparently to help pay off a parent/student loan for college."

"I talked with Cambridge detectives. They told me, off the record, Marcus is clean. No complaints from other tenants in the building. The superintendent told them he was always courteous and helpful. The detectives in Jamaica Plane said Marcus grew up around gang activity in his neighborhood. He watched his brother get into trouble all the time. The brother was a member of the Commandos, a neighborhood gang. Marcus watched his parents try to deal with his brother. They spent a lot on lawyers. They lost a house and moved to an apartment. One cop told me Marcus wanted nothing to do with gang activity. He wanted to go to college, get a decent job, and help his parents."

"So what the hell pushed this guy over the edge? Why would he kill anyone, let alone Bear? Why would he be stalking the VP?" Richard asked to neither in particular.

Steve and Phil exchanged eye contact. Then Phil said, "Look, Richard forget why. We'll find the guy, then he can explain. Let's just keep working to finding him."

"You're right. It's late. Let's call it a day."

Richard was locking the office when his cellphone rang. "Richard."

"You're not home: what are you doing?"

"Hi, Stephanie. How was your day?"

"Interesting, but nothing to talk about. How about you?

"A development in Bear's case." Richard gave Stephanie a condensed version of the day's developments. "We just finished for the day. I'm locking up."

"Let's meet for breakfast at The Kitchen tomorrow morning?"

"I'd like that. Should I call or just nudge?"

"Ahmm ... it's late. We will meet at seven tomorrow morning."

"OK, but make it seven-thirty. I should extend my run tomorrow morning."

"Seven thirty at The Kitchen. Good night. I love you."

39

The Kitchen was a neighborhood eatery in the south end of Boston. One door opened to the bakery portion of the business where patrons could view and order cakes, pies, cookies, and a variety of pastries. Another door opened into the restaurant. A U-shaped Formica counter with chrome stools bolted to the floor occupied the majority of the area. Formica tables with wooded chairs lined the walls. A fast-order chef, the owner, worked over a large griddle and stove, his back to the patrons. He often chatted with the customers as he prepared their meals. Breakfast was the eatery's main staple. The restaurant remained open until three in the afternoon serving a variety of hot sandwiches and fried foods. If Webster's dictionary wanted a picture for the definition of *greasy spoon,* The Kitchen was the place to take it.

Richard arrived five minutes late. He found Stephanie seated at one of the tables. He walked over, bent down, and gave her a passionate kiss hello. "As always, you look beautiful."

"Thank you. How was your run? You look a little tired."

"It helped some. I still can't sort out the items in my mind that keep nagging to come forward."

The waitress poured coffee and asked for their order. Richard had always enjoyed their coffee. It was strong but never bitter and the staff always made sure it was fresh. Stephanie ordered juice and whole wheat toast, dry and a side of homemade strawberry jam.

"I think I'll indulge myself today," Richard said to the waitress. "Two eggs over medium, Canadian bacon, home fries, wheat toast, and juice."

"Living dangerously, are we?" Stephanie asked.

"Just living," he replied.

While they ate, Richard told Stephanie the events of the past few days. She had heard some of it during phone conversations with Richard and with Laura. Stephanie told Richard about her investigation into the trucking discrepancies that she found while reviewing the records of the Big Dig.

Neither mentioned Rob Lee nor the dangers that their respective investigations might bring. Their conversation was light without accusations or criticism. The smiles and glow to their eyes reflected a couple in love.

"Richard, I need a favor."

"Sure. What is it?"

"Don't be so quick to say sure. As I told you, it looks as if too many truckloads of fill were billed by the contractor. One of the contractors submitted invoices for days when the others either had not or had less than usual. I checked the dates and they correspond to days with severe weather or operational problems. The severe weather and operational problems prohibited the trucks from operating on those days.

"Either the subcontract drivers were submitting forged invoices or the contractor was doctoring their invoices. On the face of it, I find it hard to believe all the subcontractors were forging invoices at the same time. I think the contractor was padding his profit."

Richard thought for a minute as he sipped his coffee. "If I remember correctly, there were reports one of the trucking contractors had dubious financial connections and accusations of money laundering. Why push this?"

"An informant told me the subcontractors never received the rates the construction contract stipulated. Subs were to be paid the union rate plus expenses. If that didn't happen, and the contractor padded the invoices, the contractor made off with a considerable amount of profit. No one picked the discrepancies up during an audit. I wonder why. The contractor took a risk padding the profit on a very profitable job. I think there is more to the story."

"A story you have to write … Hold on." Richard held up his hand to stop Stephanie from protesting. "It's what you do. I know. What do you need?"

"I need Steve's help. I know he has hacked into bank accounts and reviewed files. I don't have time to go the long way around. I need bank information now before my editor pulls the story out from under me and sends me on the campaign trail."

"I can't speak for Steve. You will have to ask him yourself."

"I know but I didn't want to ask him without first asking you."

"I think it's a bad idea. Steve could get in a lot of trouble. Talk with him. He has to decide."

"Thank you. You haven't lost the tickets for tomorrow night, have you?"

"I left them at the box office just to make sure we get in. I hired a car and driver. He will pick us up at five-thirty. Dinner at the Copley, then the show."

"It sounds great. Nothing to worry about for a few hours."

"We better get going. I have a lot of ground to cover."

"I'll see you at the office. I'm going to talk with Steve this morning."

40

Bear's office suite was not designed to accommodate the number of people coming in that morning. Richard and Stephanie found Laura, her two daughters, Steve, Phil, and Linda Pollard.

"Richard, I'm sorry about the girls. The school cancelled classes and I haven't found a sitter yet."

"No problem Laura. Don't bother finding a sitter unless you don't want the girls in here. This place will clear out shortly and you'll be able to spend some time with them. As a matter of fact, take them out to lunch on me."

"I'll see how things go," was Laura's response.

"Linda, what brings you out of the city?"

"I wanted to tell you we got the ballistics results from Eli, and Vern. The gun used was the same one that killed Bear." The room went quiet.

Richard went into deep thought mode. As he did, he looked around the room. "I'm sorry Linda; I haven't introduced you to anyone." Richard introduced Linda to Laura, Steve, and Phil. "And this is Stephanie Lynn she's—"

"She's a reporter with the Globe. Hi, Stephanie, haven't seen you for a while."

"Linda, you look terrific. How's Boston's PD treating you?"

"Between you and me, it's still a male enclave. My gold shield helps."

"You two know each other?" Richard asked. "Oh, I should have known. Linda would be involved with high-profile cases and Stephanie likes to investigate high-profile cases."

"Yes, but I haven't gotten to investigate those types of cases for a while."

"While you two get caught up," Steve interjected, "I need to talk with Richard and Phil. If you will excuse us." Steve, Richard, and Phil went into Bear's office.

"I'm no investigator, but this guy Marcus Magill can't be our killer," Steve said as he closed the door.

"Why can't he be?' asked Phil.

"I got into his finances last night. He has a student loan, car loan, two credit cards, and rent. He pays everything on time. He sends his parents money every month. He puts a little away each pay date. When he uses his credit card, he pays it in full when the statement comes in. He doesn't buy anything excessive. He hasn't used credit at a restaurant or hotel either that I can tell."

"So he's frugal. That doesn't mean he can't shoot someone," Richard commented.

"You're right." Steve replied, "It doesn't. In addition to being a suspect in Bear's murder, Marcus is also wanted as a possible threat to the vice president, soon to be president. The evidence includes stubs from three plane trips to cities where the vice president was appearing. All three flights were charged to his credit cards."

"Don't forget his journal. The Secret Service found rantings and threats written in his journal," Phil added.

"I haven't. That's why I am very confused. One of the flights puts him in Florida on the same day he did something very uncharacteristic for him."

"Like what? " Richard asked.

"As I said, Marcus always put a portion of his pay into his savings account. About a year ago, he withdrew all his funds and purchased stock. Not just any blue chip stock but cheap stock in an unknown company. The company was tanking. The stock had been sliding in price for over a year. The company was posting losses. It was a very risky investment ..." Steve paused for a moment then continued, "which was very uncharacteristic for him."

"So he lost all his savings and decided to start a life of crime. Happens. I remember—"

"Phil, Marcus didn't lose all his savings." Steve interrupted, "The company was bought by a competitor. They paid four times the price per share he paid."

"Four times? What a lucky gamble." Phil was thinking how he could use luck like that.

"Luck, maybe, but not likely. He did it again three more times. Each time he put all the money in the savings account." Steve watched the reaction of Richard and Phil to this information.

Richard looked at Steve. "Insider trading?"

"It certainly appears like it, but where was he getting the inside information? If he were doing so well, why become a murderer and a stalker of the vice president? See? This is why I don't think he's our man."

"OK, we will have to review the transactions of the four companies" Richard said. "Steve, since you already have a lot of the information, you should work on it. See if you can come up with a common link. Phil, you have a list of close friends and family for Marcus for me?"

"Right here." Phil handed the list to Richard.

"I'll interview these people. Phil you take the second-tier acquaintances."

"Richard," Steve interrupted, "You may want to look up a student at MIT. Marcus sent her flowers about a year ago with a thank you note. I checked with the florist this morning. It was around the time Marcus made his first profit on risky stock."

"Got her name and address?"

Steve handed Richard a piece of paper. "Heng Hua, she's working on her doctorate."

"All right let's hit the streets. By the way, Steve, Stephanie will be asking you for a favor. Do what you feel comfortable doing, and don't say yes unless you want to. I voiced my objections."

As Richard opened the office door, the door to the suite opened. "Well, Small-town, you had a party and didn't invite us?"

"May I help you?" Laura stood up, and blocked Detective Kelly's path.

"Move, Sister. I want to talk with Small-town." Kelly kept moving.

Laura stood her ground. "No one named Small-town here, and if there was, you don't get to talk with anyone unless you check with me."

"I don't check in with anyone, especially secretaries."

"Kelly, shut up. The lady is doing her job. Stop being an ass," Nelson, his partner reprimanded.

"I'm Detective Nelson. This charmer is Detective Kelly. We are here to talk with Richard." He gave Laura his most charming smile.

Laura looked at Nelson. "If you will wait one minute, please I have a message to give Richard. Then I will see if he wants to see you."

"Quite frankly, Sister, I don't care if he wants to or not. We will talk with him: after you give him the message of course."

Laura ignored Kelly and walked over to Richard. "Before you meet with the two detectives, I talked with the receptionist like you ask me to."

"And how did that go?"

"Better than I expected. I think she has an interest in Marcus. He either never noticed or was not interested in her. She gave me a list of names and numbers, people she remembers call or visited. She gave the same list to the Secret Service. She didn't have a good time with them. She said they were very rude and accusatory."

This information caught Richard by surprise. The agents should have been very gentle and supportive. They were trying to elicit information, not alienate the person they were talking with.

"You sure she said they were rude?"

"Yes. She said she wanted to be helpful, but they treated as if she knew more than she did. They were also pushing everyone for information as quickly as possible. She said she felt they were under a deadline. She was so rattled by them she forgot to mention one person. Marcus had a flurry of calls from and to a woman with a Chinese name. She didn't remember the name, but it might have been *Hue*. She had the impression they were close but didn't want anyone to know."

"The name is Heng Hua. Steve found some information in Marcus's financial data. Nice work, Laura. I knew you could handle the receptionist."

Richard walked out to the main office area. Stephanie and Linda had been chatting and finished.

"I need to talk with Steve," Stephanie told Linda.

"And I need to get back to my office," Linda said.

"Linda, please don't leave just yet," Richard asked.

When Linda turned to look at Richard, she saw Kelly and Nelson standing near the suite's entry door. "Well Richard you are popular today. Detectives Kelly and Nelson, what brings you two to this part of town?"

Nelson was the first to walk over to Linda and extend his hand. "Hello, Linda, as beautiful as always."

"Thank you, Nelson. Why is it you haven't been able to dump that slime of a partner?"

"Linda, we've saved each other over the years. Some people don't like his style, but we work well together. We're partners. We're family. I'd appreciate it if you remember that."

"Linda, I think you're the one out of jurisdiction," Kelly said without a greeting or handshake. "Small-town, if it isn't too much inconvenience, let's talk."

"What about Kelly?"

"My partner and I want to talk with you about the attack near Storrow Drive. The three that got away were shot with the same gun used to kill your friend. That ties the attack with our case. So, let's talk."

"Actually, Detective, the attack and the two shootings are Detective Pollard's. I gave her my statement. The three of you can use this office to compare notes. I have other work to do." Richard started to leave and Kelly grabbed him by the arm.

"Not so fast, Small-town. Why is it you always seem so eager to leave when we have questions for you?"

Richard leaned in to get close to Kelly, and in a low voice replied, "Because you never say the magic word." Then he pulled Kelly so his mouth was close to Kelly's ear. "And I don't answer to assholes." Richard walked out the door.

41

Autumn weather in New England was a byproduct of continuous skirmishes between North and South weather fronts. The jet stream pulls Arctic cold fronts down through Canada and continues south until it is blocked by a tropical front. Two days previously, the Arctic front won out and plunged Boston into freezing temperatures.

Atlantic easterly currents move tropical fronts formed in the Gulf of Mexico or the Bahamas northeast along the coast until they reach New England. The Gulf Stream then turns them more easterly and heads them to England. One such tropical front had pushed the Arctic cold out of New England. As Richard traveled south on Interstate 93, he soaked up the warmth of the sun. The temperature, just two days ago thirty-one, was a balmy fifty-nine. The forecast for the next several days included similar temperatures.

He spent several hours gathering information about Heng Hua. Since most of the information he could get directly from her, if he ever found out where she was, he finally went to the Registrar's Office. There he produced credentials identifying him as a member of Home Land Security, which was factually correct; although, he was not working a case for Home Land Security.

Heng Hua was in building thirty-nine on Vassar Street. She was scheduled to leave that building and attend a class in building seven. As he stood on the sidewalk outside building thirty-nine, he realized Ms. Hua had several exits from which she could leave. Fortune was with him, however, and she came out the front entrance.

Earlier, a class mate of Ms. Hua showed Richard a picture of her. The picture was of the cast of a troupe she had worked with the year before. Richard watched her walk down the street in the direction of Massachusetts Avenue. She was short, although probably not by Chinese standards, petite in frame, and nervous. Her black hair flowed to her waist and, as she walked, swished at her waist.

"Ms. Hua … Heng Hua," Richard repeated. She stutter stepped: almost stopping, then wanting to flee, then deciding to see who was calling her name. She eyed Richard, the only well-dressed male of adult age within voice range. Panic crossed her face.

"I'm Richard Moore, Ms Hua. I would like to talk with you about someone you know or have had some contact." He approached closer very carefully.

Heng quickly looked around. The expression on her face told Richard she wanted to flee. She looked at the passing students hoping to find one she could latch onto and escape.

"Ms. Hua, you are in no trouble and I present no harm to you." It was then that Richard realized she might not understand a word he was saying. He repeated his greeting and assurance that she was in no trouble, this time in Cantonese.

Her reply was not in Cantonese. Richard took a minute or so and smiled. "You may prefer Mandarin to Cantonese but I never mastered the dialect."

Still weary, she gave him a slight smile and said in English, "Then I will have to use English." It was almost perfect English with only a slight accent.

"That would be helpful. Marcus is in very big trouble. I think he has been framed and you might be able to help him."

"Framed as in a picture? Why would someone put a frame around him?"

Richard looked around at the busy sidewalks and traffic. "Can we go someplace to talk? I'll buy you lunch or something. I was told Bosworth's Café is in the building where your next class is scheduled."

"If we must. I would like there better than with no people." Her accent broke through and the English was less than perfect.

They sat on stools at a table apart from the crowd. Heng sipped her bottled water and picked at a sandwich. Richard had ordered a sandwich and coffee although he was not hungry. He asked her where she had learned English.

"A member of village come to America, when I was little girl. He returned and taught us. I have been here many years and improved."

Heng was speaking quickly. Richard had experienced this before. People being interrogated often spoke quickly trying to explain and get to what they believed to be the important facts.

"Heng, I present no harm to you. You are not in trouble. I am only interested in helping your friend Marcus. Will you tell me how you met him?"

"How do you know I met him?" She stopped picking at the sandwich and was now twisting her fingers.

"He sent you flowers with a thank you card."

"You are investigating me. Why?" She was nearly distraught. Richard expected her to tell him to, "Fuck off!" and walk out the door. She just remained seated.

"I am not investigating you. I am trying to help Marcus. When I tried to find some clues about where he might be, I found a receipt showing he had sent you flowers. Why are you so scared?"

"When police come to village asking questions, people disappear."

"Oh. I thought you were in the United States long enough to know that is not how we work."

"No political prisoners? No missing people? I think you are wrong." She slowed her speech. "I am sorry. My English becomes choppy when I talk fast. I will control my speech."

"Heng, I am not here to debate our political ideologies. I think someone wants the authorities to believe Marcus is a danger to the vice president. I want to find him before the authorities."

"The frame you said. Is that what you meant?"

"Yes. Someone leaves evidence or information with the intention that the authorities believe the wrong person is responsible for an act or possible act. It is called a frame."

"In my country is called business as normal."

Richard smiled and she smiled back. "Why don't you eat your sandwich," he said.

In the end, Richard learned little from Heng. He did come away thinking Marcus had contacted her recently although she denied any recent contact. Richard also came away with the feeling she would be in contact with Marcus again, soon.

Richard tried to impress upon Heng that he only wanted to help Marcus. He told her if Marcus did not shoot Bear and was not a threat to the vice president, then he should find a way to contact Richard. He hoped he made a positive impression on Heng.

42

"Andre, a friend of mine got this information. It shows two sets of books for a Papalia Construction Company that worked on the Big Dig." It was late afternoon, and Stephanie was talking with Andre Pearson, a forensic accountant she often used when checking on companies.

"Well, Stephanie, that is a pleasant surprise. I usually have to build the second set of books to find out what a company was up to. This will make it much easier.'

"Maybe not." She smiled at Andre. "I am under a very short deadline."

"How short?" he asked, skeptically.

"I need whatever you can give me, tomorrow."

"Tomorrow?" He pulled open a desk drawer, pulled out a piece of white paper and handed it to her. "Here."

Stephanie looked at both sides of the blank paper and asked, "What is this?"

"I'm saving you time. That is the report I would give you when you come back tomorrow."

"Come on, Andre, with everything I've done for you, at least you could try to get me something tomorrow."

After a few moments, Andre sighed, and said, "I'll look at the books. If I can blend the information, I'll have something for you. If not," he pointed at the blank sheet, "you have what I will have tomorrow."

Stephanie got up from her chair, leaned over Andre, and kissed him on the cheek. "You're a love. Thanks. Call me tomorrow."

Stephanie made a couple of late calls to subcontractor truckers. Most would not talk with her. As always; however, she was able to get a few to talk off the record. What she wanted was a contact that had been inside Papalia, someone knowledgeable about the company's finances. She finally struck it lucky around nine thirty, when one of the subcontractors called her back with the name of a junior accountant, a woman who had been terminated by the contractor.

43

Thursday morning started bright, sunny, and a balmy forty-five degrees. *A terrific day for a run,* Richard thought as he covered several miles along the Charles River. He mentally reviewed his schedule for the day: interview three close friends, (if anyone was really close), of Marcus, a call to Dalton Whitetail, a member of the Presidential Secret Service Protection Detail and longtime friend of Richard's, a call to Sheila to ask for a team on standby in Boston, and then some shopping.

Steve rose early determined to do more digging into the construction company's finances for Stephanie. He also allocated time for checking on Marcus McGill and the Secret Service's investigation.

Phil was still in bed. He would get a late start after catching up on some much-needed rest. Breakfast was first on his list. He and a group of retired men gathered for breakfast every morning at the local coffee shop. He had not seen them for some time. Later, he would check on the Ford Bullet he knew Richard would love to own. Finally, he would get back to interviewing the second-tier friends of Marcus.

Stephanie paced in her home office. She was officially on vacation and could not go into her office at the Globe. She did not want to run into her editor, at least not yet. She wanted to meet with Kim Myers, the terminated accountant, but, first, she needed to talk to Andre.

"Andre, will you have any useful information for me?"

"Oh, hi, Stephanie. You really are in a rush. Listen, come by late this afternoon. I think you will be very pleased."

"I have an appointment and have to be home by five."

"OK. Make it three. I'll throw you out around four-thirty if you haven't already left," Andre said, and then hung up.

"Hi, I'm looking for Kim Myers, please."

Stephanie had discovered that Myers now worked in the reimbursement department of Massachusetts General Hospital. The switchboard operator found the extension and connected Stephanie.

"This is Kim. How may I help you?" Stephanie hung up.

After confirming that she had the correct telephone number, Stephanie drove to Wellington circle in Medford. The building where Kim worked was a four-story former research facility that was now the call center and patient billing facility for MGH. The nearest restaurants or fast-food establishments were approximately a mile from the building. Ninety percent of the workers in the building went to the cafeteria located on the first floor.

Stephanie arrived at eleven-forty-five and persuaded a young security guard to point out Kim to her. It was nearly an hour later before Kim appeared crossing the lobby in the direction of the cafeteria.

"That's her," the guard said to Stephanie, "the one in the black skirt and striped blouse with ruffles." Stephanie walked up to her and introduced herself.

"Ms. Myers, I'm Stephanie Lynn. I'm a reporter with the Boston Globe.'

"Hi, Ms. Lynn." Kim shook Stephanie's hand. "If you're here to pay a bill, you have the wrong person."

"No. I 'm here to talk with you, if you don't mind."

"Sure, but you might find it boring. Most people do. I have to get lunch. I'm starved."

"We can talk while you eat if that doesn't bother you."

"OK, let's go. The food in the cafeteria is pretty good. The hospital subsidizes the cost since we are so far away from any other place to buy lunch."

Kim wandered around deciding on what to buy. Stephanie filled a cup with iced tea while watching Kim. Stephanie was amazed at how relaxed Kim was about talking with her. Stephanie had expected some resistance. After Kim got her lunch, they sat at a table removed from the rest of the crowd.

"You don't eat much," Kim commented.

"I'm going out to dinner early. I don't want to spoil my appetite."

"I have to eat. It keeps my blood sugar up. Otherwise I pass out."

Stephanie watched Kim as she took small bites of her sandwich. Stephanie guessed Kim was in her mid-thirties. Her auburn hair was cut just below the earlobes. Her complexion was clean and smooth. She wore no makeup and no fingernail polish.

"So, what did you want to talk with me about?" Kim asked, as she wiped her mouth with her napkin. Something she did, Stephanie noticed, each time after she swallowed her food.

"You haven't been working here your entire career, have you?"

"Here? No, I've had two other employers. One sold out to a competitor and most of the staff lost their jobs. I left the second one to come here."

"The job before here, it was with a construction company, wasn't it?"

"Yeah, how did you know?"

"I'm doing some research on Papalia Construction, and your name came up."

"You must have been doing some deep digging to find my name. I was just a junior accountant."

"Why did you leave?"

Kim took a bite of her sandwich and chewed it slowly. She chewed every bite slowly. She was thinking about her answer as she chewed.

"It was time for me to move on. I don't want to be president of any company, but I didn't want to stay a junior accountant either. It was time."

"While you were there, did you notice anything unusual?"

"Unusual? Like what?"

"You're the accountant, you tell me."

"Ms. Lynn, why don't you just come out and ask me what you want to know. We could save a lot of time."

"OK, Kim. I was informed that the number of invoices for trucking was greatly inflated. That money would have had to have gone somewhere. So, unusual would mean, did you notice problems with invoices and did you notice funds going missing?"

"See, not so hard. Why do you want to know the answers to the questions?"

This caught Stephanie off guard. "Why? Why do I want answers? Why not?"

"Why not? You can't do anything with the answers. Oh, you can publish a story. Maybe cause an investigation. The investigation will cost hundreds of thousands of dollars. When it's no longer newsworthy, maybe a week at best, it will all go away. The end result will be more taxpayer dollars spent on the Big Dig, but no one will refund a dollar."

"That's rather cynical, don't you think?"

"I don't deal in cynicism. I deal in cold facts."

"You did find something. You just don't want to talk about it. Did someone threaten you? Is that why you changed jobs?"

Slowly chewing the last of her sandwich, Kim studied Stephanie. Finished chewing, Kim took a drink of water and wiped her mouth with her napkin. "If you see the world in black and white, contemplating a change in jobs can be terrifying. So many unknowns: loss of wages, indefinite period of time between the old and new positions, and then the prospects for starting over. If you don't fit in, you could be unemployed again, quickly."

Kim was taking her time choosing her words. "It was time to move on. I knew it for a while. They just suggested I do it sooner rather than later. You know what was interesting? You can have all those fears, the fear of the unknown dangers, but when the time comes, you learn how to adapt and solve the problem.

"Contemplating a job loss can be like contemplating death. We fear it. We do whatever we can to avoid it. We change our lives because of it. But, when confronted with the inevitable, we fight and survive. Some people are better at it than others. Some people have no fear because they have an inner confidence based on nothing other than instinct.

"I survived. I see a little more gray than I use to and I'm comfortable with it. Let me think about what you asked. Maybe I'll call. No matter what, two things will not change: you will find something to publish and nothing will be accomplished by the publication."

"Please give some consideration to talking with me again."

Stephanie gave Kim a business card and jotted down her cellphone number. Kim promised to call and tell Stephanie her decision was.

44

Andre's office was on the third floor of the South Market building. The southeast corner offered a view of the Quincy Market building, the courtyard with outdoor dining, and Commercial Street. A small sparse office, it contained several computers, laptops, a small phone system, and assorted furniture and decorations.

Stephanie entered the office and found Andre intently working the keyboard of his computer.

"Andre, you keep squinting at the computer like that and you might go blind."

He looked up, "Sugar if I haven't gone blind by now, I never will. How are you, Stephanie? You look lovely." He got up and kissed her on each cheek.

Stephanie slumped into a chair. "I feel exhausted. I'm running against a deadline. How are you doing with my stuff?"

"You really are in a hurry. OK, let me see … yes, let's start here. A little overview; usually I have to be onsite at the company when I am analyzing financial data. Many of the notes or memos on checks or journal entries are cryptic. They will send me looking for the backup or other documents. Whoever got you these financials also grabbed some of the internal memos and electronic files."

He flipped through a pad of yellow lined paper with notes on it. "Those notes and the access to both sets of books allowed me to make significant headway, even though I do not have access to the company's offices. Ahh, here's the information I was looking for."

He started typing into his computer. "I'm bringing up a side-by-side view of some of the account entries from both sets of books. Pull your chair around so you can look at the screen."

Once Stephanie was resettled, Andre continued. "You see, companies always find some legitimate account to charge payment to. Hair care becomes advertising. A family banquet becomes a marketing expense. Even boat payments and dues at a yacht club become equipment and repair expenses.

"If you dig deep enough, the payment can be found and identified for what it really is: personal income. The check has the chauffeur's name on it. The charge card shows the name of the restaurant. The loan account number identifies the equipment as a sailboat. You get the picture?"

"I do. I've seen it all before, but not in the original finance documents. Usually it's legitimate and explained. For example: the president of the company was paying the mortgage on his second home using company funds. I never saw how it was done."

"Well, you're about to look at some of it. On this side, you check entries with legitimate expense explanations. Over in this set of books you see the same check entry with notation. I was able to find the account noted and the memo explaining the lease. Daddy's little girl got a new sports car for her eighteenth birthday and the company got the lease payments."

"Damn, daddy was good to me, but he never got me a sports car for my birthday," Stephanie said.

"Sugar, my daddy had all he could do just to let me stay in his house until I finished high school before he threw my ass out." Andre had a laugh that was infectious and Stephanie laughed along with him.

"OK, the checks are telling, but no great shakes. Much of what I found in the checks was typical for hiding personal expenses. Cash was another thing altogether. Hiding cash is tough. The best way is to have someone pay you in cash. Then you don't show the invoice or any transactions related to the cash. No one finds it as long as you don't put it in the bank.

"This company received its money from the State. It was always a check or wire transfer. The transactions were very traceable. They have big cash expenditures. Cash flowed through this company faster than water through the holes in the Big Dig tunnels.

"I haven't identified all the people who received cash, but there is an internal trail. Some of the memos name individuals and the codes to be used. Then the cash is entered as explainable expenses. See here, this guy is the president of the local Teamsters. This one here is a Boston city councilor. I wonder what her fellow councilors would think if they found out she got paid off and they didn't?"

Stephanie looked at the cash entries and the coded names. She moved the cursor and found where the names appeared. Stephanie now knew who had received how much.

"Andre, this is nice, but these amounts will be lucky to get the story next to the help wanted section of the paper."

"Oh, silly, that was just the warm-up. Look at these amounts." He scrolled down the list.

Stephanie studied the list and amounts. "Now those amounts are worth publishing."

"I thought you'd like them. They're not complete. I'm reproducing them from copies of the bank statements you provided. By the way, how did you get all these documents?"

"Sorry, I can't tell you that."

"OK, but when you see the person again; tell him I could use his expertise from time to time. I mean internal memos and notes, financial statements, and bank statements. Someone sure knows how to hack into systems."

Stephanie smiled, "Let's just stay on track, shall we?"

"OK, just keep me in mind. That's all I'm asking." Andre pulled up another screen on his computer. "Here we have what looks like some sizable cash disbursements to the Speaker of the State House of Representatives and a former State Senator. I tracked bogus payments to phantom companies. The payments were then converted into cash, and these two politicians got rich."

Stephanie reviewed the notes and figures on the computer screen. "Oh, Andre, you're extraordinary. This is what I thought would come out of this." She leaned into him and gave him a hug while she kissed him on the lips.

"Hold on, Sugar. You have to be careful. My man has a vicious jealous streak," he said when she finished kissing him. "Now, there is one more person in this mix but I can't identify him. See here?" He pointed to a new list of cash and check transactions. "If this is one person, and I suspect it is, he made out better than the Speaker of the House. I may need additional documents, if your source can find them."

"I don't know if he can go back into the files. He told me each time he goes in he runs a larger risk of detection. I'll check with him." She looked at her watch. "Oh, look at the time. I'm late. Gotta run." Stephanie got up and collected her things.

"What's so important you gotta run out on me?"

"Richard made reservations for dinner and has tickets to the theater. It's my birthday."

"I know. I sent you a card. Sugar, if you and Richard ever call it quits, let me know," Andre's body shook, "and send him my way."

Stephanie bent over the desk and gave him a kiss on the cheek. "He's my man, Andre. You have your own. Besides, Richard doesn't go your way." She walked out his office door.

"How do you know?" he yelled as the door closed.

45

Richard walked up the steps leading to the front lobby of Stephanie's building. Except for the name of the street and location in Boston, he could have been walking up the front steps to his condominium. The building and surroundings were that similar.

The security guard greeted him as he entered the lobby. "Hi, Mr. Moore, haven't seen you in a while."

"Hi, Barry. How's your mother?"

Barry's seventy-six-year old mother lived in the North End section of Boston, and was a witty and active force in her neighborhood. Several months previously, it looked as though she was going to have to move from the duplex she had occupied since her marriage. The stairs to her second floor proved to be too much for her to climb. Her bedroom and bathroom with tub and shower were on the second floor. Adding a tub and shower to the first floor was not an option. When Richard learned how depressed Barry's mother was because she had to move, and the reason she had to move, he put Barry in touch with a local council of social concern organized to help the elderly. They secured funding and donations for a chair lift designed to move her from the first floor to the second. All she had to do was sit and press a button. They also found volunteers to help make some modifications to the stairs and other parts of the house.

"Mother is doing just fine. She tells anyone and everyone about her lift chair. She's still asking when you were going to take her up on her offer of dinner. Says it's the least she can do to express her gratitude."

"You tell your mother again I didn't do anything. It was just fortunate I knew some people who were able to help. She can cook dinner for them."

"I told her. You just don't understand, 'cause you haven't met her yet. Haven't seen Miss Lynn yet. You going up to the apartment?"

"Yes, I am."

"She left a note this morning saying she was expecting cleaning from the cleaners. I have it in the closet if you'd like to take it up with you."

"It's probably her outfit for tonight. I better take it up."

"I was going to say you look sharp. You don't wear a suit and tie often." Richard was wearing a dark-blue suit, white shirt, a blue and white tie with an abstract design, and black shoes.

"It's Stephanie's birthday. We're going to dinner and then a show. I'll see you later."

He went up the stairs to Stephanie's the third-floor apartment.

Richard hung the cleaning in the foyer closet and walked to the kitchen. He placed the bottle of wine he brought with him on the counter. A shelf on a half wall between the kitchen and dining room held a fresh bouquet of red roses.

As Richard was opening the wine, he heard Stephanie coming through the front door. In a few moments, she arrived in the kitchen.

"Hey, happy birthday," Richard said, in greeting. "Would you like some wine?" He held out a glass. She took it, gave him a quick kiss, and drank some of the wine.

"Oh, that tastes good. Thanks."

"I see someone sent you roses."

"Well, you don't send flowers. They're from Roland. He sends me roses every year on my birthday. You know that. I told you about him." Roland was a classmate of Stephanie. The first time he met her, he was in love with her. She, however, did not feel the same way. She had given up telling him they are destined to be friends only. Roland had been a staff adviser to the Senate Chair of the Foreign Intelligence Committee for eight years.

"Hasn't he gotten married yet?"

"Richard, are you jealous?" She took another drink of wine. "He's been married twice. He is not married now: at least not to a woman. Maybe to his job though. I have to take a quick shower. I'll be ready when the car arrives."

Stephanie hurried to the stairs and went to the second floor. "Richard," she yelled down, "I forgot to check with Bernie. The cleaners were going to deliver my cleaning. There's a black dress need for tonight. Will you see if he received it, and if so, bring it up?" She did not wait for an answer before entering the bathroom and turning on the shower.

Richard listened to bits and pieces of the evening news as he waited to hear the shower stop. The vice president was in the news again. As usual, the media pundits were citing his commanding lead in the polls and his sizable campaign budget as evidence he would be the next President of the United States.

Richard realized the shower was off and grabbed the black dress from the front closet and took it upstairs.

Hi was laying the dress and its waist length coat on the bed when Stephanie came in. "Oh, thanks for putting that out."

Richard turned and stared at her. Stephanie was standing in front of him dressed in black stockings, black sheer bra, and black lace boyleg panties.

"What?" She asked. "Is my head on backwards?"

Richard moved closer, wrapped his arms around her, and said, "I didn't notice your head. I was thinking, however, we could catch the play another time. We could stay right here." He nuzzled her neck.

"Hey, it's *my* birthday. I get to choose and you're taking me to dinner and the play."

Richard was rubbing his hands along the contours of her back and sides. "OK. I was just giving you options."

Stephanie leaned her head back. "Are you packing or are you really that happy to see me?"

In a very serious tone, Richard responded. "You know I never carry a weapon."

"Ohh, I think I would disagree with that statement." Stephanie said with a playful tone. "Now let me finish getting read. Take one last look. You can spend the next few hours thinking about what might be in store for you later. I did tell you that maybe we both might get lucky tonight."

She broke free from him and dropped the dress over her head her arms up high. The dress slid down and the wide shoulder straps stopped the dress's fall. She looked in the mirror. "Will you zipper up the back and hook the top please?"

"Are you going to be warm enough? It's not cold but cool."

"That waist coat with the long sleeves goes with this dress. It should be sufficient, besides, I also have you."

As Richard pulled the zipper up and hooked the top, he said, "Close your eyes and don't open them until I tell you to." He took the string of pearls from his jacket pocket and put them around her neck, securing the clasp at the back of her neck. "OK, you can open them now."

Stephanie stared at the image in the mirror. She ran her fingers across the pearls and exclaimed, "Oh, Richard, they're beautiful! Thank you so much." She turned in his arms and they kissed passionately.

Downstairs, Richard held the door for Stephanie. As she walked down the stone steps, she commented, "You didn't have to hire a stretch limo."

"I didn't. I ordered a Town Car," Richard replied with a surprise tone.

46

The man holding the car door greeted them. "The Town Car was having mechanical problems. The boss decided to upgrade your service. I hope it is not a problem."

"No problem at all," replied Stephanie. "Thank your boss for me."

The chauffeur took Stephanie's hand and guided her into the car. "Ms. Lynn, please sit on either side bench. I have to wipe down the rear seats," the man told her.

He told the same to Richard. Both Stephanie and Richard sat on the bench seat on the right side of the car. Richard was turned slightly with his back to the rear door so he could talk with Stephanie. The man was wiping the rear seat. He then exited the car and another man took a seat on the rear bench. The man who had cleaned the seat sat down next to him.

"Ah." Stephanie's breathing skipped a cycle. Her face went pale and became contorted with an expression of fear.

Richard turned in his seat to see what had affected Stephanie. He moved to leap at the man in the rear seat. "You son-of-a-bitch."

The man who had opened the door for Richard and Stephanie pulled a nine-millimeter pistol with silencer. "George, put that away. Richard is not going to do anything that would jeopardize Stephanie. Are you, Richard?"

Richard sat back in his seat. "Rob Lee what are you doing here?" —The car started to move. —"And where are you taking us?"

"Hello, Richard. How are you? Direct, and to the point as always. Then, you never were very good with pleasantries or small talk."

"I asked you a question, Lee."

"I heard you. Relax. I wanted to visit and wish Stephanie a happy birthday." Adjusting his focus to Stephanie, he continued, "You look ravishing this evening. Those pearls really accent that dress. Richard has exquisite taste, don't you think?"

Stephanie was too stunned to respond.

"OK, now that you have wished Stephanie a happy birthday, where are you taking us?" Richard was carefully watching George in an effort to find an opportunity to overpower him. George for his part had not taken his eyes off Richard. He had, however, laid the gun on his lap.

"The driver is taking you to Antwan's for dinner. Then he will take you to the Long Center for the play. I have no intention of changing your plans for this special occasion." He smiled and looked at both of them.

"Richard, why don't you open the champagne and pour each of us a glass."

As Richard opened the bottle and poured, Rob Lee pulled a small box from his suit jacket pocket. "This is for you." He held the box out for Stephanie. "I think you'll like it." Stephanie studied the box with apprehension. "Please, Stephanie, the box will not explode and the champagne is not poisoned. If I wanted to do you or Richard harm, it would have been finished by now."

Richard handed out the glasses of champagne. George declined. Stephanie opened the box. Inside she found a pair of pearl earrings. "They're very nice," she said. "Thank you."

"The sales lady at Diamond's told me they were the exact match to the necklace Richard bought. I couldn't resist." He smiled and held up his glass. "A toast. To Stephanie. Happy birthday. May you have many more, and never look any older than you do today."

Richard and Stephanie took a small sip of the bubbly. Rob Lee downed the whole glass in one gulp.

"Now that the party is over, would you like to tell me the real reason you're here, or maybe we could just drive to the nearest police station and I can put you in a cell."

Rob Lee looked at Richard. "Why ruin the mood so quickly? The champagne has hardly flowed down the throat."

"Get on with it, Lee."

"All right, Richard. I'm here to give you a warning and to get you back on track. For the past year, you and I have been playing a game of cat and mouse. You have come very close to capturing me, although, I doubt you know how close, or when. It has been amusing, and without incident." He held out his glass. "Please pour me some more."

Rob Lee took an average mouthful of champagne and continued. "Bear's murder changed that. Now you have all your available resources hunting for me. The last two incidents show that it is becoming difficult to elude the hunt. They also show that many people are on the verge of getting seriously hurt.

"I have issued orders to my men to keep their weapons on safety. The two people in South Carolina could have ended up in a morgue rather than a hospital if my people had their way." He took another drink from the glass.

"How did you like the confetti? That was a neat display, don't you think?"

"Very amusing, however, the young man who was shot was not amused. Did your man forget how to safety his weapon?"

"Sometimes you get an overachiever in the ranks. No one in that house was to have a weapon. The confetti could just as easily have been C-4. If it had been, we would not be here having this conversation. Think about that. You and your men walked right into a trap rigged at the last minute.

"My men are very upset with me. They do not like being hunted at the same time they have orders to safety their weapons. I don't accept dissension in the ranks, but they have presented reasonable concerns. So, I thought I should tell you I reversed the order. The safeties are off. If you or any of your people come within range of me or any of my people, someone will be seriously hurt.

"Of course, that needn't happen. I'm here to tell you you're wasting time and valuable resources chasing the wrong man. I had nothing to do with the murder of Bear."

Incredulous, Richard said, "Do you expect me to believe you would tell me if you had? You were in Boston the night of Bear's murder. You were trying desperately to get out undetected. You telling me it was a coincidence?"

"You and I don't believe in coincidences. It is in our nature, but, they do happen from time to time, and this, unfortunately, was one of those times. I was in Boston for a meeting. I had a follow-up meeting Monday morning, but the storm raised havoc with my itinerary. As you well know, Richard, I'm not going to let something like a storm interfere with my plans, so, I hastily made other travel arrangements.

"Bear was a good soldier but not a consummate investigator. He was not a threat to me because he would never find me." Rob Lee continued, "He and I got along well back when we were all on the same team. Like you, and like just about anyone who met him, I actually liked Bear, and am saddened by his loss. Of course, the fact that I liked him wouldn't have prevented me from dealing with him if he ever interfered with my plans or became a threat to me. Unlike you, Richard, he never did, so, the simple truth is that I had no reason to eliminate him."

"You have been so intent on blaming me for Bear's murder you have lost sight of the investigation. I'm here to tell you to get your act together. I want Bear's killer identified and captured as much as you. You need to look at the facts and start following the real leads and stop chasing me. When you find and capture Bear's killer, you can, we can, go back to playing cat and mouse.

"Remember this, Richard: get me angry and I will come after you. You have to hunt for me. Sometimes you get close. Sometimes you might as well be looking on the Moon. If I want you, all I have to do is look you up in the phone book. I can find you anytime, day or night. You're vulnerable because you live in the open. You play by the rules. I live in the shadows behind forged paperwork and identities. I don't play by the rules. I make them up as I need."

The car made a left turn and came to a stop. Richard's knee was against Stephanie's and he could feel her shaking. He put a reassuring hand on her knee. Rob Lee saw Richard's attempt to calm Stephanie.

In an attempt to calm Stephanie Rob Lee said, "Stephanie, I'm sorry if I have caused you fear or unease. It was not my intention. I only wanted to set Richard straight, so he will stop chasing my shadow, and focus on finding Bear's real killer."

"Lee, that sounds so altruistic," Richard said, "but, we both know you only act if it is beneficial to Rob Lee—" Richard had more to say but he was interrupted by a tap on the side door near Rob Lee.

Lee held up his hand.

"Richard, my car has arrived and I don't want you and Stephanie to be late for your dinner reservations. Remember what I said."

The door next to Rob Lee opened. Another car had pulled in next to the limo, its rear door open. Rob Lee turned to exit the limo, then paused, and looked back at Richard. "The safeties are off. Do what you do best, and find Bear's killer."

Once he was outside the car, he stopped, and put his head inside to look at Richard again. "By the way, when I find out who gave that sheriff's deputy my location, it will be the last time that person betrays me."

As Lee climbed into the waiting car, George slid across the seat, gun in hand, and backed out of the limo. He closed the door, and the waiting car immediately accelerated away with its lights off. Before they left, however, Richard managed to get a glimpse of it just before George closed the door. It was a light brown/tan four door.

Richard got out of his sear and moved to the door.

"What are you doing?" Stephanie's voice was a mix of disbelief and fear.

"Stay here. I'll be back in five minutes." Richard opened the door.

"Are you crazy? He said he would kill you if you went after him." Richard was out the door and scanning the area. "Richard ... Richard." She was screaming. "Richard ... he'll kill you."

47

Richard was standing on Church Street in front of Antwan's. A light-brown Cadillac on Columbus Avenue was heading away from him. He gave chase. Running parallel to the Caddy, Richard was unable to gain any ground on the car. At the end of the street, traffic lights turned red and the Caddy was temporarily blocked in. Richard continued on a parallel path until he was abreast of the Caddy then he cut right and ran directly at it.

The light turned green and the Caddy was able to move forward and turn right on to Arlington. Richard was losing ground again. The Caddy took the first left onto St. James Avenue. Richard crossed left, sidestepping cars. Drivers leaned on their horns and the evening air was filled with their blaring. One driver refused to give way to Richard and Richard landed on the driver's hood. He rolled off and his butt made hard contact with the pavement.

Springing back to his feet, he ran to the intersection just in time to see the Caddy turn left into a parking garage entrance.

"I got you now, you son-of-a-bitch." Richard, familiar with the building and the garage, knew there was only one opening to the garage. If the Caddy were to come out, it would have to use the same route it used to enter.

He ran around the wooden arm barrier at the automated ticket dispenser and up the two-way drive ramp. A light-blue Honda turned the sharp corner at the second level and headed straight at Richard. The driver noticed Richard at the last second and swerved left, narrowly avoiding him, then, cursing at him in the rearview mirror, continued down the ramp, and exited the garage.

Richard continued running up the ramp, chasing the sound of tires squealing as the Caddy made tight turns on the painted floor of the garage before heading up to the next level.

Just as he was approaching the ramp to the fourth level, the noise of the tires stopped, followed by the sound of car doors opening, and then, slamming shut. He raced up the ramp, and, reaching the top, spied the Caddy stopped at the curb outside the small, windowed elevator waiting area. He ran across the garage, and, reaching the driver's door, yanked it open. The car was empty.

He turned and looked at the floor indicator at the top of the elevator as the numbers descended. He took the stairs and ran or leaped down to the lobby level. The door crashed open as he burst into the small room. To his right, two young men stood behind a counter. Everyone had to stop at the counter and pay the parking fee before going to their car and exiting the building.

Richard headed to the door leading to the building's main lobby.

"Are you Richard Moore?" one of the young men called out.

Richard stopped dead in his tracks. "Yes. What made you ask?"

"A man asked me to give you this. He said you would be through right behind him." The young man handed Richard an envelope.

"Did you see which way he went?"

"No. Just went out the door."

Richard stepped into the long expanse of the lobby. Main entrances were at both ends of the lobby. To his right was St. James Avenue. To his left was Stuart Street. He was closer to St. James Street, so he went to that entrance first. The same volume of traffic cluttered the street as when he ran along it, but there was no sign of Rob Lee or his men. He went through the lobby and stood on Stuart Street. The traffic was heavier and snarled. Still no sign of Rob Lee. In the distance to his left, he could see Antwan's. He had come full circle.

Going back to the small room, Richard asked the young man, "How many men came through here when you were given the envelope?"

"Three."

Richard was opening the envelope as he asked questions. "Had you ever seen the men before?"

"Yeah. One of the dudes came by earlier. Said he had an important meet tonight, and asked me to return his rental to Logan Airport."

"What car? Where?"

"He said it was a Caddy, tan. He would leave it on level four. He gave me five hundred bucks. Five hundred, man. Must be one important meeting."

Richard read the note: *Richard, you are so predictable. Rob Lee.*

He folded the note and put it and the envelope in his breast pocket. "Do not touch the car. Don't even go to the fourth floor. It is a crime scene. Do you understand?"

"Oh man, I got five hundred bucks. I gotta return the car."

"Do not go near the car. I'll have some people here shortly. We will move it when we're done. Someone will be here to talk with you. Do not leave."

"What about my money?"

"You should keep it. The man who gave it to you will not miss it."

48

Richard saw the limo had been moved from Church Street to Columbus Avenue. One of the valet attendants was yelling at the driver, and a Boston police officer had just arrived. Richard walked up to the limo and the officer. "Milo, how's the family?" Richard asked the officer.

"Well I'll be, Captain Moore. Haven't seen you in years. What's up?"

"This limo is waiting for me. I asked him not to move. Afraid I took longer than expected."

"The valet is pissed off. He wants the limo moved. Maybe you can have him drive around the block if you're not ready for him."

"I'll send him on his way Milo. I'm just waiting for a federal crime scene unit to arrive. "Richard had placed the call for a unit during his walk to the limo.

The driver looked ash white. "You get company like that often?" he asked Richard.

"The officer and valet?"

"Hell, no! I mean the guy who sat next to me on the drive here. He had a gun. Told me to stay right here while you chased after them. Said if I didn't stay, he'd shoot my ass. I believed him."

Richard now understood the ash white complexion and the confrontation with the attendant.

"By the way," the driver continued, "Miss Lynn got a cab. Said to tell you not to follow or to call. You know some weird people, Mr. Moore."

"Yeah, I do, and they call themselves friends."

He thought about Stephanie leaving. The anger was building in him. He willed himself to control the rage. He handed the driver a hundred dollars. "This is for your trouble. You can get lost for a while. I'll pay for the full night as agreed. You married?"

"What? Married? … Yeah."

"I have tickets at the box office for the play. You and your wife can use them if you want to play chauffeur to her. Just go to the box office and use my name. The tickets are paid for."

49

Richard watched as the FBI crime scene technicians went through the Caddy. Two agents were in the small room on the lobby level interviewing the young men. A flatbed car carrier was waiting outside the garage entrance to haul the Caddy to the crime scene unit's garage where it would receive a thorough exam.

"I don't think I've ever seen you so dashing at work before," Detective Linda Pollard said, as she approached Richard. "Suit and tie aren't your usual attire."

"Detective Pollard, what are you doing here? This is not a Boston PD case."

Linda was startled. Not only was Richard's attire rather formal for him, his reply, tone, and body language were past formal and on the edge of brisk.

"Detective Lieutenant," she corrected his use of title. She could play the game as well as he could. "The Feds are working on my turf. I thought I should check it out."

"Nothing to check out. I saw a Federal fugitive. The car is being checked for clues."

One of the technicians approached Richard. "Mr. Moore, we're finished here. We're moving the car in a few minutes."

"Thanks," Richard said.

"What's with the suit?" Linda wanted to see if she could get Richard to relax.

"I had a dinner reservation. It got cancelled at the last minute." He remained tense and curt.

"You should call Stephanie and see if she can fill in for the person who cancelled on you." She could see right away that her comment almost resulted in an explosion. This was not the Richard she knew.

"She's busy. So am I. If you will excuse me I have to talk with some other agents." He stepped toward the elevator area.

Linda stepped in front of him and blocked his path. She leaned in close. "I don't know what is happening with you, but you better get control. People in our line of work can't afford to let their emotions take control of their actions. If they do, they can end up dead. A lo of people care about you. I'm one of them." She turned and walked away.

He watched as she walked to the stairway door. Linda's short speech made him realize that his emotions were taking control. Bear's death, the situation with Stephanie, and the attacks on his life were creating more emotions than he could control. It was time to take a break. He thought about saying something, and then decided against it. He let her go.

The crime scene unit was packing. Richard had received all the information available. He would receive a call if any important evidence was discovered. He had serious doubts about any being found. Outside, on Stuart Street, he walked north.

As he walked, he tried to get a clear picture of his investigation into Bear's murder. Every time he thought he was getting a clear view of the facts, Rob Lee, Stephanie, and Lori would take over his thoughts.

He found himself on the street where Stephanie lived. He gazed up at the windows of her apartment. He saw no light, no shadows, no indicating she was home. He walked past her building to his car and drove away.

50

Stephanie woke later than usual Friday morning, her head pounding as she attempted to raise it off the pillow. She eventually swung her legs off the side of the bed and rose to a sitting position. In the process, she found that any movement was painful to her head. When the pain subsided a little, she looked around her bedroom. The black dress and matching jacket were in a ball in the corner of the room. A half-empty bottle of Jack Daniels sat on the nightstand, sans drinking glass.

"Oh, shit! No wonder I feel like crap. I haven't done Jack since college."

The events of the previous evening were slowly cutting through the alcohol-induced veil. She had the taxi stop at the first liquor store, where she bought a quart of Jack and began drinking from the bottle as the taxi took her home.

She had wanted to deaden the fear that had gripped her during the ride with Rob Lee. As the alcohol coursed through her body, she drank in anger that Richard would put her in such danger. Then she drank to erase the memory of blaming Richard and the memory of leaving him at the restaurant. She assumed that she then continued to drink for any reason until she passed out.

Coffee was the first order of the day. It was followed by a piece of wheat toast. After her shower, she felt better, but far from one hundred percent. She decided she needed to get out and keep moving. She left the apartment and headed to Faneuil Hall and Andre's office. When she arrived, there were police cruisers parked in the courtyard next to the South Market Building.

Stephanie entered the building and climbed the stairs. As she did, waves of pain coursed through her brain and broke against her skull like a trapped restless sea trying to batter its way out of her head, the crash of each wave making her duck and wince.

When she finally made it to Andre's floor, she found uniformed police officers coming and going from his office. She tried to go in but was denied entry by one of the officers. When Andre saw her standing near the door, he waddled over to her and they hugged.

"Oh, Stephanie, thank you for coming."

"Andre, what happened? Why are the police in your office?" She watched the police as she asked Andre the questions.

"Oh, Stephanie, it's horrible. Someone broke into my office last night. They ransacked the place. My computers, fax machine, copier, even the telephones are gone. Oh, I just can't believe it."

"Did they break into any of the other offices? I don't see the police going into any others."

"I don't think so. Lots of the other tenants came by. You know, to console me, but I didn't hear about any other break-ins."

Stephanie was shocked. Richard's training, however, was working in her subconscious. He never believed in coincidences. "Andre come with me." She led him down the hall out of hearing distance of the detectives. "What about the Big Dig files? Are they gone? I mean your notes and printed materials."

"What? The Big Dig files? You heartless hussy. At a time like this, you want to know about your precious files. I was violated! Violated, Stephanie! Doesn't that mean anything to you?" He was on the verge of crying again.

"Andre, listen to me—"

"No. I thought you were a friend. I was violated. I don't know if I will ever be able to come back to this office, and you're only concerned with your files."

"Andre!" She said his name as loud as she dared. "Listen to me. You were working on those files. They suggested some large payoffs; illegal activity. Your office has never been broken into before, and none of your neighbors were broken into. That concerns me, and it should concern you."

As Stephanie spoke, Andre stared at her, his eyes growing bigger as he began to realize what she was implying. When she was through, his eyes began to tear up. "Oh! Oh, Stephanie, what have you gotten me into? Oh god! Maybe I'm in danger. Oh my god!"

Stephanie wrapped her arms around him. "It's OK, Andre. We just have to look and see if they took your notes. If they did, they got what they came for, and you're in no danger. If they didn't take them, they were probably just ordinary thieves who got spooked before they could hit another office."

He wiped the tears from his face. "Yeah, they probably got spooked. No need to worry, right? I'm right; aren't I, Stephanie?"

"Yes, Andre. Let's just check on the files."

Stephanie and Andre walked back to the office entrance. "Ahh, Andre," one of the detectives said. "Please look around and give us a list of any items missing."

"Oh, yes, Detective," Andre replied. "If you do not mind, I'd like Stephanie with me. She's my moral support right now and she knows my office as well as I do."

Stephanie knew the thieves would review Andre's notes. If Andre had identified the politician who had the office burglarized, Andre might be in danger. She had to assume he was. She would have to get some help.

51

Across town, Richard had woken up at his usual time. He willed himself to get out of bed and go out for his morning run along the Charles River.

Stephanie had been right: after arriving home the previous night, Richard spent several hours trying to block mental images of her in black stockings and black lingerie. He finally fell into a fitful sleep around two in the morning. His wife, Lori and friend, Bear, both deceased, dominated his dreams.

He arrived at Bear's office determined to quickly conclude the investigation. Accomplishing that would require a laser-sharp focus. He needed to clear his mind of distractions. Entering the office, he found Laura, Steve and Phil chatting and drinking coffee. He joined them and updated them about Rob Lee's visit.

"He's got balls, I have to give him that," Steve said. "Any idea how he knew how to find you, or how he got to Boston?"

"None," Richard responded. "That's your job. See if you can find how he got in or out of the area."

"Laura if you can handle it, I'd like you to contact Austin Jarvis at Arlington National Cemetery and ask him to set up arrangements for Bear's funeral and burial."

"I can handle that."

"What about me?" Phil asked.

"Do you know if that car is still available?"

"The car? You want to know about the car now."

"Yeah. If it's available, I thought I'd take a ride and look at it."

Phil was surprised, but he made a couple of phone calls "Richard, as far as I can tell, the car is still available."

"Good. Would you like to take a ride?" Richard asked Phil.

Phil nodded, indicating yes. He was still questioning Richard's sudden interest in the car.

"OK, I have to pick up the Porsche. We can go to the shop, you can drive the Porsche to my place, and then we will go look at the Bullet." The car they were going to look at was a 1968 Ford Mustang.

Phil was getting into the Porsche, when Richard said, "I have an errand to run. I will not be long. I'll meet you at my place behind the building."

Richard pulled in front of Stephanie's apartment and parked. As he walked into the kitchen of her apartment, he saw pearls scattered around the floor. He went upstairs to the bedroom and saw the bottle of Jack Daniels. The black dress was still balled up in the corner of the room. He left and met with Phil.

52

Phil was looking out the windshield as he asked, "You sure you want to be doing this now?"

"It's as good a time as any, Phil. I have to clear my head. Besides, it will keep the tails wondering."

Phil turned abruptly in his seat. "What tails?"

"Relax. They're not with us now. One of them appears off and on. I get the feeling he knows my schedule."

As they neared the New Hampshire border, Phil, who had been watching the trees, exclaimed, "Dam, I really love New England in the fall! The colors of the trees are so beautiful. I know people who can tell you what kind of tree you're looking at just by the color of the leaves in autumn. My, I just marvel at the show Mother Nature puts on at this time of year. Did you know people come from all over the world … the world … just to see the fall foliage in New England?"

"I had heard something to that effect. I don't think I ever noticed the increase in tourism," Richard said.

"Well, you should. What's that saying? 'Stop and smell the roses.' You can smell autumn in the air." Phil was smiling to himself.

Maynard Olsen lived in an 1890 era Victorian house on Hall Road just outside Windham center. The house was three stories tall. The first floor had a living room in front, a dining area behind that room, and the kitchen, which stretched the width of the house. A hallway led from the front door to the kitchen, with the stair to the second floor bordering on the left.

The second floor had three bedrooms and a bathroom. Stairs from the second floor gave way to the third floor. The third floor was a combination attic and partially finished storage area.

Richard parked at the curb in front of Mr. Olsen's house. A gravel driveway led straight back to what at first looked like an abandoned barn. The wide double doors hung precariously on an angle caused by years of settlement. The paint was pealing and the trim was badly rotted.

"Will you look at this?' Phil was staring at the main house like a kid looking at his first bicycle or electronic game. "They don't make houses like this anymore. The gingerbread gable decorations are magnificent. The porch trim really complements the newel posts and balusters."

"I didn't know you were such an architectural enthusiast," Richard said.

"It's why I moved to New Hampshire when I retired. I can drive around the old towns and just marvel at the old houses. They tell a story, you know."

Richard had to agree with Phil, but, unfortunately, the story this house was telling was a depressing one. It had not seen a new coat of paint in twenty or more years. The fascia boards and wooden gutters were badly rotted. The porch leaned inward and down. About the only redeeming features the house had were the bushes around the side of the house. They were reasonably trimmed and shaped. In fact, at that very moment, they were being trimmed by an elderly gentleman.

As Phil walked around the house taking in the architecture, Richard approached the elderly man working on the bushes. "Good morning. I'm looking for Mr. Olsen. Do you know if he's in?"

The old man kept snipping stems on the bushes with his pruning shears as if he had not heard Richard. "Who wants to know?" he finally asked.

"I'm Richard Moore. That other gentleman walking this way is Phil Tyron. I'm here to inquire about a car."

"I'm Maynard Olsen. Don't get many people asking for me these days. Unless they want to collect on a bill." Maynard wiped his brow with a blue handkerchief. The sun was unobstructed by clouds. The air was warm with a gentle breeze. It was a delightful day in southern Maine. "Let's go in the house. I need a drink and a break."

Maynard led the way. Progress was slow but steady as he shuffled to the front porch. Climbing the stairs was even slower Maynard's left leg did all the heavy lifting. The right leg trailed behind and stayed beside the left. Left leg up, pull the right up, rest the right on the same step as the left, and hen left leg up on the next step. Fortunately, there were only five steps to climb.

Inside Richard felt as if he had fallen back to the nineteen seventies. Except for the bed in the dining room, not a stick of furniture looked newer than thirty years old. The wood trim in the rooms was dingy white, the paint cracked and pealing. Wallpaper, darker near the ceiling than the floor, was separated at the seams and dog-eared near the baseboard. The place was reasonably clean. It was just old and tired.

They reached the kitchen, and Maynard invited them to sit. The table and chairs were of chrome tub design. The top of the table was Formica trimmed with chrome. The seats of the chairs were covered in cracked vinyl. The cabinets were off-white metal. The one near the stove was charred black.

Maynard opened the door of the refrigerator. "What can I get yah? I got ginger ale, water, milk, and ice tea. I'm having ice tea."

"Nothing for me, thank you," Richard responded.

"I'll share some ice tea with you, Maynard," Phil said.

Maynard shuffled around fixing the drinks, and then took a seat, leaning heavily on the table for support as he did. "I love gardening. It's the only thing I do anymore. I get tired easily though. I forget some things sometimes too. Stairs are a real problem. Had to have my bed moved to the other room. Pushed the dining table and chairs out of the way. Haven't used then in years anyway. Don't matter none. Moving Monday." Maynard took a sip of ice tea.

"Doc thinks I can't take care of myself. Stairs the only problem. He thinks I should bathe more often. He should try walking up those stairs. I get upstairs every week or so. Still, I forget things. My daughter, Brenda, is arriving later today to help me pack. She's moving me to one of those assisted living places. Just another name for a nursing home." He drifted off for a few seconds.

When he came back, he looked at Richard. "You were in the service?"

"Yes, I was; Army, captain."

"What about you?" Maynard asked Phil.

"I was a lieutenant-colonel in the Army."

"Both brass. Ha! I was a buck sergeant. Seventeenth Regiment, Seventh Infantry Division. Ran around Korea while the politicians decided if they wanted to win the war or just bring us home. After we lost more than enough soldiers, the politicians decided we should come home."

Silence filled the room for a while.

"Brenda's coming today. She's moving me ... told you that, didn't I? I forget sometimes. You guys fight in the war?" Before either responded, he continued, "My son fought. He was Military Police. Did two tours in Vietnam. Tours, sounds like a vacation. No vacation for him. Three months left, and a month before the fall of Saigon, he was killed in DaNang."

Another period of silence filled the room. Maynard's attention appeared to be drifting again.

"Mr. Olsen, would you like us to come back another time?" Richard asked.

"What? ... Oh, no. My wife died the day we received word Gerry had been killed in action. It just took her fifteen years to lie down and stop moving. My daughter suffered the most. She never had a chance to do mother-daughter stuff. She tried, but Terry just couldn't. They drifted apart. I wasn't a dad for my daughter. I worked full time, then helped clean the house and prepare meals. Brenda left the first chance she could.

"Brenda lives in Californian. I guess she wanted as much distance from us as she could get and still be in the continental United States. I love my daughter. I don't think she knows how much I've always loved her. It's just ... Terry needed so much support after Gerry."

Silence again. Richard was sure Maynard was tearing up.

"Well, let's go show you the car." Maynard pushed himself up and stood. "Outside to the garage." He led the way.

As they walked, Maynard told them about the car. "When he was a senior in high school, Gerry saw that movie ... Oh, what was it ... the one with that good-looking actor? He died of cancer."

"You mean Steve McQueen. The movie was 'Bullet,'" Phil told him.

"That's the one. Gerry loved that movie and the car. He said he had to have one. Terry was against it; too expensive and dangerous. I made a deal with him. If he could come up with a down payment, I'd help him get a loan, but, he had to make the payments. He was a hard workin' boy. He got that car and made every payment.

"When we learned he wasn't coming back, I thought about selling the car. I just never got around to it. I started it a couple times a week, and drove it on weekends, just to keep it in shape. When I got too old to drive it, I just ran it in the garage. Had to get a battery charger 'cause it don't always start anymore. I even had the oil changed every three months. I showed the son of a neighbor how to do the oil change so he could fill in when I couldn't do it anymore."

53

They opened the doors to the garage. Richard had to pick his door up to get it to swing open. Inside the car was draped in a dusty brown cover. Richard thought he saw Maynard stand a little taller as he looked at the covered car.

"Go ahead," Maynard's voice suddenly filled with excitement and pride, "take it off. Go on. Go on."

Phil and Richard pulled back the cover from the car. Richard stood in shocked amazement. Finding an antique car and viewing it for the first time had never impressed him. The cars either had more rust than a mothballed World War Two battleship, or were spit-polished and much overpriced.

He was looking at an original green 1968 Ford Mustang Fastback. It was almost in perfect condition. "This is unbelievable, Mr. Olsen. You took great care of this."

Maynard was grinning from ear to ear. "You like it. Wait 'till you start it up. Get in. Get in. The keys are on the seat."

Carefully, Richard got in the car. He sat in the driver's seat and looked around the interior. His hands caressed the steering wheel He put the key in the ignition and turned the key. Nothing happened. He tried again. Silence.

"I think the battery is dead," Richard said, as he got out of the car. "I'll have it replaced when I get it out of here."

"No. No," Maynard said. "Use the charger. It will start. You have to start it before you leave."

Richard and Phil looked at each other and shrugged. They attached the charger and left it to charge the battery. Richard took this opportunity to look at the engine. It was a three hundred and ninety cubic inch displacement engine with a four-barrel carburetor, or quad.

"All right, try it now." Excitement entered Maynard's voice again. "Remember, Richard, pump the gas pedal. You have to feed gas into the manifold. This is not fuel injected."

"Good point," Richard commented as he got behind the wheel. He turned the key. *Arrrh arhh,* the engine groaned as it slowly turned over. He tried again. *Arrruh Arruh.* A different sound, but it still only turned slowly. Richard pumped the gas pedal several times. *Rurh, rurh, rurh.* Faster than before, but not fast enough to start the engine. Richard was concerned the battery was too old to get the job done.

"Sounds much better. This time it will catch. Be ready for it, Richard." Maynard stepped back.

Richard pumped the gas pedal again and turned the key. *Aruh aruh aruh broom.* The engine sprang to life. Richard let it idle fast for a while before he tapped the gas pedal. This caused the choke on the carburetor to adjust and the car idled.

Phil was looking at and listening to the engine. A small amount of water started dripping from one of the radiator hoses. The engine had settled into a purr. As the heat rose in the engine, Phil noticed the water drip was becoming a stream. He took a closer look. Suddenly, a series of noises erupted from the front of the engine: a snap followed by a pinging as the blades of the fan came in contact with something. Then Phil heard a swish as something flew past his head. Richard shut the engine off as soon as he heard the fan clatter.

"Must have broken the fan belt," Richard said.

"Almost took my head off." Phil was still startled. "By the way, there's a leak in one of the hoses."

"Most of the rubber is unreliable," Maynard said. "Been on the car too long. It does rot and weaken. I bet if you check the walls of the tires under the car you'll find they have cracks. I wouldn't drive on them. But that engine ... Didn't I tell you it would start? Gerry had a great car." It was as if Maynard had received a shot from the fountain of youth.

"Maynard, the odometer says thirty-two thousand miles. Is that right?"

"Well, Gerry drove it a lot. He was always in it. He even slept in it until I got after him. The engine has more use than that. Remember, I used to run it here in the garage."

Richard was not concerned about the number of miles on the odometer or the amount of time the engine might have run while in the garage. He could not get over the condition, and how few original miles were on the car.

"I have to get back to the house. I'm feeling a bit tired," Maynard said. "Richard, you have to have the car picked up by Monday. That's when I have to be in the home."

"OK, Maynard. How do you want payment? You never said how much you want."

"Did I ask? The paperwork is on the kitchen counter. Fill it out. The car is yours."

Phil looked at Richard in disbelief. Richard could not imagine anyone giving a car like this away. "Maynard, I can't take this car, it's quite valuable. I don't want to take advantage of your situation."

Maynard stopped his shuffling toward the house. "Have you heard what I've told you? I'm going to a home. I have no need for your money. If you think you could take advantage of me when it comes to that car, well, you underestimated me."

"Yes, but what about your daughter? I'm sure she'd be upset if she found out you just gave the car away."

"She lives very comfortably in California. She and her husband have very well paying jobs. She doesn't want anything to do with the car. She told me the car might be worth a hundred thousand dollars. She said it could be worth a hundred million, she still didn't want any part of it."

"Maynard, there must be something I can do. I couldn't just take it. I'll have to decline the offer."

Maynard's face went pale. "You'll do no such thing. You were an officer in the military. My son was killed while serving. Honor his memory and take the car. Put it back on the road. If you want to do something, promise you will not sell it. When you get too old to drive it, assuming it is in decent condition, find another soldier and give it to him or her. You keep the memory of my boy alive. Honor a fallen comrade by putting his car back into use. That is the deal, and you can't back out now."

He started his shuffle again. "I have to rest. My daughter will be here later. You've made me very happy. Take the car." He left Richard and Phil standing in the driveway.

54

They drove back to Bear's office in relative quiet. Phil assumed Richard was as shocked by the find and by deal as he was. Phil was not a collector of cars. He had no interest in getting his hands dirty fixing a car, let alone trying to recondition one. For Richard, however, everything associated with the process of reestablishing an old car to its prior condition was therapeutic.

As they got closer to Boston, the weather changed. The sky darkened, and the air cooled. A light mist was evident on the windshield as they pulled into the parking lot at the office.

In the office, Richard asked Steve, Laura, and Phil to join him in Bear's office. He had some thoughts he wanted to share. He stood in front of the whiteboard and began. "If we assume Rob Lee was telling the truth about not having been involved with Bear's murder, and I think it's a logical assumption, we can cross him off our list of suspects." Richard drew a line through Rob Lee's name on the whiteboard.

"We have to look closely at Bear's most recent clients. I know what was happening at Container International. I don't know why. Unfortunately, our only suspect there was murdered." He crossed off Container International. "I would like to know who set up the theft operation and who killed Martin King, but we don't have leads here."

He looked at the next name on the list. "We know what Bear was doing for the Boston Archdiocese and how that client came to Bear. We should eliminate the Archdiocese and add Catholics for Equal Justice." He drew a line through the Archdiocese and added the Catholics for Equal Justice.

"The Salvatore brothers and their cousin, Vern, are dead. This looks like another dead-end. I would like to know who killed them and who sent them after me." He placed a large question mark next to Catholics for Equal Justice.

"Now we come to Congressman Willard. Bear was investigating threats against Willard's life. Those threats appear to be bogus. Even the congressman didn't take them seriously enough to notify the Secret Service or the Capitol Police. Something here is not right. We need more information about the congressman." Richard placed a star next to Willard's name.

"Phil, I'd like you to visit Willard. Tell him we know the threats are phonies. Rattle him and see what falls out."

He wrote *Higher Credit Score* on the whiteboard. "We cannot ignore this company. Bear was in the parking lot of this company when he was killed. He might have been there for any reason unrelated to the company, but, until we know differently, we investigate its operations and Holly Cook, its president.

"Steve, I would appreciate it if you would do your magic on this company. We should know their financials, bank accounts, contracts, anything."

Richard wrote *Marcus McGill* on the board and placed two stars next to the name. "This guy is mine. He's holding the keys to this investigation. The information Steve and Phil pulled up on this guy suggests he couldn't have killed Bear. It also suggests he's prepared to stay hidden for some time. I want him before anyone else catches him."

"Laura, I'd like you to stay in touch with Linda Pollard. She's working the Salvatore brothers' incident and a few other leads she hasn't disclosed. We need to keep updated on her investigations."

Richard looked at the clock on the wall. "Oh, one more thing, Laura, pull together whatever you can about Senator Noonan, his daughter, and her father-in-law. All right everyone, any questions?"

Phil looked around. "Not a question, just an observation. You really knew what you were doing when you decided to go look at that car. Didn't you? I mean, I thought you were crazy, but here you are laying out a battle plan to get this guy. Welcome back."

"Thanks, but save it until we succeed."

"By the way, Richard," Phil added, "tomorrow is Saturday. I doubt the congressman will be in his office."

"You're probably right. He might have an office or study in his home or someplace where you two can have a private chat." Richard paused as he thought about what everyone was assigned. "Anything else?" he asked.

"One thing, Richard," Steve said. "I'm picking up Sheila at the airport. She arrives in an hour."

"Sheila, what brings her to Boston?"
"She thought you might like more assistance."
"I certainly will not refuse her help. Tell her I will call her later. Maybe we can get together in the morning."

55

Warren Avenue runs perpendicular to Richard's street. A row of buildings facing Warren Avenue backs up to the public alley behind Richard's building. The first floors of the buildings are mostly shops, including a convenience store and a small takeout place specializing in ethnic food. Two thin separations between these building were often used to get from Warren Avenue to the public alley.

When Richard's car pulled into his parking space, a pair of eyes was watching from behind a large maple tree diagonally across the public alley and behind Richard's parking space. After several minutes had gone by, and the driver's door of Richard's car had not opened, the eyes grew tired, and a cold mist penetrated the watcher's light clothing.

"He's not coming out until I tell him it's OK to do so." Richard stepped out from between the two buildings.

The voice came from behind, and the young man jumped and let out a quiet yelp. After a moment's hesitation, he started to move in an attempt to run away.

Richard grabbed the young man's shoulder and spun him around. "Don't run away. You came here to talk. Let's talk."

"Who ... who are you?" To the young man, Richard was nothing but a shadow with a strong hand grasping his shoulder like a vice.

"Richard Moore. I assume you came to talk with me."

"Moore? But ... but how ... you're in the car. Who's in the car?"

"That's Regis. He's the security guard in my building. We switched places when I went into the convenience store."

Thoroughly confused and fearing for his life, all the young man could think about was fleeing. Little of what Richard was saying was getting past his confusion and fear.

Sensing this, Richard made a decision.

"I'm going to let go of your shoulder. Then, I'm going to get Regis out of my car. We both are going into my building. If you really want to talk, you can follow. If not, you can leave. Just remember, the police will eventually catch up with you."

Richard let the young man go, and started walking toward his car.

"I didn't kill your friend," the young man said. "I don't know who did, but I didn't." His voice quavered with gut-wrenching fear.

Richard turned, and looked back toward the young man, now almost invisible in the shadows.

"I know you didn't. I suspect you couldn't even find the safety on a nine millimeter handgun. However, you may know who did kill him. You just haven't had time to figure it out. Why don't you come inside with me? We'll get you some dry clothes and something to eat."

After a few moments of indecision, the young man stepped out of the shadows, and reluctantly followed.

Richard tapped on the trunk of his car. "Regis, you can come out now."

"Jesus, Richard. How long was you goin' to leave me in there? We never said anything about how long I should sit. I thought—"

"Regis, say hello to Marcus McGill." Marcus, the young man, was now nervously standing beside Richard.

"So, you're the guy Richard was so worked up over. Made me wear this vest under my shirt and sit still in his car. Dam fool that I am, I agreed." Turning to Richard, Regis continued, "This young puppy, here, could have killed you; you with no gun and no vest of your own, and then come over and put a bullet in my head. What the hell good would that vest have done me then? " After a few moments, during which he gave Marcus a thorough appraisal, he finished in a much softer tone, "Well, maybe not."

Richard smiled, and said, "I'd hardly call you a dam fool, Regis, but, if you are, you're one brave dam fool," then turned on his heel, and headed into the building.

Marcus hesitated until Regis said, "I suspect, young feller, the fact that you're still alive, undamaged, and not under arrest, means that Richard meant you no harm. And, if he harmed you now, he'd have to get rid of me as well, 'cause I'd have to tell everyone that you were alive and well when you went into the building with him, and Richard wouldn't hurt me."

As the three walked up the ramp from the alley, another set of eyes watched. The eyes moved back and forth as the man shook his head. "Amateurs," he said to himself.

56

Richard gave Marcus a pair of jeans and a dry shirt, then prepared sandwiches and coffee as Marcus rambled on. "Mr. Moore, I wouldn't kill anyone. I don't know why the police think I killed your friend, Bear. I don't own a gun. I never touched a gun. Why is everyone convinced I killed him? Heng said you were a good guy. Said you and Bear were close friends. She said I should trust you. Why does anyone think I killed him?"

"You were there, Marcus. You saw what happened."

"What? I never said I was there. What makes you think I was there?"

"Whoever killed my friend, Bear, expected to find you at the same time. When you didn't show, they assumed you saw what happened. They planted evidence in your apartment. They want you on the run or someplace they know they can get to you. But, Marcus, this conversation isn't helping either of us. You have to tell me everything, starting at the beginning. Let's start with your insider trading."

Marcus was startled. "You know about that?"

"I know you made some insider trades, but I don't know how you got the information."

Marcus was pacing the kitchen floor. "Oh, Jesus what a fucking mess. I just wanted to tell you I didn't kill your friend. Then I was going to leave. Now, this ... how do you know this?"

"Marcus, pour yourself some coffee and fix it the way you like it then we'll go into the living room. You will sit down and tell me the story. No pacing, no jumping around."

Marcus fixed his coffee. Richard pushed open the swinging door between the dining room and the kitchen. They walked through the dark dining room to the living room. Marcus sat on the couch which was against the wall to the right. Richard went to his favorite chair in the left corner from the couch. He had a clear view down the corridor to the main entry door.

Richard settled in and took a bite of his sandwich, his actions deliberately relaxed and leisurely.

Marcus, on the other hand, was obviously still uncertain and agitated. He was chewing his sandwich with difficulty, and his body was tensely poised on the edge of one of the couch's cushions.

In his best calming manner, Richard said, "So, tell me about the securities trading."

"Oh … oh, yeah … sure. I dropped out of school, college. I couldn't afford it anymore. So, I got a job. You know, at Improve Your Credit. I've been sending money to my parents and trying to keep ahead of my bill. I still want to go back to school.

"One of the clerks from upstairs at the law office and I were having lunch one day. He mentioned this acquisition the law firm handled. He said they helped one electronics firm acquire another. He said he wished he had bought some stock in the company before the acquisition. Said the stock doubled overnight once the deal was announced.

"I got the idea I could make some extra money if I knew what companies the law firm was working with. So I bugged the conference room of the law firm. They don't do a lot of deals and many of the ones they handle are privately owned companies. No stock available for the public. Still, I made a few bucks.

"I couldn't listen to the conversations as they were happening, because I had to work, so I had a receiver record what the bug picked up onto a CD. When I had some time, I would sit and listen to what was on the recording. The bug was voice activated, so it was hard to follow the conversation, but I got enough to complete some deals.

"One day, god it seems like a lifetime ago, I was listening to a conversation. I recognized Ms. Cook and Attorney Hurshberg but not the others. Someone was on a speakerphone. One of the people was kind of complaining and saying that they should hold off any more contributions. He said that an investigator was looking around and might be getting close. The guy on the speakerphone told them the investigator was not a problem because he was being kept busy."

Richard leaned forward. "He said that, 'was being kept busy,' his words?"

"Well … yeah … was hard to get it all, and it was a while ago."

"OK. Did this guy on the speakerphone say who the investigator was?"

"No, but sometime during the meeting, someone tried to joke about a big black guy called Bear. That's how I got to know his name."

"OK. What was the meeting about? Do you know?"

"Yeah, I know. Wish I didn't. It was about some political campaign. Someone was checking on the campaign contributions. Wanted to make sure the funds were ready and the donor list complete. Forty-million dollars: that is what they were talking about. They were contributing forty-million dollars to the campaign. Another man argued they had contributed enough. The candidate had the election locked, he said. Why did he need forty-million more? Someone else said because he wants it for a final push. Or something like that."

Richard was stunned. "Are you sure they were talking about just one candidate, and the figure was forty-million more, and not forty-million total?"

"Absolutely, nobody said how much had been given already, but that amount was mentioned several times as the amount that was needed now, and there was no question they were talking about just one candidate?"

If what Marcus is saying is true, if this is all about one campaign that's leading in the polls spending this kind of money, we're talking about the presidential race, and we're talking about the vice president, Richard thought. Nonetheless, he asked, "Did anyone mention which candidate wanted the money?"

Marcus didn't answer right away. He seemed to be deciding how to respond. Finally, he sighed, and, almost as if he were putting down a great burden, said, "I don't know. I assumed it was the vice president but I don't remember if anyone came out and said it. Besides, I was thinking about the forty-million dollars, and all the money that went before it, and the fact that someone was investigating all this, and these people were nervous about that. Something illegal had to be going on. Maybe there was something illegal about contributing that much money, or something illegal about the way they got it all. I mean, where the hell did they get it? Right? So, I figured, if they could contribute amounts like forty-million as an add-on, they could spare a hundred thousand or two hundred thousand for me."

"The way I saw it, I had a small window of opportunity. I could threaten to expose the scheme, which might seriously undermine the vice president's chances of winning, or they could pay me a sum of money. Once the election was held, my threat and its value would be diminished. The approach would have to be to Hurshberg, because I only knew two people in the meeting.

"I couldn't approach Hurshberg directly myself. He might recognize me and figure out how I learned about the meeting. I would probably get fired, and end up in a worse position. I needed someone to help.

"I come from a tough neighborhood. You probably already know that. My best friend was a kid named Zima. Zima and I grew up together. We never joined a gang. I use to get shit all the time about not joining because my brother was in one. One day, a guy comes by and starts giving me a lot of shit, starts pushing me around, and threatening me. Zima got between me and this dude. Gets right in his face and tells him to get lost. The dude pulls out a gun, but Zima just keeps staring at him. After a while, the dude gives us the finger, says, "You two punks aren't worth the trouble," and walks away. Man, I knew then that, if I was ever in that kind of trouble, I wanted Zima to be with me.

"So, I told Zima about the gig with the veep, and he said he's in. I told him to go for two hundred grand and we could split fifty-fifty. 'Deal,' he said." Marcus paused, closed his eyes, and slowly shook his head. "I should never have contacted Zima. He was my best friend."

57

After a few more moments of silence, he went on. "Hurshberg and Zima met in the food court of the mall in Burlington. I watched from a distance. I knew something was wrong from the way Zima was talking and acting. They almost got in an argument. They finally settled down and they left together. I couldn't figure out what was happening. I had told Zima not to push the guy. If Hurshberg didn't want to play, then let it go. No sense in getting in major trouble. I still have the bug and stock buys. I could cut Zima in on that.

"They went out to Hurshberg's car. I recognized it, a big ass Caddy Escadrille with a lot of chrome. Opening the back door on the driver's side, Hurshberg showed Zima something in the back seat. It must have been a package of money. Zima didn't move from the back of the car. He was standing near the bumper. Hurshberg threw a stack of bills at him and started walking away. That's when it all went to shit.

"Zima went to the open car door and looked inside. The side door of the white van parked next to Hurshberg's Caddy slid open and two guys grabbed Zima and pulled him into the van. They drove out of the parking lot and I haven't seen them since. It happened so fast, I couldn't do anything if I had wanted to."

He had been doing a good job of holding himself together, Richard thought. It didn't take much imagination for him to figure out what the rest of the story was going to be, and how hard it would be for Marcus to tell it.

Marcus was slipping. His body was shaking more than it had earlier. He was surprised, however, at how detached he had become by telling the story.

"That was Thursday evening. I stayed away from work Friday. I didn't call in either. Friday night, the cops found Zima's body. As far as I know, the police said he was a victim of a hit and run."

"Where did they find him? Do you know?"

"Oh, I don't know. ... Somewhere in the neighborhood."

"Your old neighborhood? The Boston Police found him."

"Yeah, my neighborhood."

Richard thought for a moment. He would have to call Linda and ask her for the information about Zima and his death. He would also have to have the security tapes at the mall checked.

"So, what was your involvement with Bear, Marcus? Or was there any?"

"I knew enough to hide. I also knew I couldn't hide forever and I should get some help. I thought that if Bear really was the investigator they were talking about in the tapes, maybe he could help me. You see, I knew who Bear was, because my cousin once got in a heap of trouble, and found himself looking at some serious time. Bear approached him in the courthouse, and said he could cut him a deal if he committed to getting his life back on track. My cousin isn't really a bad guy, and he promised he would stay on the straight and narrow if Bear got him off the hook. Bear kept his word, and my cousin kept his. Now he owns a small repair shop and does OK. I called him and asked for Bear's number.

"It was late Saturday when I talked with Bear. I told him I was Ricky's cousin, and that I was in trouble, the kind of trouble that a guy like him might be able to help me with. I didn't give him any of the details. I mean, he could have brought the cops. I suddenly saw extortion and blackmail as my ticket to time behind bars. Even so, he agreed to meet me, maybe because I was Ricky's cousin. We agreed to meet in the parking lot of Improve Your Credit."

"Why there? Why not someplace more public? If people were after you that was one place they'd be sure to be watching."

"I don't know. I just wasn't thinking too straight after I heard about Zima. My only copy of the conversation I recorded was in my office. I figured that when the cleaners arrived around ten that night, I'd get them to let me and Bear into the building, and then I could play the CD for him, even make him a copy. In the end, of course, none of that happened.

"I parked up the street, and watched the parking lot, waiting for Bear to show up. I saw him pull in, but before I could even start my car, someone came out from behind the building. The guy said something, and waved, and Bear got out of his car.

"Bear and I have never met, but he told me what kind of car he would be driving. He told me I should wear a red short-sleeve shirt, so he would know it was me. It wasn't until afterwards I realized the guy that waved at Bear had a red short-sleeve shirt on.

"As Bear and the guy walked toward each other, Bear suddenly stopped. He looked to his right, moved a little, and then went down on his knees. He flopped on his back and stayed there. I was shocked. What the hell happened? I never saw anyone get shot or die before, so I couldn't figure out what was happening.

"Another guy came out of the bushes, the ones on the berm next to the building. He was in black; all black, and he was carrying a gun. He walked around Bear, just watching. Then he put his gun in the belt of his pants. You know, in the back. He bent down for some reason and, suddenly, Bear came alive. He hit the guy in the left shoulder. The guy jumps up and pulls the gun out and points it at Bear. I never heard the shot, but Bear went down again, and, this time, he stayed down, and he never moved. I saw the guy take Bear's wallet, but, by that time, I was hightailing it out of there without any lights on. I've been hiding ever since."

When Marcus was finished telling his story, Richard was confident that it was the truth. Despite that, he still had many questions, and he intended to check and recheck the young man's tale.

Marcus started to get up. "I need some more coffee."

Richard got up. "Stay there. I need some water. I'll get you coffee."

58

As he stepped away from his chair, the telephone rang. Richard looked at the caller ID information. It was Regis calling from downstairs, and Richard answered.

Regis was saying something, but Richard could barely make out the words. "What Regis? What did you say?"

"Richard, two ... two ... armed—" The phone went dead.

"Shit!"

Richard looked down the hall and saw the flapper handle on the front door moving.

His voice urgent, but low, he said, "Marcus, get behind the couch and stay there until I pull you out."

"What! What did you say?"

"Get back behind the couch. We have company, and I didn't invite them."

As Marcus scrambled behind the couch, Richard took cover in the shadows just as the front door of his condo swung slowly open, and two men cautiously entered. Both men were casually dressed in slacks and pullover tops covered by sport jackets. Both carried nine-millimeter Glocks fitted with silencers. One intruder went right down the hall to the kitchen. The other turned left toward the living room. Both moved quietly, their bodies tensed, and their weapons held up in assault position.

Sliding toward the hallway entrance, Richard prepared to assault the man who was coming toward the living room. Before entering, however, the intruder suddenly stopped, turned, and moved up the hallway toward the dining room. Anticipating the man's next move, Richard moved into the dining room, then slunk low in a corner, a position that put him on the left and below the line of sight of anyone coming into the room.

A moment later, the intruder appeared at the entrance to the dining room, peering cautiously to his left, but missing Richard when he failed to lower his gaze. Then, swinging toward his right with his gun raised, he stepped further into the dining area.

Richard catapulted himself out of his crouching position, and, completely extending his right arm, grabbed the intruder's gun hand while circling his left arm around the man's left side and pinning his left arm. Taken by surprise, the intruder initially struggled wildly, inadvertently pulling the trigger on his weapon, which made two quick burping noises as it fired two silenced rounds. Quickly regaining his composure, the man back-pedaled, forcing Richard to stumble backward, hitting the wall behind him with a loud thud. The move did not have its desired effect, however, because Richard, though he had the wind knocked out of him, did not release his grip on the man or his gun hand.

In the kitchen, the second intruder heard the struggle and kicked open the door between the kitchen and the dining room. Seeing the struggling figures, he instinctively stepped into the opening, thus, unfortunately for him, making himself clearly silhouetted by the lights in the kitchen behind him. As the first man struggled to move forward with Richard still clamped to his back, Richard forced the man's gun arm to point at the silhouette, and then, squeezed the trigger finger of the hand that was holding the gun. The weapon burped once again, and the silhouette fell to the floor.

Raging, Richard's man let out a low growl and back peddled with the force of an over-revved truck. Richard sidestepped as he went backward, causing both men to fall over the coffee table. Richard rolled to his right, and, as the intruder tried to stand, Richard used both hands to try to twist the weapon out of his grasp. The sound of two burps from the gun was followed by splinters flying into the air from the floor. Richard twisted the wrist some more, and the intruder yelped in pain, and the gun fell to the floor. When Richard moved to pick it up, the man kicked it gun away, and it skidded under the couch.

Having missed the weapon, Richard turned his lunge into a roll, and was regaining his footing when he saw the man taking a small twenty-two pistol from an ankle holster. Richard stepped into him, and drove him back. They hit the side table and then the attacker hit the wall and went limp. Richard saw blood on the corner of the windowsill, and blood was running down the back of the man's head and onto the floor.

Richard stepped on the limp figure's outstretched hand, and, getting no response, turned to assess the status of the other intruder, when a voice said, "Put your hands up, and turn around, real slow."

Richard did as he was instructed.

A man dressed in a suit and tie stood just inside the entry from the hall. He was holding a nine-millimeter Glock with a silencer attached.

"Do we know each other?" Richard said.

Ignoring the question, the man looked down at the inert bodies lying on the floor, and said, "Too bad about these bozos. I told them they shouldn't underestimate you."

"No, Richard, we don't know each other." The man smiled at Richard and continued. "I do, however, know enough about you to be cautious. You're not the person I'm here for. I want Marcus McGill, and, as far as I'm concerned, once I have him, my involvement with you is finished. Now, he's either here, or somewhere else in this building, and I'm going to find him, with or without your help. So, why don't you just tell me where he is so I can just go about my business, and you can continue to go about your life."

"I'm afraid I don't know—"

Before Richard could finish speaking, the Glock spit, and a bullet lifted splinters from the floor in front of Richard's feet.

The man took several steps into the room, and the look on his face hardened. "I don't need you, Moore. I will find Marcus with or without your information. So, tell me where he is and live, or don't, and die."

Richard maintained eye contact, and mentally ran through a list of options. None of them looked very promising. Richard's silence was interrupted by the man with the gun.

"I thought so. Goodbye, Mr. Moore," he said, aiming his weapon at Richard's head.

Richard heard the familiar burp of a silenced weapon, and, then, the sound of a body hitting the floor. In the living room, Marcus dropped the Glock he had just fired, and slumped back against the couch.

Richard reached down and grabbed the weapon that had his would be executioner had dropped when the slug from Marcus's Glock had slammed into the man's now inert body. A quick check told him that the man was dead, and then he went right over to Marcus.

A cursory examination showed that the young man was unhurt, and, relieved, Richard gently shook him, and called his name. "Marcus. Marcus. It's Richard. Talk to me, boy."

Marcus's eyelids fluttered, and then opened wide, as he sat up with a start.

"Mr. Moore?" he asked, propping himself up against the couch. He looked at Richard with a dazed expression. "What happened? That man was going to kill you. Where is he?"

Mindful of the fact that Marcus, who had probably never even fired a gun before, had just killed a man the first time he ever pulled a trigger, Richard said, in a gentle, but matter-of-fact manner, "He's lying over there on the floor, and he's not going to hurt anyone at the moment. Marcus, tell me what you remember about what just happened."

Marcus began to tremble. "I got behind the couch just like you told me, but I didn't know what was going on, and why I was hiding. It was very quiet at first, and then I heard what sounded like a fight … a lot of crashing and grunts. Then, there was this series of funny noises like someone was firing an air gun; that seemed to happen several times during all the crashing and grunting, then something clattered onto the floor, and, a moment later, something hit me on the knee. I looked down to see that it was a gun that had slid out from under the couch. I picked it up, and just then there was a very loud crash, and it got very quiet for a few moments. Then, I heard a strange voice say 'Put your hands up,' or something like that, and I was about to raise my hands when I heard your voice, and I realized that he was talking to you. I peeked out from behind the couch, saw you standing with your hands raised, and this guy pointing a gun at you. … He was just going to shoot you. I really wasn't thinking, I aimed the gun at him and pulled the trigger. When he fell down, I realized that I had probably just killed the guy. The next thing I knew, you were calling my name, and I woke up here on the floor with you shaking me."

He paused, then, with a plaintive look on his face, asked, "Is he dead, Mr. Moore? Did I kill him? I couldn't let him shoot you. I couldn't. Two people are already dead because of me. I couldn't."

Richard, afraid that Marcus would go into shock, said, "If you hadn't shot him, Marcus, I would be dead, and so would you. The police will be coming, and I don't want them to take you in. I have to get you out of here right now. Do you hear what I'm saying?"

Marcus was looking off into space.

Speaking firmly, Richard said, "Marcus. Marcus. Let's go. I have to get you out of here."

Richard pulled Marcus to his feet and walked him out the door of his condo. He banged on his neighbor's door. Harmon Stump, Richard's friend and neighbor, a sixty-two-year-old retired widower, opened the door. Harmon was a Vietnam combat veteran, and like many other combat veterans he and Richard shared a special bond.

"Richard, are you OK? I called the police. Sounded like a fight or something."

"Harmon, I need a big favor. This is Marcus. I need you to hide him in your apartment until some of my people come to get him out of here."

"What? Hide him? Why? How long?"

"Not more than eighteen hours. You can't tell anyone he's here. Not even the police. A woman named Laura will bring some men to get him out."

"What's this about, Richard? By the way, you're bleeding."

Richard looked down at his side. The knife wound had opened again. "He's a key witness in a case I'm working on. Some really nasty people are looking for him, and they've convinced the police to help them. Once he's in custody, they'll make sure he doesn't live to testify against them. You know the kind of people I'm talking about, Harmon; 'respectable' people with dirty secrets, and a lot of political clout. Don't worry, though, you'll be safe as long as you don't mention Marcus to anyone."

Harmon knew a little about what Richard did for a living, and, had made some educated guesses about the rest. He considered

Richard one of the "good guys." His experiences in Vietnam had also left him with a deep anger about any kind of duplicity by anyone connected with the government. It only took him a moment to decide that, if Richard was fighting people like that, he would help. "I've got your back, pal," he said to Richard, and, turning to Marcus, said to him, "Come on in, young man."

"Thanks, Harmon. I'll explain it all later."

Returning to his condo, Richard went into the living room and picked up the Glock Marcus had used to shoot the third intruder. He wiped the weapon down and, then, placed it in the hand of the man with whom he had been struggling. Then, he dropped the weapon, and kicked it across the room. Next, he wiped down the weapon he had picked up off the floor, and put it back in the hand of the man in the suit coat and tie. Finally, he grabbed the cup and dishes Marcus had been using, threw them in the dishwasher, and turned on the machine.

"Oh, shit! Regis!" He suddenly remembered Regis, and headed to the door. He opened it to find a police officer just about to knock. Before the officer could speak, Richard said, "I'm Richard Moore. I live in this condo. I'm going down to check on our security guard."

59

Using his bulky body to block Richard from getting past him, the officer said, "Whoa, slow down, pal. My partner is attending to him. The guy is awake and talking. Now, we got a call about a disturbance in your condo." Looking at Richard's bloody shirt, he continued, "Just what the hell has been going on here?"

"It's OK, Officer; I'll take over from here."

Turning around, the officer saw an attractive, well-dressed, middle-aged woman with dirty-blond hair.

"And just who the hell are you, may I ask?" said the officer.

Pushing aside her stylish jacket to reveal her gold shield and gun, Linda said, "Detective Pollard, Officer ..." she peered at his nametag, "O'Bannion, and, as I just said, I'll take over from here. Now, will you get the EMT's up here before Mr. Moore, here, bleeds to death in the hallway."

"Yes, ma'am," O'Bannion replied, somewhat abashed, and started calling in on his radio.

"OK, Richard. Now, as the good Officer O'Bannion was asking, just what the hell has been going on here?"

Richard told Linda about the call from Regis and the ensuing struggle with the three intruders, without, however, mentioning Marcus, or placing anyone other than himself and the three intruders at the scene. When the narrative was interrupted by the EMT's caring for Richard's wound, Linda surveyed the scene, and examined the three bodies.

"Get over here, guys," she called to the EMT's, and, pointing to the man with whom Richard had struggled, continued, "This one's still alive."

Going back over to Richard, she said, "I knew, as soon as I heard the address of the disturbance call, that you had to be involved, and I hauled ass getting over here as fast as I could. I didn't expect it to be a routine call, but this ... this, Richard; this is a bit much, even for you."

Sitting down next to him, she said, "Let me see if I've got this straight. You say these guys shot your doorman, who just happened to be wearing a Kevlar vest, so he wasn't killed and was able to call you and tell you that you were about to have company. Then two of these guys came up here, picked the lock to your front door and snuck in, only, thanks to your bullet-proof and mind-reading doorman, you were ready for them. You got into a struggle with that one," she pointed at the man on whom the EMT's were working, "during which the guy over there by the kitchen door was shot a couple of times by the gun of the guy you were dancing around the room with. Then, this guy," she pointed at the man in the suit and tie, "shows up out of nowhere waving that pistol in his hand around and he gets shot, again by the gun of your dancing partner. After he goes down, you and bozo number one decide to call it quits, and he winds up flying headfirst across the room into the wall, which, if I'm reading the signs from the EMT's correctly, might make him just as dead as the other two. Finally, you think this little episode might— just might—be connected with your current case." She paused, looked Richard squarely in the eye, then said, "Have I left out anything important?" Before he could answer, however, she leaned over, and, putting her mouth next to his ear, whispered, "I'm not stupid. This didn't happen the way you told it. Some—"

"Well, Small-town, did your diner guess criticize your cooking?" Detective Kelly and his partner, Nelson, walked into the living room.

Richard ignored Kelly, but Linda could not ignore him. "Detectives Kelly, Nelson, what are you doing here?" Linda asked.

"We heard someone paid Small-town a visit and things got ugly. Since your friend here is associated with two homicides we're working on, we thought this might be relevant to our investigation." Kelly was clearly enjoying himself.

"So, what do you think Small-town? These bodies have anything to do with your friend's murder or the murder of King?"

Richard ignored Kelly. "Linda, I'll go downtown and give my statement."

As Richard started to walk out, Kelly blocked his path.

"Kelly, get out of his way. He's going to my office to give a statement. This is my jurisdiction." Linda wanted to defuse any confrontation, knowing that the longer it went on, the more likely someone would get hurt.

Kelly was staring at Richard with a smile that was too broad. "Two murders and Small-town is in the middle of them. Now he gets attacked and there are two more dead. He's a material witness. I have a lot of questions for him. We'll take him with us. You can have him after we're finished with him."

Richard started to walk around Kelly. Kelly put his hand on Richard's right shoulder. No one was sure how it happened, but, in an instant, Kelly's hand was locked under Richard's right arm, and Richard's right arm was wrapped over and under Kelly's outstretched arm. Richard raised his arm a little creating intense pain in Kelly's shoulder, causing Kelly to cry out, and rise up on his toes.

"Now that I have your attention," Richard said, "I suggest you and your partner leave this crime scene. If you want to talk with me, call my attorney and set up an appointment." He let Kelly go.

Humiliated, and in pain, Kelly began sputtering, "You're mine Small-town. You're under arrest for assaulting an officer. You have the right to remain—"

"Kelly, I am ordering you and your partner to leave. This is my investigation. If you want any information, you can request it through the regular channels. Do you understand, or do you want me to call up my chief so he can come over and arrest both of you for interfering with my investigation. Then, he can call up your colonel to get you out, and you two can explain to him why he had to come downtown and embarrass himself by bailing out two of his misbehaving little boys." Linda was tired of all this macho bullshit, and she was furious.

"Bullshit," Kelly began sputtering again, "this man assaul … Where are you going?"

Nelson, who was headed out the door, turned, and said, "I'm headed back to headquarters, partner. I want this jurisdiction thing straightened out as much as you do, but, we don't seem to be making much headway here, so, I'm going to go right to the top with it. I think we can make a stronger case if we go together, don't you?"

"But what about—"

"Come on, partner. We're just spinning our wheels here."

Kelly was going to object, and then thought better of it. Glaring at Richard and Linda, he growled, "You two lovebirds haven't heard the end of this." Then, he turned on his heel, and followed his partner out the door.

"Thanks, Linda," Richard said.

Linda glared at him.

"OK, Richard, we'll do it your way," she said. Then, she got in his face. "But, if you fuck me over and hang me out to dry on this, friendship or no friendship, your ass will be grass, and I'll be the biggest dam lawn mower you ever saw. Now, get some clothes, and get your macho kiester out of here. This isn't your home anymore, it's my crime scene."

When he got in his car, Richard called Sheila.

"I have our man." He gave her a condensed version of what happened. "You need to get him to a safe location but you can't take him until the police leave the scene. Even then, you have to assume my place is being watched."

Richard took a room at Kings Inn, the same hotel were Steve was staying. Steve and Richard talked about the attack and the information Marcus had provided. They decided Steve would run detailed electronic searches into the campaign finances of the vice president and into the finances of both Higher Credit and Hurshberg and Stein Attorneys at Law. Steve would also set up wiretaps on Hurshberg's phones.

60

Glen Hurshberg backed his Cadillac Escadrille out of his driveway and drove down the street. Richard watched from two streets away. Saturday morning remained cold, overcast, and damp. It was a bleak day. Richard followed Hurshberg, waiting for a good place to confront him.

Hurshberg made several stops: dry cleaners, office supply store, and coffee shop, and, eventually, arrived at his office building.

Richard followed a few minutes later, located Hurshberg's office on the directory, and headed there. When he arrived, he found the door partially open and tapped on it. If Hurshberg was surprised to see him, he did not show it.

"Mr. ah … Moore, isn't it?"

"Richard Moore, Mr. Hurshberg."

"Well, Mr. Moore, I don't conduct office visits on the weekend. If you have some need to talk with me, you should come back Monday. I just stopped by here to finish a few things before taking the family out for the day."

Richard entered the office and sat down. "I just wanted to ask you a couple of quick questions. You can continue what you are doing while we talk."

"Is this about that mugging in our parking lot? How are the police doing with their investigation?" Hurshberg continued to review some papers as he talked.

"The police are a little behind in their investigation. They now have two murders to investigate. That's why I'm here. I was hoping you could help."

"Help? I'll help in any way I can, but I really don't know anything about your friend's murder."

"Well, I was thinking more about Zima."

Hurshberg dropped his pen and the papers he was reading. 'Zima … I don't think I know anyone named Zima."

"Zima or Zachary Bairos, as he was known to his friends and killers. Turns out, he wasn't a victim of a hit and run. He was murdered."

"Again, Mr. Moore, I don't know anyone named Zima. Now, if you don't mind, I really do not have time for this."

"Well, maybe you don't know Zima, but here's where I need your help. See, Zima had some information he thought might have value. He tried to sell that information for two hundred thousand dollars. Unfortunately, the guy he tried to sell the information to didn't want to pay. Instead, he had Zima kidnapped. Zima was found the next day on the street in his neighborhood. The police thought he had been a victim of hit and run."

"Mr. Moore, are you getting to a point? I don't know who or what you are talking about."

"Not a point, just a question, maybe more than one. Zima and this guy met at the mall in Burlington. Zima was kidnapped in the parking lot of the mall. Here's my question. How many security cameras do you suppose were operating at the time of the kidnapping? How good an image do you think I will get of the man Zima met?"

Richard sat back and observed Hurshberg, and several long moments passed before the attorney spoke.

"I think the police will have to answer those questions for you. I'm sure they will tell you after they do their investigation, if they decide they should share the information with you. I certainly can't answer your questions. I haven't been to the mall in some time. Now, if you will excuse me—"

"The police will not be looking at the tapes. Bear was a very dear and close friend. I want the killer or killers, and anyone involved with his murder and cover-up. My people are reviewing the security tapes. The man in the picture either talks or—"

"Mr. Moore, you cannot be talking about taking the law into your hands. You certainly should not be telling me you might harm someone involved with Bear's murder. I am an officer of the court. It would be my duty to report such statements."

"I wouldn't harm the man in the video. I'll give him the opportunity to tell me who, what, when, and why. If he refuses, he like anyone else involved, will just disappear. Think about it. I want information. I already know whose face is in the security video. I you do not want to talk now, you will when I bring the video with your image."

Hurshberg was white. Perspiration had formed on his brow. He could no longer look directly at Richard. He really thought he would be sick. Hurshberg got up to leave. "Mr. Moore, I can't help you. It's time you leave. I have a family outing to go to."

"OK. I'm leaving, but I will see you later, and I'll show you the video."

Using a disposable cellphone, Richard called Sheila's high-tech, anti-eaves-dropping phone supplied by Steve. "Sheila, what's the plan for our man Marcus?" Richard had not spoken with Sheila since calling her the previous night.

"Well, he's still asleep. Apparently he hasn't slept much lately. We'll give him a good breakfast when he gets up then start debriefing him."

"You have him already?"

"Sure. Did you think I was going to have your neighbor pissing his pants for twenty-four or thirty-six hours wondering if someone was going to kick in his door?"

"I'm sure Harmon has done some door-kicking of his own in his day, but, thanks for the quick response. You are incredible."

"No problem. Wait until you get my bill. We went in as a three-man BPD biohazard unit, two technicians, and a driver. All the two guys watching down the street saw was two BPD biohazard technicians go into the building, and then come out about twenty minutes later, dressed head to toe in full biohazard suits and masks. The techs put the Biohazardous Evidence box they were carrying into the back of the biohazard van, climbed into the van themselves, and away they went. All perfectly normal and routine, except of course, that the techs never went near your place. They went into Harmon's, where one of our fake techs changed places with the kid. A few hours later, the guy who had swapped places with the kid said goodbye to Harmon, walked out the front door of the building, got into a waiting car, and was driven off. ."

"Thanks, good news. Do you have any idea who the two guys were, or who they were with?"

"None, we didn't want to get too close. They were still there when our guy left. Now that we have Marcus, the longer they stay watching your place, the better."

"OK. Thanks, Sheila. I'll call later to see if Marcus had anything useful to add."

Richard watched the office building for over an hour before Hurshberg came out. He tailed the attorney until Hurshberg pulled into the driveway of his house. When he got out of his car, he appeared to be arguing with someone on his cellphone as he walked to the front door, and he did not go into his house until the call was finished. Twenty minutes later Richard saw a woman, whom he assumed was Hurshberg's wife, storm out of the house and speed of in another car, leaving Hurshberg home with the kids.

Richard had hoped Hurshberg would meet with someone, but it now appeared the man would be home for some time.

61

Before getting on Route 95 North, to head for the Woburn office, Richard called Maynard Olsen. His daughter, Brenda, answered. "Who's calling please?"

"Brenda, my name is Richard Moore I—"

"Oh, Mr. Moore. You met my father yesterday. You're taking the car."

"Well, yes. I really don't want to take it. I'm willing to buy it, but your father wouldn't set a price. Maybe you can talk with him."

"We had a very long talk last night—" She began to sob.

Hearing her crying, Richard said, "Brenda, if you don't want to part with the car, I won't mind. It must have some sentimental value."

She was sniffling now. "Oh, excuse me, Mr. Moore. It's not the car ... Dad passed away last night in his sleep."

After a few moments of silence, Richard said, "Brenda, I am so sorry. He talked so much about you."

"Thank you, Mr. Moore. He talked about you all evening. I haven't heard him so happy in a long time. You see, that car was as much his as Gary's. Dad couldn't let go of it. Then, he didn't know who to give it to. He wanted someone who would put it back on the road. He said you promised him you would—" She was crying again. "It made him so happy. Thank you."

Richard was still processing the fact of Olsen's death. "Brenda, you know he talked about how much he loved you."

"Oh ... know. We talked about it before. I'm very happy with my relationship with dad. Listen, I have a few things to take care of. Would you mind waiting until later in the week to pick up the car?"

"Not at all, call me when you know a good day and time." He gave her his cellphone number.

62

As soon as he finished talking with Brenda, Steve called. "Richard, Phil wants you to give him a call. He met with the congressman."

"OK, Steve. How's the research on campaign contributions coming?"

"I'm crossing-checking the list against various databases of deceased voters. That will take a while. I had to borrow some computing space on a local college system."

"I'm not sure I want to ask how. I expect to come by the office soon."

He disconnected and called Phil. "Phil, Richard. You got something for me?"

"Hi, Richard, I met with Congressman Willard at his house. He went from cordial to downright nasty. He denied any knowledge of Bear's murder. He claims the threats were real. He just didn't want any publicity associated with notifying the Secret Service or Capitol Police. The man can't lie. He stammers and gets confused. I stayed down the street watching his house. I can see his kitchen and study. The man's been on the phone since I left. He's pacing like a lion in a cage. He's going to break."

"Good job, Phil. Willard or Hurshberg or both will make a mistake. They didn't sign up for this type of heat."

"Just be careful, Richard, you may be controlling the heat now, but whoever's behind this might want to take your hand off the control … permanently."

"I know. Keep me posted about Willard."

63

Stephanie had arranged to meet Andre and Kim for lunch at The Market Eatery, a restaurant in the northwest corner of the Quincy Market building. On a nice day the umbrellas above the metal tables in the restaurant's outdoor courtyard section, shaded patrons from the sun, and tables were at a premium. On this day, however, only eight hardy souls were sitting outside, defying a constant drizzle, cool temperatures, and occasional wind.

Andre and Kim were not among them. They chose the warmth of the indoor section next to the windows. Andre pointed up and across the courtyard to show Kim where his office was located. The lunch meeting was scheduled for eleven thirty. It was now twelve fifteen. Stephanie was late.

"I have to order," Kim said. "I get light-headed and faint if I don't keep my blood sugar balanced."

Andre agreed. "I'm famished. I didn't eat breakfast. So let's order. Stephanie should be along soon."

Andre and Kim compared notes on the Big Dig company. Except for the identity of the primary benefactor, Kim possessed exactly the kind of information that Andre and Stephanie wanted to know. They discussed the notes Kim had left on the company's computer, and Kim explained that she had left the notes there, hoping the company would be audited and the payoff discovered. That didn't happen, of course, but, she hoped, Stephanie's investigation would lead to the same result. They became so focused and intent on their conversation, that they hardly registered that their lunch had been served, they had eaten, and the table had been cleared until Kim finally looked at her watch. "Oh, look at the time. I can't stay any longer. Tell Stephanie I'll talk with her later."

They both got up to leave. As Kim stooped to pick up her pocketbook, the window shattered. The man sitting at the table behind Andre leaped and slip across the table. He knocked Andre to one side and drove Kim to the floor. A patron walking past their table yelled and dropped to the floor.

Stephanie just could not imagine her day going more badly. She had gone to her office at the Globe to use her computer to complete some research. When her editor saw her, he ordered her into his office, and the ensuing discussion, heated at times, lasted until after noon. When it ended, she was unable to reach either Kim or Andre by the cellphone, and the restaurant's phone was busy.

Her drive to downtown Boston would have been quicker if she had walked. The completion of the Big Dig had done little to mitigate the often-snarled Central Artery traffic. The streets around Faneuil Hall Market were clogged, and a parking space, as usual, was impossible to find.

She was walking at a quick pace through the center of Quincy Market when two police officers nearly knocked her and others down as they ran to the north end of the building. Running police nearly always signaled a story of some kind, and, she was a reporter. Instinctively, she ran after them. When she saw that they were headed toward The Market Eatery, however, another set of instincts took over, and her reportorial curiosity turned into concern. When she actually got to the restaurant, and saw that, not only had the police sealed the entrance, but also that an ambulance was pulling in to join two others already in the courtyard, her concern turned into alarm.

Pleading that her friends were inside, and, even showing her reporter's credentials, got her nowhere with the officers at the door, and, stuck in the growing crowd of onlookers, she was forced to wait for news about Andre and Kim.. After ten increasingly anxious minutes, the restaurant doors opened, and two EMT's emerged, rapidly guiding a stretcher toward one of the waiting ambulances. From her vantage point, she had to stand on her toes just to get a fleeting glimpse of the stretcher, but, it was enough to tell her that that the man on it was a stranger. A second stretcher followed a few minutes later, but, once again, its occupant, a woman, was unknown to her.

It was several more minutes before the restaurant doors opened once again, and a third stretcher was propelled across the courtyard Its occupant, a man, had one of his arms bandaged, but, seemed otherwise unharmed. As the EMT's lifted the stretcher into the back of the ambulance, Stephanie got a clear view of the man's face. It was Andre.

"Andre! Andre!" she shouted, jostling her way through the crowd, trying to reach the ambulance. She had nearly broken through, when her progress was suddenly stopped by the bulky body of a tall, burly, and, very immovable policeman.

"Sorry, lady," he said, not looking in the least sorry at all, "you can't go near the ambulances."

"Listen, officer, my friend is on that stretcher, and I need to know what happened to him."

"Look, lady, I'm sorry about your friend, but, I have orders not to let anyone near the ambulances. If you want to know what happened to your friend, and where they're taking him, you can go inside the restaurant, and talk to the detectives. They'll be able to tell you what happened to your friend and what hospital he's going to."

Stephanie was on the verge of showing him her credentials, when she heard the doors of the ambulance slam shut, and it started to drive away. Resignedly, she turned around, and headed back toward the restaurant's door. When she got there, alerted by the officer she had just left, the officers at the door let her in. Instead of looking for the detectives, however, she looked around for Kim. A few minutes later, she found her talking with a police officer.

Stephanie ran to her. "Oh, Kim, are you all right? I saw Andre taken out on a stretcher."

"Hi, Stephanie, I'm OK."

Stephanie could see that Kim was shaken, and that she had cuts on her face. In addition, her blouse was torn and stained with blood.

Without any preamble, she said, in a tremulous voice, "The glass shattered and sprayed us. Cut my face and hands. I'm going to have some serious bruises from where the guy hit me and landed on me."

"A guy hit you? What guy?"

"Ah, if you don't mind, ma'am, I'd like to finish getting this woman's statement, and, then, you two can talk."

Realizing that the sooner the officer finished questioning Kim, the sooner she would be able to find out what had happened, Stephanie nodded her assent, patted Kim on the hand, and left her and the officer to finish the interview.

She found several servers, and tried talking to them, but they were either too shaken by what they had seen, or had not seen anything. She spied a police officer she knew. Stephanie said high and asked the female officer if she could share any information. The officer told her that they believed someone had shot out one of restaurant's windows. The resulting shower of glass had left some patrons with minor cuts, and three patrons seemed to have sustained minor gunshot wounds.

When she returned to Kim, the policeman was gone, and Kim had a large drink in front of her. She looked up at Stephanie, held up the drink, smiled weakly, and said, "For my nerves."

Stephanie hugged her, sat down beside her, and said, "From the looks of things, you deserve it. I'm sorry I wasn't here. My pinheaded boss held me captive in his office until twelve-thirty, and then I couldn't get through to Andre or the restaurant. By the time I got through the traffic and found a parking space, the police were already on the scene. Can you tell me what happened?"

"Well, when you didn't arrive, we ate lunch and talked about what I had discovered about the company's phony bookkeeping. By the time we got through eating, I had to leave. Just as we got up to leave, the window shattered, and, as it did, the man sitting behind Andre launched himself out of his seat with his arms outstretched, and landed on Andre and me, pulling us both to the floor. I had the wind knocked out of me and couldn't move. Andre must have tried to move, because the man yelled at him to stay still. He had to yell, because people were running and screaming, dishes were crashing, tables were being knocked over; the whole place was in chaos. In the middle of all this pandemonium, I heard a moan, and, when I turned my head toward the sound, I was staring right into the face of a woman who was lying on the floor. She had this unbelieving look on her face, and she said, 'I think I've just been shot.' I thought, *What the hell is she talking about?* Just then, the man on top of us rolled over onto the floor, and stayed there. Andre tried to get up off me, but when he tried to brace himself with his arm, it collapsed, and he yelped in pain. We both looked down at his arm, and it was bleeding. By that time, some people were beginning to come to their senses and a woman nearby grabbed a napkin, shoved it into my hand, and told me to press it against Andre's arm and not let go until the EMT's arrived. I'm glad she did that, because focusing on that simple job kept me from coming apart. It turns out that the woman is a nurse, and she quickly examined the woman on the floor, and found out that she really had been shot. She had someone else hold a napkin against the woman's wound. When she finally turned to the man who had been on top of us she found that he had been shot in the side, but he was already holding a bunched-up corner of a tablecloth against the wound. The whole time she was doing this, she was giving orders to call an ambulance, call the police, clear a space, back away; she was a real take-charge person. She really managed to keep things organized until the police and emergency personnel arrived on the scene and took over."

She took a drink from her glass.

"Who was the man who jumped on you and Andre?" Stephanie asked.

"I honestly don't know. I just kept pressing on the napkin for all I was worth until the EMT's came. When I looked up, they were already wheeling him out on a stretcher. The police officer I talked to didn't know who he was either, he just said that he didn't think his wound was life-threatening. He said that Andre and the woman on the floor were shot, too, but, as far as he knew, none of the three was in serious danger from their wounds. Thank God for that." She paused, took another drink, and then, looking Stephanie directly in the eye, said, "Someone connected with your investigation tried to kill us, didn't they?"

Stephanie thought about her answer, then said, "I'm not sure, It's very possible that whoever did this was just trying to get Andre. I'm certain that they know about his involvement. Of course, if it were someone connected with the investigation, they know now that you and Andre were together, and they'd have to be awfully stupid not to figure out why. Look, Kim, if you want to back away from this right now, you can."

"Would that make me any safer? I mean, even if they knew I was not going to cooperate with your investigation anymore, would they leave me alone?"

"The truth is, probably not."

"I was afraid you'd say that. It looks like my best hope of putting all of this behind me and getting on with my life is to help you expose these people, so, what do you want to know?"

Kim was helpful with the answers to the other questions. Stephanie was very skeptical, however, so she decided she would have to verify the information for herself. If what Kim told her was true, the vice president, while a congressman, sold his approval for federal funds for the Big Dig.

When she and Kim had finished, Stephanie called Steve, and started to tell him about what had happened, but he interrupted her.

"We're way ahead of you there, Stephanie. As soon as you told us about the break-in at Andre's, we put a man on him. He was the man who jumped on Andre and Kim in the restaurant, and he managed to call us before they took him up for surgery; it's nothing serious, by the way. We already have someone headed to the hospital to watch over Andre, and another person is headed your way to guard Kim. She should be arriving any minute, so, don't let Kim go until her minder gets there. We're also working on a safe-house for both of them, if that seems necessary."

Stephanie thanked him, and, after telling Kim what he had said, she looked at Kim's drink and said, "All of a sudden, that looks like a good idea. I'll join you while we're waiting."

64

The response was quicker than Richard expected. Congressman Willard called and asked that Richard contact him by noon. Richard returned Willard's call, and they arraigned to meet in the Boston Common.

Boston's Common gets its name from the fact that, until the early eighteen hundreds, it served as the common grazing area for Boston's livestock. In fact, it is purported that the wandering narrow streets that wind through the area were created by the meanderings of the herds being driven to and from its sloping fifty acres. Today, the grazing herds have been replaced by people hurrying back and forth, or enjoying leisurely walks on its many paths. These paths, laid out in a crisscross pattern, have divided the area into a series of lawns populated by stately trees, which create a scenic barrier between the State House and the brownstones on Beacon Hill above, and the busy commercial and shopping district below.

Richard walked the paths in the Common for half an hour before making his way to the Boylston Street end. Various hues of orange, yellow, red not only colored the trees, but also the paths themselves, littered as they were with fallen leaves. The colors, so radiant in the bright sunlight of October, seemed out of place in the gray overcast which hung over the city, now, and occasional gusts of wind drilled the light drizzle against exposed skin like grains of sand.

Not that any of this made much of an impression on Richard. In his mind, he kept going over his conversation with Congressman Willard. Willard had sounded agitated. He still denied any knowledge of Bear's death, and disputed Richard's contention that the death threats made against him were fictitious, but said that he wanted to meet and set the record straight.

When he got to Boylston Street, Richard spent time studying the area and the people in it, noting details that the untrained, inexperienced, and unwary eye either ignored, or did not even see. When he was through surveying at ground level, he looked up at the building across Boylston Street, noting that behind three of its closed windows, there were strings of lit incandescent lights of the type used by contractors, an indication that renovation work might be taking place inside.

Not far from him was one of the kiosks that provide pedestrian access to the Boston Common Underground Garage, and after a few minutes, he saw Willard emerging from it. Before heading in the congressman's direction he took one more look around, and then upward. In an instant, he knew something was wrong, the lights were out in one of the three windows, and that window was now open in spite of the fact that the wind was driving the light drizzle inside. Instinctively, he turned, and started running toward Willard, yelling at him, to hit the deck. The words had hardly left his mouth, however, when a woman walking behind the congressman was suddenly splattered with a spray of blood, brain tissue and bone slivers. Willard dropped to his knees and then flopped face forward to the sidewalk, revealing a gaping crater in the back of his head. The woman began screaming hysterically

By this time, Richard had reached Willard and the woman, and, grabbing the latter, drove her to the ground, turning his body so that he absorbed the impact of their fall. Once on the ground, he continued turning until they had rolled around the corner of the kiosk, out of sight of the building on Boylston Street. Having had the wind knocked out of her, the woman, whose horror was now coupled with bewilderment, was whimpering instead of screaming.

Richard quickly said, "You're safe as long as you stay right here and remain quiet until I can get help." With that, he took out his cellphone, and, calling 911 told the dispatcher that he was a federal officer, and that a federal official was down, shot by a sniper. He gave the location of the building and the room from which he thought the shooter had fired the shot that killed Willard. When he hung up, he could see that a crowd was beginning to gather. The fact that, with all those convenient targets, the shooter was not firing, told him that this was no random attack by an unbalanced person or a terrorist. Willard had been deliberately targeted by a professional killer, and, the chances were that he was a target as well. As long as there was no risk to anyone else, he reasoned, there was no point in exposing himself to the possibility that the killer was waiting around to finish the job. For the next few minutes, therefore, Richard occupied himself helping the woman clean off some of the gore, and determining that, with the exception of a few abrasions and bruises, she had no further injuries. Just as he was finishing, the air began to fill with the wail of sirens as police cars and trucks came in from every direction, quickly followed by a small parade of ambulances.

Among the first to arrive was a black outfitted SWAT unit in full combat regalia totting h menacing weapons. They secured the streets around the Boylston Street building then stormed into it, rousting occupants as they moved from floor to floor. In the end, they found no sign of the sniper.

The crowd that had started to gather just after the congressman was shot, was now growing exponentially larger, and while emergency personnel were busy with the congressman, Richard and the woman, uniformed officers were busy setting up a cordon around the area, and, with the help of hastily summoned mounted officers, were moving the crowd backward. By the time Linda Pollard arrived to take over the investigation, the area around the kiosk had been cordoned off with yellow crime scene tape.

"Richard, are you single-handily trying to keep my team busy? If you are, you're doing a good job."

"Hi, Linda I'm fine, thank you. Haven't got a scratch on me but, thank you for asking, just the same."

Linda was in no mood for levity. "You want to save the sarcasm and tell me what happened?"

"Congressman Willard was coming out of the kiosk, when someone shot him. I saw him go down, and I saw the woman behind him covered with blood. My instinct was to grab the woman and roll both of us out of the field of fire. I saw the way the congressman was hit, which made me peek at that building," he pointed to the building on Boylston Street, "I saw the open window. I figured that was where the shot came from. Then I called 911."

"Why was the Congressman meeting you here?"

"Did I say he was meeting me?"

"You're here. He's here. No coincidence. You two were meeting. What about?"

"Sorry, Linda, I was just passing by."

Linda grabbed Richard by the collar. "You listen to me," she hissed, "I've been willing to go along with your bullshit up until now, but, that was no ordinary dude lying over there with his brains splattered all over the sidewalk, that was a United States Congressman who was killed in broad daylight on my watch and in my backyard. The chief, the mayor, the governor, and, maybe, even the president, are going to breathing down my neck so hard, my skin is going to blister, and that doesn't begin to say what the FBI and the Secret Service are going to be doing, so, don't fuck with me, Richard.

"Linda, I'll talk to you off the record, but not out here in the open. Someone is getting nervous, and being seen with me is becoming hazardous."

Linda took a quick look around, then turned back to face him. She was on the verge of saying something flippant, when she saw that he was deadly serious. "OK, Richard. We'll do it your way. It will take me a while to clean things up here. I'll call you when I'm through, and we can have a nice talk in my office. And, Richard," she paused, "if, by some chance, I can't reach you, you'd better be dead or in a hospital, because, if you aren't, I'm going to throw your ass in jail for obstructing justice, withholding evidence, and anything else I can think of. Now, get your cute, but troublesome butt out of here before I change my mind and put the cuffs on you."

After Richard left, it was another two hours before she could leave the scene. During that time, between fielding phone calls from the chief and the mayor, and riding herd on a small army of local, state and federal officers, she somehow managed to get her investigative team up and running They immediately discovered that the sniper rifle had been left behind by the shooter, and appeared to be free of any fingerprints or identifying marks. She shipped it off to the State Police Crime Lab for testing. They also discovered that a workman had been observed leaving the building just after the shots had been fired. It was later determined that there had been no construction workers in the building that morning. She sent out an APB based on the description given to her by the witness.

65

Richard sat down in Linda's office at the headquarters' building of the Boston Police Department. The office, barely one hundred square feet, gave out a clear message: This was a work office. The only personal items visible were framed copies of Linda's Bachelor of Law degree from Northeastern University, and her Master of Law degree from Suffolk University. The office was void of pictures, knickknacks, or other nonworking items in the room. Even the books on the shelves were related to law enforcement or law. Precariously stacked and bulging file folders occupied on one half of Linda's desk. Other piles sat on the four-draw file cabinet. Linda sat behind her desk in a short-back-swivel chair that squeaked when she moved too far to the left.

Before Linda could speak, Richard said, "Look, Linda, I know what a fix you are in with this Willard thing, but there is a lot more going on here, and it is all connected with Bear's murder somehow. I haven't put all the pieces together yet, but the best way for me to do that is to keep playing my game my way. Now, you can throw me in a cell, and you might get some satisfaction out of doing that, but we both know that I'd be back on the street before you could complete the paperwork, and you wouldn't know any more than you know right now. You're a hell of a cop, Linda, and a good friend, and I know that I'm asking a lot, but I promise you that the only way for you to get to the bottom of the Willard murder and the others is to let me do my thing."

66

The sun broke through the clouds and the wind subsided. It was still cool but overall weather was changing for the better. As Richard started to walk up Stuart Street in the direction of the Boston Common, two men got out of a Crown Victoria sedan and blocked his path.

"Mr. Moore, Agent Teeling, this is Agent Stinger, Secret Service." They both held up their picture IDs.

"What can I do for you, Agent Teeling?"

"Special Agent Yeltson asked us to bring you to his office. He wants to talk with you."

"Did he say why he wants to see me or what we will talk about?" He knew the answers, but he wanted to stall.

"No, sir. He just told us to bring you."

"OK. My car is in a garage the other side of the Common. I'll meet you at the federal building in say thirty minutes."

"No, sir. We were told not to let you out of our sight. We'll give you a ride to the meeting. Special agent Yeltson will arrange a ride back."

"I'll tell you what, you call Special Agent Yeltson, and tell him to call and make an appointment. I'm sure we can coordinate our schedules." Richard moved as if to walk away.

Agent Stinger blocked the path. "I sorry, sir, but although Special Agent Yeltson did ask us to try to persuade you to accompany us voluntarily, he did make it clear that we were not to return without you. You are, after all, a witness to the murder of a member of the United States Congress, and we do have a right to bring you in for questioning."

Richard thought about calling their bluff and just walking away anyway, but, having just left Linda's office, he decided that he needed to avoid a public incident in the case that they really would just grab him and throw him in the car.

"All right, let's get this over with."

Teeling opened the rear door for Richard while Stinger went around to the other rear door and got in. As Richard got in, he saw that there were two other men in the front, one behind the wheel, and the other in the passenger seat. As Teeling settled in on Richard's right, Stinger drove a needle attached to a syringe into Richard's neck.

"Jesus, what the hell?" Richard swung his left elbow toward Stinger's face. Stinger had expected the reaction and blocked the blow, then Teeling and Stinger pinned Richard's arms and torso. Richard kicked with both legs but could not break the grip the two men had on him. Slowly Richards's movements and resistance were subdued by the effect of the drug. He fell into unconsciousness.

67

The flat-bed car carrier rumbled and bounced down the dirt and gravel driveway. Ahead was a Quonset style metal building with a garage door and a standard door. To the left of the building, a dozen cars in various states of disrepair sat in a parking area of dirt, rocks, and oil. The man behind the wheel of the truck chewed on the plastic tip of his thin cigar. He wore a sleeveless T-shirt and a Boston Red Sox cap with the bill turned sideways.

Two men stood outside the building. As the truck neared, the two men moved to either side of the vehicle. They were in casual slacks, pullover shirts, and windbreaker jackets. The man on the driver's side put up his hand and told the driver to stop.

"Howdy," the driver said as he stuck his head out the window, a big friendly smile across his face.

"No one allowed here," the man said, as he got closer to the driver's door. "Turn around and get out of here."

"OK, I just have to pick up that blue wagon over there." The driver pointed in the direction of the parking area.

The man did not turn his head. "I said turn around and leave."

The driver opened the door and stepped down as he said, "Come on, man. I don't get paid unless I bring the car in. See it says right here I got to get that car." He pointed to the clipboard in his hands.

The man on the passenger side of the truck opened the door and looked around. "Hey, hey, don't go taking any tools," the driver warned, "the boss deducts them from my pay if I lose any."

The first man grabbed the driver by the collar. "I said turn around and leave." He produced a nine-millimeter pistol with a silencer.

The driver looked at the pistol, and a shocked expression crossed his face "Wow, I guess you don't want me to take that car! Will you sign my paperwork? Maybe the boss will pay me if you sign." The driver dropped the clipboard as he held it out for the man to take. The man moved as if to pick up the clipboard, and then hesitated. The driver went down to pick it up, but grabbed the man's gun hand during the momentary hesitation. Driving an elbow into the man's solar plexus, he wrenched the pistol out of his hand. The man on the passenger side saw the scuffle and pulled out his pistol. Before he could fire, the driver shot him in the face. The first man was moving to attack but the driver sensed him coming. The driver again delivered a blow to the man's midsection. He doubled over and the driver brought his elbow down on the back of the man's neck. The man landed sprawled on the dirt.

The driver picked the man up and threw him against the hood of the truck. He frisked him for weapons. "I am going to ask you a few questions," the driver said to the man. "I want a straight answer." He grabbed the man's right hand, pointed the pistol at the hand, and pulled the trigger. The man screamed when the pain registered. The driver had placed his left hand over the man's mouth and muffled the sound.

"Now, that was to let you know that I mean what I say. You have only one chance to answer my questions. Do you understand?"

The man nodded his head.

"Good. How many are inside?

"Three."

"Where?"

"One roaming around. Two in the right rear."

"You're doing very good. Are they all armed?"

"Yeah, same as me."

"OK, get up in the truck."

The man's eyes indicated fear and confusion.

"Get the fuck up in the truck, asshole, or do you want me to blow a hole in your other hand?"

The man climbed up and got into the truck.

"Good, now, you're going for a little ride. Hold the steering wheel and don't turn it. Put your foot on the gas pedal, and rev up the engine. That's good. Now drop the shifter into drive, and let it rip."

The man just stared down at the driver. The driver pointed the pistol at the man's left foot. "I will not tell you again. Rev it up, and drive through that garage door."

As the truck leapt forward, the driver back away from the truck and ran around the right side of the building to the window at the back.

68

The cold water shocked Richard into a dark consciousness. He felt cloth on his face, but, with the exception of his boxer shorts, the rest of his body was naked His hands were bound together and resting on his chest. His legs were bound at the ankles.

"Ahh, Richard, you're awake. See, Archie, I told you it was about time for him to wake up. Let's get started. Shall we?" Richard felt his arms being pulled up over his head, and his back coming off a stiff hard surface. In a few moments, his whole body was suspended in air from his wrists, and his shoulders were screaming for relief.

"There, now we can hold your attention. You won't be drifting off because of the drug. By the way, Richard, you have a nasty cut on your right side." The man slid a knife along the wound. It opened up and started to bleed. Richard tightened his muscles and moved his body slightly away from the sting of the knife.

"Don't worry; we're not going to let you bleed to death."

Richard tried to control his senses and emotions. The black hood was thick enough to block out the light but thin enough to allow him to breathe. Deprivation of sensors was a typical and effective interrogation technique. Stripped almost bare left the subject humiliated and feeling vulnerable. Hanging without contact of any kind added to the isolation and feeling of hopelessness. Richard also felt something on his right biceps and left calf.

"Now my partner, Brutus, thinks you're going to be a very stubborn person. He said we should go right to a high level of persuasion. I, on the other hand, think you're a logical person. I said you'll cooperate and we can all leave quickly. What do you say, Richard?"

Richard made no response. He was trying to lift himself up and relieve the strain on his shoulders.

"Well, I really didn't expect you to answer that question. Before we get started, Brutus will give you a small sample of what is in store for you if you do not answer the rest of our questions. Ready, Brutus?"

"Why give him a sample? We should go straight to the max."

"My partner; always in a hurry. Brutus, a sample please."

Richard felt a tingling run through his body, and realized that there were wires attached to his right biceps and left calf, wires that undoubtedly ran to a low amperage variable voltage source operated by Brutus. The low amperage would allow Brutus to increase the voltage, and therefore the amount of his discomfort without danger of killing him. Even at this low level, he could feel some of his muscles jerking involuntarily. Survive what was coming, would require use of all the anti-interrogation techniques he had been taught.

"OK, Brutus. I think Richard gets the picture. Turn it off."

Richard's body convulsed. Every muscle in his body contracted and then snapped loose sending his body bouncing on the end of the rope.

"What the hell?" Brutus's partner shouted. "Brutus what happened?"

"Sorry, Julius, I turned the knob the wrong way."

"Don't apologize to me. Apologize to Richard. He's the one you almost killed with that shock."

Julius grabbed Richard by the feet and steadied him. "All right, Richard, now, all we want to know is where Marcus McGill is being hidden. We want to know where and how many guards you have watching him. Do you understand, Richard?"

Richard was trying hard to retreat to a place of safety in his head, a place largely removed from any outside stimulus. He held his head firm between his arms, and remained silent.

The next jolt of current hit hard and lasted ten seconds. "I don't want to do this, Richard. I would like to go home to my girlfriend. Maybe have a nice relaxing dinner and some wine. So tell me. Where is Marcus and how many are guarding him?"

Again, Richard remained silent.

Another jolt came, more intense and longer, and Richard's whole body convulsed uncontrollably, causing him to dance at the end of the rope like a puppet on a string. It even ripped open his hiding place, and he gritted his teeth behind the black hood trying to keep from screaming.

"Come on, Richard; tell us what we want to know. I'll let you lie down on the board again. No more shocks. You can get dressed and pull that hood off. Just tell us. Where is Marcus, and how many are guarding him?"

Julius had hardly stopped talking when the next jolt came. Brutus or both of them were getting impatient and not waiting for a response. Richard bounced with such force he was sure his shoulders would break. The muscles and tendons burned with pain as the fibers of each slowly broke.

Brutus turned the power off again and Julius began. "Much too long, Richard. No one is going to help you. You have to answer our—" The sound of a tremendous crash came from the garage work area. Julius and Brutus pulled out their pistols and ran to the door. Looking into the garage, they saw that the huge door had been smashed in by a flat-bed car-carrier.

69

A moment later, the sound a crash came from behind Julius and Brutus. They turned around in time to see shattering glass, and a small boulder bounding across the floor. Before they could react, a figure appeared in the shattered window, and shot them both.

The driver hopped through the window and checked the bodies on the floor. Satisfied that they were both dead, he crept to the door that led into the garage. When he got there, he opened the door enough to creep low into the main garage area. Metal counters lined the rear and side walls. He saw that a car had stopped the truck's forward movement, and four bullets fired through the windshield had stopped its unwilling operator who was now lying, unmoving, on the garage floor Not far from the body, a man with a weapon was talking lowly on a cellphone, while watching the front of the garage.

He moved to get a better line of fire on the man. "Drop the weapon," he called out.

The man swung around, his weapon up and pointing in the driver's direction. The driver fired two rounds, and the man slumped back. He walked over, kicked the weapon away, and then checked the man. He was dead. "Fucking amateur," he said, and then returned to the back room.

Once inside, he found the opposite end of the rope from which Richard was suspended, and carefully lowering him, laid him on the table.

Removing the hood, the driver said, "Hi, Richard. I'm Craig. Steve sends his regards." He placed his weapon on the table next to Richard's left side, and began to untie Richard's hands. "We have to move fast. The guy in the garage was talking on his phone. I don't know how far away his backup might be."

He bent down to untie Richard's legs. When he stood up, Richard was pointing the weapon at him. "Oh shit, Richard. We don't have time for this. There may be more on their way."

Richard's hands were shaking. The muscles in his upper body were still twitching and moving involuntarily. With three quick moves, Craig disarmed Richard and pointed the weapon at him.

Craig pulled out a cellphone. "Steve told me any button would connect me with him." He pushed send and listened. "It's ringing." He handed the weapon and phone to Richard and waited.

"Craig, what's happening?" Steve asked.

"Steve?"

"Richard? How did you get this phone?"

"Describe your man Craig."

"He's young, twenty-seven. Too self-assured. Lean build and in excellent condition. He's about five feet seven inches tall with sandy hair cut like a Marine recruit."

Richard placed the weapon on the table and nodded to Craig.

"Richard, what the hell is going on?"

"I'll explain later, Steve. You and Craig just saved my life but we aren't out of this yet." Richard disconnected the call.

"Your clothes are over there." Craig pointed to a table at the rear of the room. "Get your pants on. I'll get the truck ready. But move quickly."

Richard got dressed, picked up Julius's and Brutus's weapons, and then raced to the truck.

Craig had backed the truck out of the garage and raised the flat bed up on an angle until the rear of the bed was a foot off the ground.

"I hear cars coming. Get in, Richard."

As he was speaking, a four-door sedan raced down the dirt driveway.

"Hold on," Craig said as he pressed the accelerator to the floor. The truck bucked as it spit up gravel and hurled itself backward toward the oncoming car.

With men leaning out three of the windows firing weapons, the car veered to the left in an attempt to avoid driving up the oncoming ramp. The move proved to be a fraction of a second too late. The right wheel of the car hit the truck-bed; the vehicle became airborne and turned over several times before coming to rest upside down.

A van had followed the car and arrived as the truck was nearing the street end of the driveway. Instead of entering the driveway, the driver of the van stopped to block the truck's path. The side door of the van opened and three men with automatic rifles opened fire on the approaching truck, only to have their bullets ricochet off the raised truck bed.

One of the men jumped out of the side door of the van and leaped to his right just as the end of the ramp slid under the side of the van, raising the van up and rolling it over. He opened fire on the passenger side of the truck, shattering the window, and showering Richard with glass fragments, but was knocked to the ground when Richard returned his fire. Craig turned the steering wheel sharply to the right, slewing the overturned van sideways across the street before shifting into drive and swerving around the front of the van and speeding off down the street followed by the sound of blaring horns and cursing divers.

After turning down several side streets, Craig slowed as he approached a parked tan Camry. "That's our next ride," he said, pointing to the Camry, and coming to a stop. "Let's go."

Leaving the truck angled enough to block any pursuit, he ran over to the Camry, and a moment later, he and Richard were speeding away.

Richard found that he still had his cellphone, so he called Sheila and warned her that activity to find Marcus was intensifying. She assured him no one would find the young man, and, even if they did, they would not get within one hundred yards. He then called Linda Pollard and told her she could find at least six dead at the garage where he had been held. She insisted he go to the nearest police station. He disconnected the call.

When he was through, he asked Craig, "So, how did you know where to find me?"

"Steve was concerned about your safety. He's had me tailing you for a while."

"How long is a while?"

"Long enough to see you fight off some guys carrying baseball bats in your backyard, sneak up on some young guy while someone else drove your car for a diversion, chase some car through the streets of Boston–if you don't mind me asking, by the way, who was that good-looking chick who got out of the limo?"

"I think I'll let Steve fill you in." A pause filled the car as they weaved their way through the streets of Boston. "Thank you for saving my life back there. I couldn't be sure who you were with. That's why I held the gun on you."

"You're welcome. I would have done the same thing if the situation were reversed."

70

Sunday morning Richard woke in a cheap motel just north of Boston. The night clerk was not in the habit of asking for identification as long as the room was paid for in advance in cash. As Richard attempted to get out of bed, his body rebelled. He was tired and in some pain. His muscles had stopped shaking and twitching around two. He'd fallen asleep after that, but had obviously not slept long enough or deep enough.

Richard called Vivian Davenport and asked her if she knew who had recommended Bear to her father-in-law.

"I don't know. I don't think he ever mentioned anyone specifically. I could ask him when he calls in. He's out of town. I'll be meeting him on Wednesday in Washington, DC"

"You'll be in DC on Wednesday?" Richard asked.

"Yes. I'm thinking about running for my father's congressional seat. I want to talk with some of his former colleagues. My father-in-law has offended to make some other introductions."

"Maybe we could meet. Bear's funeral will be at Arlington National Cemetery on Wednesday."

"I would like very much to attend. He seemed like such a good man. If I talk with Earl before Wednesday, I'll ask him if he remembers who recommended Bear." After some pleasantries, they disconnected the call.

Later, Richard met Steve in a small room in a warehouse owned by a friend of Richard. They went over the details of the kidnapping and subsequent rescue, and Richard made a somewhat grudging admission that Steve had made the right move in having him tailed by Craig.

He then mentioned his call to Vivian Davenport.

"Why do you want to know who recommended Bear to investigate her father's death?"

"As I checked Bear's clients, something kept gnawing at me. I didn't know what it was until I thought about something Rob Lee said. He said Bear was not a threat to him because Bear was a soldier, not an investigator. He was almost right. Bear provided security and threat assessments, and investigative services. But Bear was not a gifted investigator. Someone ran him around to keep him off track. Whoever it was did the same thing to me. The attacks kept me going back to Bear's clients. The lead at the container company is gone. The congressman is dead. I know who recommended Bear to the Boston Archdiocese and I know it was a cover. I don't know who made the recommendation to Earl. In fact, Earl said that Bear was second only to me. That is what has been bothering me. No one familiar with investigators would have put Bear or me in the top twenty let alone first and second. Earl's the only one left who can provide an answer to the question."

"Well, while you're waiting for an answer, you might be interested in what I have been able to uncover. First, do you know how much revenue credit companies and their side business produce?"

Richard smiled and said, "I was told recently. Credit card companies generated around thirty-two billion in revenue last year."

"Yes, but that is just the credit card companies doing business as credit card companies. There's whole other side-business making money for them. You see, in 2003, Congress passed the Fair and Accurate Credit Transactions Act which required credit reporting companies to free provide credit reports to consumers once a year. Credit card companies and the reporting companies immediately set up affiliated companies advertising free credit reports. Once the consumer signs up for the free report, they then try to sell them additional services, and they've become so successful at it that it's generating billions in additional revenue."

"What kinds of services?"

"Unlimited access to your credit scores, monthly updates, notices of changes to your score, counseling services, even so-called identity theft protection. The thing is that most of these 'services' cost the company little or no additional overhead, so the charge to the consumer is largely profit."

"So, the credit card industry and credit reporting companies and these other consumer reporting companies are all in this together?"

"That they are, and the total revenue they collect exceeds thirty-two billion by almost double. I can't find reliable figures that are all inclusive."

"And Higher Credit Score is one of these companies?"

"Bingo!"

"Sounds like a nice scam. How do they get away with it?"

Steve smiled. "It's perfectly legal. Congress didn't say the companies couldn't sell the information. They only said they had to provide one free report per year, if the consumer asks for it. If the consumer wants to pay for the report or buy any other 'services' Congress doesn't want to know about it."

Richard thought about this for a few moments, and then said, "And there are at least thirty-two billion dollars worth of incentive to keep it that way, which is why they have pumped so much money into Vice President Lampert's campaign."

"Speaking of which," Steve said, as he pulled some notes from a soft carrying case. "Higher Credit Score has been skimming revenue off and depositing it into an offshore bank. The funds then come back and go to credit card companies. Card holders of these companies, some alive and well, others deceased, have made substantial contributions to the VP's campaign right after the funds arrived from the offshore bank."

"So all we have to do is find out who set this operation up. Talking with Holly Cook won't do us any good; she won't talk without Hurshberg, her attorney. Fortunately, we have him under surveillance and have his phones tapped. We have to wait and see what Hurshberg does next."

Richard thought about this for a while. "We pushed and they reacted. We have to assume whomever is behind this scram is working on their next move. We'll need to be careful."

Steve abruptly changed the subject. "Richard, you should know Stephanie has stepped in harm's way."

"I assume this has to do with her investigation into the Big Dig contractor."

"It does. I put a man on a consultant she hired. The consultant's place was broken into and Stephanie asked me to have someone keep him safe. Both the consultant and my man were shot yesterday. Not seriously."

"You have someone on Stephanie?"

"Yeah, I put someone on her the same day I put Craig on you."

"OK. Aside from locking her in her room, is there anything else we can do?"

"Nothing she will agree with. I asked her."

"I warned her to be careful. Maybe I can talk her into taking more protection. I'll call her."

71

Monday morning Richard woke in a different cheap hotel. He had slept better than the night before, and although his upper body still ached, the involuntary muscle movements had stopped. He felt good enough to take his morning run, but decided the area was not conducive for it. Instead, he drove his rental car to a restaurant, ordered breakfast, and began making phone calls with the secure phone Steve had given him.

"Richard, Are you all right?" Laura asked when she recognized his voice. "I heard you had a harrowing weekend. Did you get that knife wound taken care of?"

"Yes, Laura, I did. A doctor I know stitched it up for me. Thanks for asking. I don't want to stay on the line long. Any messages and is Steve in yet?"

"No and no. Steve called and said he's finishing some research in his hotel room. He'll be in later. No calls for you here or in Boston."

"OK, Laura. Thanks. I'll be in touch later this morning."

Next, he called Special Agent Dalton Whitetail. "Dalton, Richard Moore."

"Richard always a pleasure to hear from you, but I'm a little pressed for time. What can I do for you?"

"Just a couple of questions, Dalton. You got anyone looking for me?"

"Why would I do that? I know where to find you. What makes you ask?"

"Second question: How serious are you about Marcus McGill?"

"I know that he is a suspect in Bear's murder, and I'll give you any help you need off the record to track him down, if that's what you mean."

"No, Dalton. I'm not talking about tracking down McGill for Bear's murder. He didn't murder Bear. I don't know who did, but it was not Marcus. I'm talking about the VP connection."

"Jesus, Richard. You're not supposed to know about that."

"Just tell me, Dalton. How serious?"

"It's not our baby, Richard. The VP's detail is actively pursuing it. They have a couple agents up your way. Now, how do you know McGill didn't kill Bear, and how do you know about the VP connection?"

Richard ignored the question, saying, "They're wasting their time. McGill isn't a threat to the VP."

"Richard, if you know something about McGill and he does turn out to be a threat and gets to the VP, you'll have more than me and my people looking for you. You'll be in deep shit."

"I'll keep that in mind, but I can assure you that isn't going to happen. I'll talk with you soon." Richard disconnected.

Richard then called Steve. "Can you tell me where Stephanie is?"

"I just talked with Hawk. She's in work."

"OK. I'll take a ride out and talk with her."

"Before you do that, you might want to hear about Hershberger. Phil called and told me he went to the office. The office tap told us he had a call from someone about attending a meeting tonight. He and Holly Cook have been instructed to attend."

"This evening. Any idea who called him?"

"Yeah, sounded like the VP's campaign manager. The meeting is being held at his cottage in Connecticut."

"Any idea who else will be in attendance?"

"He didn't elaborate. Our guy protested, saying it was too soon to hold another meeting. He was overruled."

"I think I'll pay our man another visit." After a few moments of thought, Richard continued, "Steve asked Laura to call Cullen Avery. His name and number should be in Bear's file. If it isn't, Marcella has it. I would like Cullen to be prepared to take a trip to Connecticut."

"You going to crash the meeting, Richard? I'd like to come with you."

"All depends on what I learn later today. You can join me if you want' but it could get dicey."

"For Bear, I'll do dicey."

72

Richard drove to the Burlington Mall to meet with Quinton Rivers, a retired Burlington Police Captain who was chief of mall security. Rivers had been reviewing the security tapes of the parking area for the day Zima disappeared.

"Here's your man, Richard. You can see two guys pulling him into the van. Got a good shot of the guy standing next to the Caddy."

Richard took the still prints and studied them. *Hurshberg will have a difficult time denying these photos,* he thought to himself.

"Thanks, Quint. I owe you."

"Want to tell me what this is all about?"

"The guy being pulled into the van is dead. This guy," Richard pointed to Hurshberg, "set up the grab. I think he was involved with the murder of my friend."

"You find out anything, call me. Can't let mall management find out through the media someone got snatched in our parking lot and killed. Won't look good for business."

"I'll keep you informed. Thanks again, Quint."

Richard walked past the receptionist and Hershberger's secretary and entered the man's office. The secretary followed behind Richard. "I'm sorry Mr. Hershberger, this man just barged past me."

"That's all right Millie. Mr. Moore thinks he owns the world. I'll deal with him."

Millie left the office, closing the door as she did.

"And what can I do for you today, Mr. Moore? I hope you are not going to make more statements that I might have to report to the authorities. As I told you Saturday, I am an officer of the court and am bound to report threats or other criminal activity."

Richard sat in one of the plush side chairs. "I understand you're taking a little trip with Ms. Cook late this afternoon."

Hershberger was caught off guard. "How ... how do you know that? Do you have my phones tapped? If you do, I'll have you arrested for invasion of privacy."

"Are you taking a trip?"

"I think you should leave. I'll have my phones checked. If I find a tap, I'll notify the authorities. They can deal with you. Now, please leave."

Richard took the pictures from an envelope and handed them to Hershberger. "You might want to look at these.."

Hershberger looked at the pictures and his face went pale. He slumped forward over his desk. He had no response.

After several minutes, Richard broke the silence. "I want to know if you are going to a meeting this evening. I want to know who will be attending. I also want to know if this group had anything to do with Bear's murder."

"I ... I had nothing to do with Bear's murder and I had no idea what happened to the young man in the photo."

"But you did meet with Zima in the food court after he tried to extort two hundred thousand dollars. Correct?"

Hershberger was sweating and fidgeting in his chair.

"Two hundred thousand! Try one point one million. He wanted one point one million. He thought I would just walk in, hand him the cash, and forget he ever existed. I had others I had to tell."

"The others you had to tell, who were they?"

"I told Sidney Meas, the VP's Campaign Finance Manager. He runs the meetings. He said he would take care of the problem."

"Did he say the same about Bear?"

"No, no. I didn't even know about Bear. No one did. I don't even know if Bear was murdered by anyone associated with ..."

"OK, what about tonight?"

"What about it?"

"I want to know where the meeting is being held. I want to know who will be attending and I want to know about security."

"What, are you going to crash the meeting? It's just a business meeting. Some people might find a few decisions questionable, but there is nothing illegal."

Richard frowned. "Killing at least two and hunting a third is not just questionable, it *is* illegal. Violating campaign finance laws is illegal. So, who, when, and where?"

73

After Richard left Hershberger's office, he called Charles at his Washington FBI office.

Tim opened Charles's office door. "I have Richard Moore on the line."

"OK. Put him through and close the door, please."

Charles listened to Richard's justification for crashing the meeting. The more Richard talked the more Charles tried to interrupt. Finally, Charles grew frustrated and started yelling into the phone. "He's the campaign manager for the next President of the United States, for crying out loud! You can't just go barging in without probable cause and a warrant issued by the Chief Justice of the US Supreme Court."

"I don't have time to get a warrant, Charles."

"Now, listen to me, Richard, you stay away from his cottage in Connecticut tonight. That Rob Lee screw-up you pulled nearly got me fired. If you go through with this stunt tonight, you're on your own. Something like this will not only get me fired, I'll end up in a cell next to you. I don't care what evidence you think you have, you do not have enough to tie him or the others in–Richard? Richard? Richard?"

Charles threw open his office door. "That damn idiot, he's gone too far this time!"

"What happened?" Tim asked.

"Richard is taking three of his guys down to Connecticut. The VP's campaign finance manager is holding a meeting with some company presidents. Richard thinks they were involved with the murder of his friend Bear. Damn fool has lost his mind. Get me the DO for the Connecticut area. I don't want him helping Richard."

After putting the DO through to Charles, Tim left for lunch.

Hawk was half a dozen cars behind Stephanie. He did not have to worry about her spotting him. She was not looking for a tail, and probably could not spot one if she were looking. After a while, he realized that she was taking the usual route home after leaving work, and made a mental note to talk with her about varying her routes and routine.

At that moment, he was about to pass through an intersection when a tractor-trailer ignored the stop sign and came screeching through it from his right. Hawk stood on his brakes to keep from slamming into the vehicle, just as the truck driver slammed on his own brakes. When both vehicles came to a stop, Hawk's hood was nearly under the trailer, which was now blocking the intersection.

The truck driver rolled down his window and stuck his head out. "Sorry. I wasn't paying attention. I'm real sorry. Are you OK?"

Hawk told him everything was fine, backed up to allow the trailer to pass, and then sped up to catch Stephanie.

Hawk could find no sign of Stephanie, so he drove straight to her apartment. When he got there, however, her car was not parked in its spot behind her building.

"Shit," he said, pounding on the steering wheel, "I've been had."

He took out the cellphone Steve gave him and punched send.

Steve was in a car with Phil and Craig, heading to Connecticut.

"Hawk, I hope you're not calling with bad news. We have a very busy evening planned."

"Steve, I hate to admit it but I've been had. I got cut off following Stephanie home. I lost her and she has not arrived home."

"Let me make a couple of phone calls. I'll get back to you. In the meantime, retrace and find her."

"Will do."

Steve disconnected.

74

Putnam Lake in Fairfield County, Connecticut is situated in the middle of a small forest. Its densely wooded shoreline is punctuated by widely separated cleared areas occupied by mansions set back from the lake by gently sloping lawns. A small, well maintained, two-lane road circumnavigates the lake about one-half mile from the shore, and off it radiate long narrow private drives which access both lakeside residences and those that are landlocked on the other side of the road. At the end of one of the lakeside drives stood Sidney Meas's three thousand square foot "cottage." Complete with an indoor swimming pool, a basketball court, and two outdoor tennis courts, the rear of the house overlooked a play lawn that stretched some six hundred feet to a boathouse, dock, cabana, and man-made sandy beach.

When Richard arrived, the fragrance of fall foliage filled the air beneath a diamond-filled black night sky scarcely lit by a thin sliver of Moon. He found Steve, Phil, and Craig already geared up for a night operation, and watching the entrance of the Meas drive from the hidden drive of a vacant estate on the opposite side of the road. Steve told him that they had observed the arrival of three limousines, and that Phil had just returned from reconnoitering the house and grounds.

While he was talking, Richard was suiting up in his own night ops gear: black outfit, Kevlar vest, night vision goggles, and a radio attached to an earbud and lip mike.

When he finished, Steve said, "Ah, Richard, before we proceed, you should know that Stephanie went missing this afternoon. A trucker cut Hawk off and then Stephanie disappeared. It could not have been a coincidence."

"I assume that Hawk's working on it up in Boston?"

"Yes, he is. He contacted Linda and asked for help from the Boston Police Department."

"OK. We can't do anything from here, and this operation has to go down tonight or never"

Turning to Phil, he asked, "What's the story, on the layout, Phil?"

Holding up and pointing to a rough sketch of the house and grounds, Phil said, "There are two armed guards outside. One is just inside the woods here about halfway down the drive. The other one is near the front door. Three limo drivers are loitering around their cars, which are all parked here next to this thickly overgrown area. I saw another armed guard inside in the kitchen, which is here. Unfortunately, I wasn't able to determine if there are any other guards inside."

Richard said, "Hmm." After a moment, he continued, "Is this right? Are the limos parked at the side of the house out of sight of the front door?"

"That's right. Cars coming down the driveway turn on to this circle in the front of the house and, after letting off their passengers, park in this area on the side of the house."

"Do you think the limo drivers are armed?" Richard asked.

"As I said, the limos are parked next to this heavily overgrown area which provides perfect cover right into the woods. I was able to crawl right up to them and got a good long look at the drivers. Two of them are older guys, and the other is very overweight. They just don't look or act like bodyguards, and I didn't see any sign that they were carrying."

"Good job, Phil," Richard said. "Let's see what goodies you have for us, Steve."

Steve opened up his trunk and handed each man a loaded MP5 submachine gun and two spare clips of ammunition. He also pulled out some small cans, some facecloths and several prefilled syringes.

"What's with the cans, the rags, and the syringes?" asked Craig.

"We don't want any fatalities if we can help it, so we planned to neutralize any outside guards by knocking them out by tranquilizing them," replied Richard.

Oh shit, thought Craig, *this is what I get for fooling around with amateurs.* Aloud, he said, "With all due respect, this is real life, not a movie. Nobody's going to go out like a light just because you stick a needle in them. Even the fastest tranquilizer will take at least several minutes to send someone off to la la land. What are we going to be doing in the meantime, have them count backwards while we take their pulses?"

With a wink to Richard, and a twinkle in his eye, Steve said, "What, do you think we're amateurs?"

He grabbed one of the cans and one of the facecloths, and motioned Richard over.

"The cans contain a chemical which shocks the nerve endings in the eyes, mouth, and nose, causing them to send a jolt to the brain. This jolt fools the brain into thinking it's having a convulsion, and it loses consciousness in self-defense. You wet the cloth with it, and slam it over the face, making sure to cover the eyes, nose, and mouth like this."

He mimed the act of pouring the contents of the can on the cloth, and then reaching over Richard's shoulder, held the cloth to his face.

After several seconds, he let Richard go, and continued, "Be prepared to inject your guy with the tranquilizer right away, and he'll stay out for several hours."

"If he's already out, why do we have to use the tranquilizer?"

"The initial loss of consciousness is almost instantaneous, but it only lasts a few minutes, so you have to finish the job a fast acting tranquilizer that will take over before your guy can fully recover."

He paused, and then asked, "Any more questions?"

"Well, yes. Just where did you get this stuff?"

Steve gave Craig a bemused look, then said, "Anyone else have any other questions?"

Resisting the impulse to be sarcastic, Richard responded, "I have one. Craig, do you think you can do the guard in the woods?"

A moment went by before Craig said, "What, do I look like an amateur?" Then, he smiled, and said, "You can count on me."

Richard handed him a syringe, a cloth, and a can, saying, "I was sure I could." Then, he gathered everyone around Phil's map, and told them the rest of his plan.

75

Fifteen minutes later, Craig was pulling an empty syringe out of the arm of an unconscious man lying at his feet on the forest floor. Speaking softly into his mike, he said, "This is unit one. My guy is down and I am headed in."

A few minutes later, a limo driver came around the side of the building and started walking toward the guard at the door. He appeared to be in some distress, as his gait was a bit erratic, and he was bent over clutching his gut. The guard watched him approach, and when the man was a few feet away, said, "Stop right there, fella, and tell me what you want."

When the limo driver looked up, the guard was startled to see that his face was all discolored, and it was a second or two before he realized that the man's face was painted with night camouflage paint. By then it was too late, for someone had grabbed him from behind and shoved a wet, odd smelling cloth over his face. He felt a tingle like a small jolt of electricity, then the lights went out, and he felt nothing.

After taking down the man in the woods, Craig had crossed the road, and then worked his way down to his next position on one side of the house. In the meantime, the other three had infiltrated down to the parking area on the other side of the house and neutralized the limo drivers. Phil was able to fit into one of the driver's jackets, and it was he who distracted the guard while Craig slipped up behind the man from the other side of the house.

When the guard slumped back against Craig's chest, Phil step forward and grabbed the man's weapon before it clattered to the ground. He then pulled a syringe out of his pocket, plunged the needle through the man's pants into his thigh, and pushed down or the plunger until the syringe was empty. A moment later, he lifted the man's legs off the ground, and he and Craig swiftly and silently carried the inert form back around the corner of the building to the limo area.

Richard and Steve were just finishing depositing the unconscious drivers' bodies on the back floors of their limos. Craig and Phil laid the body of the guard against the side of the house, where he would be out of harm's way. Then, with Richard leading the way, the four melted around the rear corner of the house.

The rear lawn had been flooded with light ever since the security lights had come on at dusk. The guard in the kitchen at the rear of the house had just finished scanning the area with a set of binoculars, when one of the limo drivers staggered on to the patio just outside the kitchen door. The driver was already bent over, when, just a few feet from the door, he suddenly stopped, clutched at his stomach, and nearly doubled over. Instinctively, the guard quickly opened the door and stepped out onto the patio to grab the man. He had only taken a couple of steps when a wet white cloth was clamped on to his face from behind him. He felt a tingling in his face and scalp, and everything went black.

Richard, who had been concealed beside the door when the guard had hurriedly stepped out on to the patio, dropped the wet facecloth he had been holding over the guard's face, and held the man upright until Phil had injected him in the thigh. As he lowered the body on to the patio, Craig and Steve slipped past him into the kitchen, and covered the two doors leading into the rest of the house. When Richard and Phil followed, Steve gestured that he was hearing voices on the other side of his door, which was the type of swinging door used by servers carrying food from a kitchen to a dining room. Craig indicated that all was quiet at his door, which was a regular house door.

Steve pulled a fiber-optic snooper out of one of his fatigue pockets, and, squatting down, slipped one end under the door. After taking a good long look at the screen on the viewing end, he slid the device out from under the door and put it back in his pocket. He signaled the others that their quarry was just on the other side of the door, and that it looked safe to move in. Richard nodded once, and the team assumed assault positions. When he nodded again, Steve pushed the door open and they stormed in.

They found themselves coming out of a doorway in the middle of the wall at one end of a twenty-six by eighteen-foot room. At each end of the long wall on their left was a doorway opening on to a hall. The long wall on their right was all glass. Stretching almost from one end of the room to the other was an enormous dining table around which were seated a group of people, who, at the moment, were staring in shock at four camo-faced men dressed in night assault gear who were pointing loaded automatic weapons at them.

After a moment or two, the spell broke, and one of the people, Congressman Hale Brown, yelled, "What the hell is this?"

"They've got guns," screamed a woman.

"Sidney, where the hell is our security?" shouted someone else.

"Oh, shut up, all of you," said Sidney Meas, in a disgusted voice.

Directing his comments to Richard and his men, he said, "Mr. Moore, please excuse the rude manners of these people. They really have no sense of decorum. Won't you and your men come in and have a seat?"

"I think we'll stand for now."

"Have it your way, but I really would prefer you take a seat."

"Isn't this so nice and civilized," Congresswoman Hanson said sarcastically, but the sarcasm could not hide the fear in her voice. "You two obviously know each other. I think I'll leave you alone so you can talk." She started to get up from the table, but stopped when Craig took a step toward her and leveled his weapon at her.

Richard kept a close watch on Meas. The man was not nervous about being confronted by four armed men. Clearly, he thought he had the upper hand.

"If you wish to adjourn this meeting and send these folks on their way, I have no objection," Richard said. "You're the one I came to deal with."

Meas seemed to think for a moment. "Yes, it might be better if some of them did leave. The meeting is adjourned. Holly, Glen, and Troy, I'd like you to stay for a few minutes, if you do not mind. The rest of you are free to leave. Please forgive me if I ask you to find your own way out. As you can see, at the moment, my other guests are taking up all of my attention. Oh, and please don't trouble yourselves by foolishly notifying any law enforcement agencies about my unexpected guests. I can assure you that all is well and that they pose no real threat to the safety of anyone here. "

Richard added, "Those of you who arrived in limos will have to drive them home yourselves. You'll find your drivers sleeping off a sedative on the back floor. Don't worry, the drug won't do any permanent damage, and they will wake up nice and refreshed in a few hours."

As people were leaving, Richard looked around the room. The walls were a pastel blue with wood trim that included a two-section crown molding, and they were adorned with framed oil paintings. The hardwood floor was covered under the long table by an oriental rug. Two serving centers were evenly spaced along the wall on either side of the doorway behind Richard and his men.

After everyone had gone, Richard pointed to the glass wall and said, "Sidney, this must be a nice view in the daylight. What type of glass is that? Does it get cold in the winter?"

"Cold doesn't penetrate that glass. It is not your common two-pane glass. It's triple thick with LowE2 coating on two panels and krypton gas fills the space between the panes. But, I'm sure that you're not here to collect material for *Better Homes and Gardens*, so why don't we get down to business. And, Richard, as I said before, I'd really rather you and your men sit down."

"And as I said, for now, we'll stand. You're right though, we should get down to business. Why don't you tell me who pulled the trigger on Bear?"

"I can do better than that. I'll introduce you to him and to a few other professionals." Meas raised his voice, "Rand, please join us."

76

Meas smiled as four men carrying automatic assault rifles came through the kitchen door.

Once inside the room, they took no further action, and, after a few tense moments, Richard said, "Looks as if we have an old-fashioned standoff, but, since you would be the first to go down if any shooting starts, Sidney, I think you should tell your men to lower their weapons."

Meas laughed. "No, Richard, that's not going to happen. In fact, it's you and your men who will surrender your weapons and sit down."

"And why would we do that?"

"Because I hold the trump card." Once again, he raised his voice. "Jilmara, bring your friend in and join us, please."

The door from the kitchen opened again, and Stephanie was pushed through into the dining room. A piece of duct tape ran across her mouth, and another strip bound her wrists in front of her. Following her, was a tall, well-muscled man with short, curly dark hair, and a golden-brown complexion. He was holding a nine-millimeter Glock aimed at her head. Richard started to move toward them, but stopped when the man stuck the barrel of the gun against the back of her head.

"How good of you to join us, Ms. Lynn. Richard, I believe you and Agent Winslow of the vice president's Secret Service detail have met before"

It was a moment before Richard realized that he had indeed met Jamal Winslow. The man had attended a special operations course taught by Richard. The course was part of the Elite Law Enforcement Training Program at the FBI Academy in Quantico Virginia. The discovery that a member of the Secret Service was mixed up in this affair staggered Richard. Was Winslow a rogue agent working on his own, or were other agents involved in this web of political fraud, kidnapping, and murder?

Meas continued, "Rand, you can relieve Richard and his men of their weapons and make them sit."

When they finished collecting the weapons, the four then stood behind and to the side of Richard and each of his men.

Richard said, "Let Stephanie go. She has no more to do with this than the people who left a few minutes ago."

"You're right, Richard," Meas replied. "She doesn't have anything to do with the meeting I was having tonight. She's here because she got too nosey while rummaging through records associated with that hole in the ground you Bostonians refer to as the Big Dig. She was about to write an article describing the role my boss, the future President of the United States, had in that enterprise. I'm afraid that it would not have put him in a very flattering light. We couldn't have that now, could we?"

He got out of his chair, and continued "So, Richard, you have been a major pain in my ass. At the same time, I have been impressed by the way you operate. You always seem to land on your feet. Tell me, how do you expect to get out of this situation?"

, "Before I tell you how I will get out of this, and I will get out, maybe you would answer some questions for me."

Meas smiled. "Only seems right to give a condemned man his last request. What would you like to know?'

"Who is Ted?"

"Oh, Richard, I am sorry but we never talk about him. Few people know the identity of Ted."

"Does the VP know who Ted is?"

"No, Lambert does not know the identity of the man."

"Why was Bear killed?

"We wanted Marcus; still do. We knew he had arraigned to meet Bear. We figured Marcus would turn over a recording or documents with information about the VP's campaign finances. We decided to substitute Jimar for Bear."

"So, you killed Bear," Richard said to Wilson.

Wilson did not reply, but his look was one of confirmation.

The man's a stone killer, Richard thought. *He looks as if he might enjoy killing Stephanie right in front of me.*

"How much of all of this does the VP know?"

"Jimar reports to him. I report to him. What can I tell you? He's a greedy son-of-a-bitch. But he will be the next POTUS. We will all be rich."

"How did he get his hooks into the credit industry?"

"The same way he got his hooks into the Big Dig. He sold his vote. He spent time on the Senate Banking Committee. He stopped regulations proposed to curb credit company abuses. Naturally, they are very grateful to him."

"And when another member of the committee lines up enough support to enact significant changes, they have an unfortunate accident." Richard said it as a point of fact.

"Yes, yes. But, Richard, this is getting boring. I have other things to do…"

"Just one more question before I tell you how I'm going to get out of here. You knew I was coming tonight. How did you find out?"

Sidney walked over to Hershberger. "You want to tell him, Glen?"

"Me! I don't have any idea. Why ask me?" Hershberger was visibly disturbed.

"No, I'm sure you don't. Rand, what type of weapon did Richard and his men bring with them?"

"They're MP5s, Sidney."

"Let me see one." He took the weapon and studied it. "I don't think I've ever seen one of these. Have you, Glen?"

Hershberger nervously shook his head.

"Do you know how to use one of these, Glen?"

Again, Hershberger shook his head.

"Rand, you know how to use one of these?"

"I sure do, Sidney. It's a nice weapon."

"Pick up that other one in front of you and show Glen how it works."

Rand explained what he was doing as he checked the magazine, pulled the bolt back, and switched off the safety. "Now, all you have to do is aim and pull the trigger."

As he pointed the weapon at Hershberger, Richard interjected, "Sidney, you didn't answer my question and I haven't answered yours."

Sidney showed annoyance as he asked, "What question didn't you answer?"

"I think it's time I tell you how I'm going to get out of here."

"Richard, I was sure you realized there is no way out for you and your companions."

"Oh, you underestimate me, Sidney. Not a good move. Let me see ... Wilson has his weapon pointed at Stephanie. I assume he will pull the trigger without hesitation. So, he has to go first. Then we have our guards. This one to my right will go second. He looked at the man. "Sorry, you pulled the short straw. Next is our show-and-tell friend, Rand. Steve, Phil, and Craig will neutralize the remaining two, and then, we'll go home. Of course, Sidney, you have nothing to worry about. I want you alive."

"Very interesting fantasy, Richard, just when do you expect to have all this happen?"

"As soon as I say the magic words ... 'Fire at will.'"

77

The pane of glass behind Wilson exploded into tiny pieces. He froze, and then collapsed to the floor. A second pane of glass shattered and the man to Richard's right rocked back against the wall and slid down. Richard grabbed the man's weapon.

Rand comprehended what was happening almost immediately, and tried to move out of the line of fire. As he made his move, his right temple crossed the path of the third bullet. His torso dropped to the table, and then gravity pulled on his legs and butt. He slid backward off the table and landed on the floor with a bang.

The two remaining guards turned out to be even slower, and by the time they tried to react, Steve, Craig, and Phil had put them down and taken their weapons. Just as they did, black clad figures all armed with assault weapons stormed into the room.

A burst of automatic gunfire fire erupted, and Meas let out a high-pitched cry. Richard turned his head and saw that Meas was still holding the MP5 pointed directly at him. Then, the weapon fell to the ground, and Meas toppled to the floor. Richard ran over to him, but he was dead. *I really did want you alive*, Richard thought to himself.

Richard went to Stephanie. With no easy way to remove the tape from her mouth, Richard cut the tape binding her wrists, and let her take care of removing the rest. She hugged him and he could feel her shiver.

"Hey, Shorty, aren't you lost? This is a crime scene," one of the agents in the room said.

Richard look at the man in the doorway, the man the agent had just addressed. Cullen Avery was wearing a pullover long-sleeved-knit shirt, fatigue-style pants with eight pockets, and, on his feet, sneakers. His whole outfit was black. It matched his thick, shortcut hair, two-day growth of facial hair, and the hair of his eyebrows and lashes. His barrel chest extended from just below his chin to just above his pelvis, and his arms bulged beneath the tight shirt. The black eyes set deep in their sockets showed an intensity not found in any of the other men in the room. The custom-made sniper rifle with suppressant that he was holding was almost as long as Cullen was short.

Another agent went over to the one who had just made the remark. "I suggest you keep your mouth shut when you have no idea what you're saying. The man is Cullen Avery. He is one of the best sharpshooters in the world. He trains the Secret Service shooters as well as most of the military's shooters and FBI. If you tell him you don't like your right eye, he can shoot it out at twelve hundred meters. Show some respect."

Cullen was all of sixty inches tall. His body was standard issue, but someone gave him short legs and arms. He made up for his size with a skill few could match. Richard looked him in the eyes and gave a slight nod of his head. With that OK, Cullen went directly to Jimar and looked at the entry wound. Then he measured the distance from Jimar to where the glass had been. He went to the guard slumped on the floor and checked the entry wound. Then he checked Rand.

"What is he doing?" one agent asked another.

"He keeps a book on every shot he takes. He knows where the bullet should have gone, and now he's checking where it actually hit."

"This one almost made it," Cullen said to Richard. "Bullet caught him in the right temple but was traveling almost parallel to the right side of his head. A fraction of a second and it would have been a miss." Cullen shook his head.

Richard said nothing. Cullen was a perfectionist, and Richard had had more than one occasion to be thankful that he was. Looking down at Stephanie, he knew that his was one of them.

Cullen closed his notebook and looked at Richard, who gave him the slightest of nods. It was the only thanks the man wanted or needed, and, saying, "Ma'am," to Stephanie, he slipped out of the room passing Charles White, who was just entering.

"Hi, Richard. Stephanie how are you holding up?" White asked.

"Charles, were you in on this with Richard?" Stephanie was still shaking and it was noticeable in her voice.

"I think I'll let Richard explain." Charles replied.

"It's something everyone learns in the military: Always have a reserve force, and never commit it until you have to." Richard looked over at Meas's body. "I guess he was never in the military."

"Well, I'm sure glad you were." She hugged him closely.

After a moment, White said to Richard, "After our phone conversation, Tim left the office and, a few minutes later, used a 'safe phone.' Of course, he didn't realize that we had planted a bug on him and were listening in to his part of the conversation. He reported what I had told him about you and the raid. He's been working for the senator all the time, helping him to make the Bureau look bad. So, what's the connection between the senator and Rob Lee?"

"I'm sure you'll figure that out, Charles." Richard turned to Stephanie. "Are you OK?"

She nodded her head yes. "I'll be fine. It's been a long day and I have to get to the office in the morning."

"In the morning!" Richard said. "Why don't you take some time off? You will need to relax."

"I will, but first I have a series of stories to write. I just might earn a Pulitzer. The vice president sold his vote on the Big Dig. He probably had the auditors look the other way when the contractor over-billed for trucking and other services. That's how they were able to afford to pay him for his vote. Now it looks as if the vice president received tens of millions of dollars from the bank and credit industries. He may even have directed the murder of Bear and others." Her energy was coming back quickly as she thought about the implications of her story. "I need to get back to Boston. I was hoping that you could come with me."

White spoke up. "I'm afraid that will be impossible, Stephanie. Richard has an appointment in Washington in the morning."

"You were able to arrange for a meet?" asked Richard.

"It took some doing, but I got you on the schedule for 0800. I'll give you the details, and then I'll clean this mess up and arrange for Stephanie to be escorted safely back to Boston."

78

The following morning, Richard pulled open the drapes covering the window of his eighth floor hotel room. The sun was low in the cloudless east sky. Off in the distance, obscured by tall buildings, were Lafayette Park and the Whitehouse. More northward and also obscured was One Observation Circle: the official residence of the Vice President of the United States, the site of Richard's appointment.

Richard thought about what he was about to do. He was going to confront the Vice President of the United States in his own lair. If the meeting was not successful, the vice president, cheat, crook, extortionist, money grabber, and possible murderer, would be the next President of the United States. Not only that, it would probably be the end of his life, as he knew it, and, quite possibly, be the end of his life, period.

A few minutes later, he closed the door to his room and headed to the elevator. As he stepped into the elevator, two men in suits stepped in behind him, and rode down to the lobby with him. When the door opened at the lobby level, Special Agent Dalton Whitetail was waiting.

"Good morning, Richard. Allow me to introduce Agent Underwood and Agent Finn." The two men from the elevator were suddenly standing on either side of Richard, and one of them was speaking into his wrist mike.

"Dalton, what are you doing here?" Richard was apprehensive. He was on his way to meet with a murder suspect and the suspect's security agency was intercepting him.

"The president asked me to escort you. He thought, in light of your recent encounter with Secret Service Agents, you might feel less apprehensive with me around."

"And where exactly are you escorting me to?"

"Oh, yes, sorry I failed to mention it. The president has requested your company for coffee in the Oval Office."

Just goes to show, I can be surprised. Richard thought to himself. "Dalton, I have an appointment with the vice president. I'm on my way to the residence now."

"I know, The president rescheduled that meeting. Let's go. We do not want to keep the president waiting." He gestured toward the front door of the hotel.

"I don't suppose I could follow you in my own car?" Richard asked, somewhat in jest.

"I assure you, Richard, you are safe with me."

Richard had been in the White House before, and had even met the man who had been president at that time, but he had never been in the Oval Office. He was surprised to find that its anteroom was a small alcove that contained only a desk and a few chairs.

The woman behind the desk put down the phone, smiled at him, and motioning to a door to her right, said, "Please go right in, Mister Moore, the president is waiting for you."

Richard was surprised to find that the president was alone, and walking toward him with his hand outstretched.

"Mr. Moore, I'm pleased you could accept my invitation and join me for coffee."

"I wasn't aware that I had a choice, Mr. President." Richard was still puzzled by what was happening, but not intimidated.

The president smiled and said, "Yes, well, I do apologize for the manner of the invitation, but, I assure you that I am pleased that you are here, and I hope that, by the end of our business here this morning, you will be as well. In the meantime, would you like coffee or do you drink milk at this time of day as well as in the evening?"

Whatever is going down here, thought Richard, *he's letting me know that he's done his homework.* "Coffee will be fine, Mr President."

"All right Mr. Moore, why don't you pour us both a cup. I am expecting some others to join us, but they're running a few minutes late."

Richard poured the coffee. "Do you take anything in it Mr President?"

"Thank you, Mr. Moore, I'll fix it myself."

"Mr. President, if I may speak frankly."

"By all means Mr. Moore, please do."

"With all due respect, Mr. President, what the hell am I here for? Does this have anything to do with the vice president?"

The president smiled again, and then pointing to a chair said, "Why don't you sit down, Richard?"

Richard sat down in the indicated chair, and the president sat in the couch across from him. After a few moments of thought, he leaned forward and said, "You have been very busy the past couple of weeks. I was saddened to hear about the murder of your friend, Bear. I really should have expressed my condolences when you walked into this office. My apology for the oversight."

"Thank you, Mr. President."

"Mr. President." The voice of the president's secretary came through the speakerphone.

"Yes."

"The attorney general is here."

"Have him come in."

A moment later, the door from the anteroom opened, and the attorney general entered. Unlike the president, who was tall and patrician looking, the attorney general was short and pugnacious. He and the president were an unlikely duo, but they had been best friends and political allies since they both met as Harvard undergraduates. With a scholar's mind, and a street fighter's instincts, he was sometimes referred to as the president's consigliore, a reference to both his Machiavellian operating style and his Sicilian heritage. It was a title that secretly delighted him, and which he even encouraged by occasionally swearing theatrically in bad Italian, using a few phrases he had memorized.

The President got up, but waited for the attorney general to walk across the room, before extending his hand. "George, good timing. I hope you have everything."

"Yes, Mr. President."

"Good. This is Richard Moore. Richard, George Cantini, attorney general."

The two men exchanged handshakes and greetings.

"George," the president started, "Richard was just asking me why he was here. He wanted to know if it had anything to do with the vice president. What do you think?"

"If you don't mind, Mr. President, I would first like to get a cup of coffee. It has been a long night."

He fixed himself a cup of coffee and, after taking a generous sip, said, "Mr. Moore, you haven't got a thing you can hang on the vice president."

Richard's body language signaled that he was going to respond until Cantini held up his hand. "I know what you're going to say, but in the final analysis, you would never get the vice president or anyone else, if they were in his shoes, into a court of law. All your evidence is hearsay, innuendos, and speculation. No prosecutor in the country with any brains is going to touch the case, and anyone who will take it is going to end up trashing his or her career and yours as well. Don't waste your time."

Richard watched the president and Cantini as they watched him. He wondered if this was a game of *Who Blinks First*. "Mr. Attorney General, I have a recording in which the vice president's campaign manager implicates the VP in the murder of Jan Polaski."

The president looked at Cantini. "Is this true, George. Does such a recording exist?"

Cantini responded, "I'm afraid there was some mechanical problem with Mr. Moore's equipment, Mr. President. Nothing said at Sidney's cottage last night was captured."

Richard finally understood, and it made him furious. The next President of the United States was responsible for murder and the current president was using the attorney general to cover it up. He was not sure which one he disdained more.

"Mr. President" The secretary's voice broke the silence.

"Yes"

"The Secret Service is here with your other guest."

As the president got up and walked toward the door he responded, "Good, show them in." The door opened and an agent stepped in, followed by Stephanie.

"Ms. Lynn, thank you for coming," the president said, rising and extending his hand in greeting.

"Thank you, Mr. President," Stephanie said as she walked into the Oval Office and looked around. Her face registered surprise when she saw Richard.

The president had a few quiet words with the Secret Service agent. The agent then left the room.

As he walked back to the group, the president dropped a computer CD on his desk. "Stephanie, you of course know Richard. This is George Cantini, the attorney general."

"Mr. Attorney General," Stephanie shook hands with the AG. "We have met."

"Yes, I remember: several years ago. It was at a conference the president sponsored."

"I'm flattered you remember."

Stephanie then addressed the president, "Mr. President, I believe your agents took some files from my computer. Would you like to explain their actions to me?"

The president smiled and fixed himself a cup of coffee, before he sat back on the couch and answered. "Only a reporter would come into the Oval Office at the invitation of the president and ask me to explain anything. You haven't even joined me for coffee. By the way, how was your flight?" He sipped from his cup.

Stephanie smiled. "I think it is the only way to fly: a sleek corporate jet with no one but me, a secret Service agent, and a steward. Oh, and of course, the pilot. Every woman should have one of them." Still smiling, she added, "You haven't answered my question, Mr. President"

The President looked at the attorney general. He, in turn, leaned forward and made a steeple with his hands. Holding them close to his face, he seemed to take a few seconds to gather his thoughts. Finally, he said, "Ms. Lynn, you have been doing a fine job of investigating for a story about the vice president selling his vote when he was a senator, in favor of funding for the Big Dig up in Boston. You could run the story, and it would cause quite a stir for a while, but, considering the resources at his disposal and the power of the people backing him, I seriously doubt it would ultimately keep him out of the White House.

"You and Richard have also unearthed information, unsubstantiated mind you, that the vice president was directly involved in or had knowledge of the murder of Jan Polaski, AKA the Bear. The same information also insinuates violation of campaign financing laws.

"As I have already pointed out to Mr. Moore, none of this information, largely unsubstantiated as it is, will stand up in a court of law. What it may do, however, is destroy what little faith in our system of government that the public still has. What it almost certainly will also do is destroy both you and Mr. Moore in the process. The powers behind the vice president will make certain of that."

"What do you mean, 'unsubstantiated'? I have my files and I'm sure that Richard has his."

"Mr. Moore's material suffered from a technical malfunction, as, I am afraid, did your files. I've already checked with my people, and they were unable to retrieve any usable information from them."

"Richard," Stephanie almost shouted the name, "do you go along with this pretense for trying to gag us from revealing the truth?"

The president responded before Richard could. "The truth is not always what you want it to be, Miss Lynn."

"Maybe not, Mr. President, but, in this case we know what is the truth. I want my files returned. With or without them, I will publish my story. The only question will be whether or not I include your feeble attempt to silence me."

Richard added, "Why don't we all forget we had this meeting and go our separate ways? Mr. President, the voting public will be informed about what we discovered about vice president. I am sure there are no threats you can come up with intimidating enough to keep Stephanie from publishing her story. A Secret Service agent held a gun to her head last evening. What do you intend to do?"

At that moment, the intercom buzzed and the secretary's voice interrupted. "Mr. President, he really is getting impatient."

"Good timing. Send him in."

79

The door to the anteroom opened, and Vice President Lampert entered the room. Neither the president nor the attorney general rose to greet him, and he headed straight toward the president.

"Jeb, what the hell is going on? First I get summoned here, and then you keep me waiting like some common salesperson."

"You know Stephanie Lynn, and George. Have you met Richard Moore? I understand you two were scheduled to meet earlier."

The color drained from Lampert's face as he said, "Jeb I still don't know what is going on. Why am I here and why was I made to wait while you sat with these people?"

"Have a seat and I'll tell you. Want some coffee?"

"Just get on with it, Jeb. I have a campaign to get back to."

"Well, this will prove to be well worth the wait. Stephanie was getting ready to publish an article about you selling your vote on the Big Dig."

"What! I never—"

The president held up his hand. "Now just hold on. Let me finish. I said she was about to publish. She hasn't yet. She was also going to write about your knowledge of campaign finance irregularities, extortion of some credit card and bank companies, and the murder of a gentleman affectionately known as Bear.

"Mr. Moore was involved in a raid of your campaign manager's summer home last night. Several people were killed when Sidney threatened to kill Stephanie, Richard and some of Richard's men. Richard wanted to meet with you this morning because he is convinced you were responsible for the murder of his close friend, Bear.

"George was just explaining the legal niceties of all this and, in light of the fact that the files supporting their claims have yielded no useful information, he was advising them that their case against you is quite weak, and, should they make these allegations public, it might do more harm to them than to you. So, I think you can feel secure that these accusations will not make it to the public or the press."

Lampert's face showed relief, and his body relaxed. "Thank you, Mr. President." The vice president said. "I appreciate your confidence in me. I can't imagine how the unfounded allegations might have affected the election. I'm sure I would not have had enough time to adequately dispute the story or allegations."

Lampert started to get up from his chair. As he did, he continued, "I need to get back on the campaign trail. You should see if you can put these two under house arrest so they can't spread their vicious lies."

"Funny you should mention house arrest." The president said with a slight smile and chuckle. "Sit down. I haven't said we were finished." The President's tone left little doubt that he had just ordered the vice president to sit down. Again the color faded from Lampert's face as he sat.

"I didn't invite Ms. Lynn or Richard here in an attempt to ensure that they did not destroy your chances of winning the election. And George isn't here because he likes my coffee. The three of them are here at my invitation so they can attest to your withdrawal from the race for president."

"What?" Lampert was stunned. "Are you crazy? Withdraw from a race I already have won? Never happen. I'll see you on Inauguration Day." He got up and headed to the door.

"Victor." The President called the name loudly. The door opened and the Secret Service agent in charge of the presidential security detail entered and blocked the door.

"I don't care if you sit or listen to this standing, but you will not be leaving until we are finished. Victor can stay in the office with the door closed, or he can leave and close the door behind him. Which shall it be?"

The vice president looked at Victor. The man was not visually imposing, but Lampert knew he was built like iron. The president was not offering options. "I think I'll have some coffee," he said, and walked to the coffee table.

"Thank you, Victor. I don't think I'll need you now."

When Lampert had his coffee and sat down, the president resumed speaking.

"For a man who has spent the last few years a heartbeat away from this office, you have proved to be woefully ignorant of the amount of information that flows through it, or you would never have assumed that I would not eventually become aware of the type of behavior you have been engaged in. And you are also woefully ignorant of the type of person I am, if you thought that, once having that information, I would just ignore it out of political expediency."

"Mr. President, I have no idea what you are talk—"

"Shut up! What kind of an idiot do you think I am? Sidney clearly implicated you in the murder of Bear. Significant amounts of your campaign contributions have been traced to offshore banks. Your campaign committee claims to be getting funds from deceased individuals. The fund's bank account the money came from can be traced to credit card and bank companies.

"Your relation with the banks and credit card companies goes back to your days as a congressman and senator. I suspect you had involvement with or knowledge of the accidental death of members of the bank finance Committees. You corrupted a member of your security detail and had him engage in criminal behavior that included kidnapping. —Your Secret Service people have all been replaced, by the way— I also know that you have a network of informants in various government agencies, including several staffers in this very building. Oh yes, I know every person who reports to you, and I know everything they report to you. If you'd like, I'll give you a list. In fact, it was because of the need to keep your informants from learning that I was investigating your activities, that I engaged the help of some outside operatives to do some of the investigation. I made sure that they could not be traced back to this office until I was ready to confront you. In fact, I made so sure of it that they themselves did not know who they were really working for."

With that, he turned to Richard and Stephanie, and said, "I must admit, you two have done an excellent job."

For a few moments the room was silent, and then Stephanie, Richard and Lampert all started talking at once.

"Hold on. Hold on," said the president, holding up his hand for silence. When he got it, he said, "Let me explain."

"George, here had a couple of his most trusted people looking into the vice president's activities, but, frankly, since they worked for George, they couldn't do the kind of probing that we needed without the inquiries being traced back to us. Then, you, Richard, began looking into the death of, Mr. Pulaski, a killing that seemed to have a connection with our own investigation. After looking into your background, we decided to encourage and help you in your inquiries."

"And just how did you do that, Mr. President?" asked Richard with some skepticism.

"Really, Richard, you don't think you were getting all that cooperation from federal and local agencies, or having them turn a blind eye to your more questionable operating methods just because of your charming demeanor, do you? Some of the assistance you were given could have cost people their careers if it had not been authorized by this office."

"Point taken, Mr. President."

"As for you, Ms. Lynn, it was no coincidence that the vice president, here, decided to ask your editor to assign you, an investigative reporter, to do that interview with him at the same time you got a tip to look into the Big Dig's finances. The tip came from us and the suggestion that you do the interview was made to the vice president by one of my people."

Suddenly, Lampert shouted, "This is outrageous! I've heard enough. You have nothing here but rumors and innuendos cooked up by a muckraking reporter and a nutcase private eye."

The president gave him a withering look, and then said, "Oh, George here agrees that it might be hard to convict you in a court of law, but this isn't a court of law, and I am not a judge. What I am is your boss and the leader of the party that you are set to represent in the forthcoming elections. As your boss, I am ordering you to return to the vice presidential mansion, and to remain there. You are not to come to your office or to perform any private or public functions as the Vice President of the United States from now until the day the two of us leave office. As the leader of your party, I am telling you that if you do not withdraw as a candidate for the presidency and give us an opportunity to replace you on the ticket, I will ensure that you will find yourself a political pariah without the support of the party. Now, on my desk is your letter of withdrawal from the race due to ill health. Oh, yes, your latest examination has revealed a heart condition so severe that you have been told that the stress of being president will almost certainly kill you within the first year. Ms. Lynn, here is just about to break the story as an exclusive. Now, sign the paper and go home to follow your physician's orders to refrain from doing anything stressful until the day you leave office."

"You can't do this. The party will be all over you. We can't field another candidate in time to hold on to the office. You're giving the presidency to the other party."

The anger that the president had been controlling suddenly erupted. "No, Mr. Vice President," he shouted, startling everyone and causing three Secret Service agents to burst into the office. The president ignored them all. "You gave this office to the opposition, to the other party. You sold it with the blood of innocent people of friends and colleagues. Sign the fucking papers! Sign the papers and get out of here before I change my mind and have the Capitol Police or FBI or someone throw your ass in a cell."

The President turned and looked at Victor. "Victor is the vice president's new detail waiting outside as planned, and do they understand their orders."

"Yes, Mr. President. They are ready to escort him directly to his mansion, and they are not to permit him to leave without your direct orders."

"Good. And, Victor, if the vice president resists, throw him in a cell somewhere."

The president sat down. It took several minutes for him to gain control of his anger and breathing. Meanwhile, Lampert read the withdrawal letter. The paper shook in his hand as the reality of his situation struck home. As he signed the letter, he said, "There I signed. You haven't heard the last of this from me. I'll find a way—"

"George, get him the fuck out of here," the president said.

Cantini tried to take Lampert's arm, but Lampert shrugged him off and stormed out with Cantini and the three agents following him.

80

After they'd gone, all the energy seemed to drain from the President. He remained silent for a minute or two, and when he turned to Stephanie, he looked older and sadder. "Ms. Lynn, you now have a decision to make. You can leave here with an exclusive story about the Vice President ending his campaign for reasons of health, or, without any corroborating evidence, try to convince your editor to publish a story alleging criminal misdeeds on the part of the Vice President, and a cover-up on the part of the President and the Attorney General. Speaking for George and myself, considering that we were between a rock and a hard place in this situation, we think we've done the best that we can for the country. We're going to be out of office and writing our memoirs in a couple of months regardless of what you do. As for the Vice President, for a man who wants to be President as bad as he does, the realization that he blew it will make the rest of his life miserable. Destroying your career in a futile attempt to punish him further would only give him the satisfaction of knowing that he took you down with him. My advice is to declare victory and go write your story about his resignation. My secretary will show you to a room where you can write your story and call your editor and anyone else you care to call. You can take a copy of the written withdrawal with you. I'll make arrangements for you to fly back to Boston later today."

Stephanie looked at the President for a few moments, before saying, "I think that I will accept your offer, Mr. President, on condition that I have an exclusive interview with you to get your reaction to the Vice President's withdrawal. Also, I am staying in town to attend Bear's funeral at Arlington tomorrow, but I will gladly accept your offer of a ride back to Boston after the funeral."

"Thank you, Ms. Lynn. Please tell my secretary to put you on my calendar for later today, and tell her to move your flight arrangements to anytime tomorrow that is convenient for you."

The President then got up and extended his had to her. "Now, if you don't mind, I need to have a few words with Richard in private."

"Thank you, Mr. President." Stephanie said, as she got up, shook his hand, and left.

Richard sat sipping his coffee as several minutes of silence passed.

The President was rubbing his eyes and gathering his thoughts. "Well, Richard," he finally said, "it has been a hell of a morning. I think Ms. Lynn finds the arrangements satisfactory, but what about you?"

"I think you know my feelings," Richard responded. "I got Bear's killer and the Vice President is not going to occupy this office. ... Your solution may not be perfect, but it's not a perfect world. I think that some form of justice has been served."

"Thank you, Richard. I'm glad you feel that way." The President paused for a moment, and then added, "I really am sorry about Bear. Damn, who knows how many lives have been wasted as a result of this."

"That reminds me, Mr. President. Several members of Congress were implicated in the credit scheme. I think—"

"I know. I have several other letters of resignation waiting to be signed. They can't all be done at once, of course, but by the time I leave office, they will all be gone, and along with them, most of the Vice President's government operatives. As for those outside the government, the Attorney General is already moving against them in his own fashion. I doubt that many of them will escape unscathed as well."

Richard got up to leave. "I'll leave now. I'm sure you have a full schedule, and I have a funeral to take care of."

The President got up and shook Richard's hand. "I would like to attend Bear's funeral, but it would invite too much speculation. Please know that my thoughts are with you and the rest of his friends, and that my prayers are with him."

"Thank you, Mr. President. I know Bear will appreciate it." Richard headed toward the door and left.

81

In the Vice Presidential Mansion, the following morning, Lampert was seated at his desk, seething. He had been on the phone all night and most of the morning, attempting to contact the party's power brokers. The trouble was, most of them were not returning his calls. In addition, when Stephanie had broken the story of his withdrawal the previous afternoon, his wife had immediately packed herself and the children off to her parents in Florida. She said it was because she didn't want to face the media storm that had erupted, but, he knew, that now that she was no longer going to be the First Lady, she had no reason to remain married to him.

Just as well, she'll be very disappointed when I make my comeback and finally occupy the Oval Office. I'm well rid of the bitch and the brats, too. I'll show her and all my other fair-weather friends.

The steward knocked on the door at exactly ten o'clock. Whenever he was in residence, it was his custom to have fresh coffee and toast at ten.

"Come in, Jerry."

The steward entered. "Good morning, Mr. Vice President."

"Where is Jerry?" Lampert asked.

"I'm Glen. Jerry was rushed to the hospital about a half hour ago. They think it's appendicitis."

"I hope he's all right."

"Yes, sir. They got him to the hospital quickly. I have some towels for the bathroom. I'll just be a minute."

When Glen returned, Lampert was finishing his toast and was on his second cup of coffee.

"Will there be anything else, Mr. Vice President?"

"No that will be all ... No, wait. Ask my secretary to send a card and flowers to the hospital for Jerry."

"Jerry will appreciate the thought. I'll have her take care of it."

Glen closed the door behind him and addressed the Secret Service agent posted in the hallway. "The Vice President said he didn't get much sleep last night. He wants to get some rest. He asked that you wake him at noon if he hasn't already come out."

82

Outside the Old Post Chapel in Fort Myer, Arlington, Virginia, Richard,

Stephanie, Laura, and other mourners watched with teary eyes as members of the 3rd US Infantry, the Old Guard, ceremoniously and reverently loaded Bear's casket on to a caisson that was pulled by six pairs of white Percheron draft horses. Mounted on each of the left side horses was a member of the Old Guard, while a forth was mounted on a horse standing just to the left of the lead pair.

After they had finished, the eight members Casket Team formed on either side of the caisson, and the cortege started the slow walk to the grave site about a mile away. The procession was lead by the Color Guard, followed by the Army Chaplin, and then the caisson. Richard, in dress blue uniform and white gloves, followed the caisson. Uniformed mourners followed in a formation of four columns, and civilian mourners made up the final group. Those mourners unwilling or incapable of making the long walk drove by way of a different route and met the procession near the grave site.

The graveside service was short. Although it was expected, the three volleys fired by the firing party seemed to shake most of the mourners, perhaps because it was a reminder of the sudden and violent way Bear had died. As the bugler played Taps, Richard fought back tears as he thought of Bear and the other friends he had buried with military honors. As the final notes echoed off into silence, the Casket Bearers folded the flag covering Bear's casket, and handed it to the Officer in Charge who inspected it, and then headed it to the Chaplin, who, in turn, presented the flag to Richard.

Moving smartly to the seated mourners, Richard stopped and turned to face Laura. Her bloodshot eyes fixed on Richard in some confusion. Barely able to contain his own tears, Richard knelt down and extended the flag to Laura, saying, "This flag is presented on behalf of a grateful nation as a token of our appreciation for the honorable and faithful service rendered by your loved one." He then leaned closer to Laura's ear. "You were the closet family Bear ever had. He wanted you to receive this flag."

As they left the graveside, Richard walked several passes behind the other mourners. He preferred the solitude and the others realized this fact and gave him space. He also enjoyed watching the interaction of some of the people he knew well. Stephanie was in deep conversation with Laura and her husband. Steve was flirting with Sheila. Vivian, the Senator's daughter, was listening intently as Sergeant Livermore, a former member of Bear's unit, recounted a rather unforgettable encounter between Bear and a scantily clad Major's daughter.

At the Chapel, a groundskeeper walked up to Richard. "Mr. Moore?"

"Yes, I'm Moore."

"A gentleman came by earlier and asked me to give this to you." He held out an envelope with Richard's name on it. "Do you know Stephanie Lynn? I have an envelope for her also."

Richard directed the man to where Stephanie was standing still in conversation with Laura. Richard then opened his envelope and read:

> *Richard,*
> *I had an interesting conversation with Earl Davenport. Did you know that Earl is really his second name? His first name is Theodore. Theodore Earl Davenport or TED for short. He's the guy who gave the tip to that sheriff about my location. Just before he took his last breath, he told me he arraigned for Senator Willard's accident.*
> *You can tell the Senator's daughter you solved the mystery of her father's death. Bear was apparently a better investigator that we realized. He confronted Ted about the accident several weeks before his murder.*
> *By the way, do you think the Vice President was remorseful?*
> *Cat or Mouse*

Richard searched the crowd for Vivian and Stephanie. Stephanie was just opening her envelope. Vivian was walking toward the parking area apparently ready to head back to her hotel.

"Vivian." Richard called out as he walked briskly to her.

"Richard, I was just leaving. I'm going to the—"

"Where is your father-in-law?" Richard's voice betrayed his concern.

"I don't know. He didn't meet me when I left the hotel this morning. He left a message that he was running late and would catch up with me at the gravesite. What's wrong?"

As he handed her the note, he asked what hotel. Vivian read while Richard called the hotel and asked them to check on Davenport's room.

"That son-of-a-bitch. Who wrote this? Is it true?"

"I believe it is. I'm sorry." Richard replied.

"You believe the guy who wrote this?"

"Yes, I do."

"Well that son-of-a-bitch better be dead when I get to the hotel or I'll kill him." Vivian ran over to her rented Chevy and sped away.

Stephanie suddenly appeared beside him, talking rapid fire into her cellphone. She pushed her envelope into his hands.

He opened it and read.

Stephanie,

I thought you would enjoy having another early exclusive. At 12:05 PM Eastern time today, the Secret Service found Vice President dead in his study. Unconfirmed reports indicate he died of an overdose of prescription medication. He left no note, but, undoubtedly he was distraught at the news of his grave medical condition, and the fact that it had cost him the White House. No further word is available.
Cat or Mouse

Richard looked at his watch. It was just noon. He called the White House, and, after identifying himself asked to be put through to the head of the President's security detail.

"Mr. Moore, what can I do for you?" said Victor.

Richard read him the note, and Victor told him to hold while he checked with the Vice President's detail.

When he came back on the line, he sounded shaken.

"Mr., Moore, stay where you are. Someone is on his way right now to get you and that note."

"You mean the Vice President is dead." It was a statement not a question.

"Mr. Moore, you know that I am not going to divulge information about the Vice President to you. Just stay where you are, and someone will be there in a moment. Is Ms. Lynn there with you?"

"Yes, she is."

"Please bring her along with you. Tell her the President is waiting here for confirmation of an important piece of news, and he would like her to be here when it comes."

"OK I'll see you shortly."

Stephanie looked at Richard. "Is Lampert dead?"

"They wouldn't confirm or deny, but the President wants to see us at the White House ASAP. They're sending a car for us."

Fifteen minutes later, they were escorted into the Oval Office, where a shaken President greeted them with words, "I'm afraid that I've just received confirmation that Vice President Lampert is dead, and, since you, Ms. Lynn, are the only member of the press here at the moment, I'd like to release a statement to you."

Later that day, as they sipped a drink in the private jet taking them back to Boston, Stephanie asked Richard, "Why did Rob Lee sign the letter *Cat or Mouse*?"

"It is his way of telling me the chase is back on."

"You can't be going after him again. You're out in the open. Lampert had more security around him than you could ever hope for and Rob Lee got to him. He could be lying in wait for you anywhere."

Richard gave no response.

"Shit," she said, "you are going after him!"

Richard gave no response.

Made in the USA
Middletown, DE
02 December 2015